WALL OF FIRE

"It is called the Nazca plain."

"What's happening there?" Dane asked.

"We're not exactly sure," Ahana said. "But the muonic activity is worldwide, all the power being drawn to that spot."

Foreman slapped his hand on the tabletop. "How much time do we have?"

"Two days, maybe three," Ahana said.

"And then?"

"When it reaches critical levels, everything we've seen so far—Iceland being destroyed, the tsunami in Puerto Rico, Mount Erebus erupting—will seem like child's play. There will be massive destruction all along the tectonic lines."

"The bottom line?" Foreman asked.

"The end of the world."

ATLANTIS GATE

Greg Donegan

BERKLEY BOOKS, NEW YORK

ATLANTIS GATE

A Berkley Book / published by arrangement with the author

PRINTING HISTORY
Berkley edition / August 2002

Copyright © 2002 by Robert Mayer.
Cover design by Judy Murello.
Cover art by Craig White.
Interior text design by Julie Rogers.

Visit our website at
www.penguinputnam.com

ISBN: 0-425-18572-9

BERKLEY®
Berkley Books are published by The Berkley Publishing Group,
a division of Penguin Putnam Inc.,
375 Hudson Street, New York, New York 10014.
BERKLEY and the "B" design
are trademarks belonging to Penguin Putnam Inc.

PRINTED IN THE UNITED STATES OF AMERICA

10 9 8 7 6 5 4 3 2 1

prologue

The Present

"Some say the world will end in fire, some say in ice." The voice was deep, resonant with power, echoing off the walls of the Oval Office. *"From what I've tasted of desire, I hold with those who favor fire. But if it had to perish twice, I think I know enough of hate to know that for destruction, ice is also great and would suffice."*

The act of speaking wore out the old man, and his head slumped back on the chair's high back. President Kennedy was behind his desk across from the old man. The hallway outside the closed door was full of advisers and Secret Service agents, everyone on edge given the current crisis with Cuba, but there were only the two of them in the room.

The old man's voice lost some of its power as he continued. *"The words. The words are the key."*

Kennedy leaned forward. *"Did Khrushchev really say we were too liberal to fight, Mr. Frost?"*

Robert Frost's deep blue eyes turned toward the president. *"You're not listening. No one listens."*

Kennedy frowned. "What are you talking about?"

"Khrushchev isn't important," Frost said.

"One of our U-2 spy planes was shot down over Cuba yesterday," Kennedy said. "He's very important. You met the premier two months ago. I need a feel for him. He sent a letter yesterday agreeing to pull out the missiles if we agree not to invade Cuba. Then his people in Cuba shoot down a U-2. Can I trust him? That's the key."

"Khrushchev isn't important," Frost repeated. "I hear voices. I always have. Since I was a child. Some of the words I've written aren't exactly mine. They come through me." He blinked, his gaze regaining some focus. "No, Khrushchev didn't say that."

Kennedy leaned back in his chair, relaxing slightly. "Why did you say it then?"

"It got your attention. I'm here, aren't I?"

"And why did you want to see me?"

"The voices of the gods," Frost murmured. His voice firmed. "I've been told things. Some that have happened, some yet to happen."

"You predicted my election in '59," Kennedy acknowledged. "No one else gave me a chance that early." He checked his watch. "Why did you want to see me?"

"There is a man. In the CIA."

Kennedy half turned in the seat away from Frost. Ever since the Bay of Pigs, those three letters had brought such a reaction.

"His name is Foreman. He works alone. Studying gates."

"Gates?"

"We're not alone," Frost said. "In the universe. There are gates on our planet. To other places. He studies them."

Kennedy half stood, ready to end the meeting, but Frost's next words froze him.

"I will die soon. So will you. Within a year. Maybe sooner, if you don't listen."

Kennedy sank back into the seat. "How do you know?"

"The voices tell me."

"Whose voices?"

"The voices of the gods that I hear inside." Before Kennedy could respond, Frost waved a frail hand. "Not God, as in the traditional version. But some thing, some beings, some presence, beyond our world. Just like the Shadow, the force that seeks to destroy our world."

"Wait." Kennedy turned slightly toward the right side of the office. "Bobby, come in here."

A hidden door in the middle of the wood paneling swung open, and the president's brother entered.

"What do you have on this Foreman?" the president asked.

"He's being held at Langley. He tried to transmit a message to the Russians over the CIA emergency landline to Moscow six hours ago."

"About?"

Robert Kennedy shrugged. "I don't know."

"He listens in on your conversations?" Frost asked, indicating the hidden door.

The president nodded. "Of course."

"Foreman needs to send that message," Frost said. "It is probably already too late."

"Why?"

"To save the world."

The president frowned. "Mr. Frost, you've had five minutes of my time. You're not making any sense, and I'm afraid there are pressing matters I must attend to."

Frost looked confused, as if he were trying to remember something, but it was eluding him. Bobby Kennedy went over to the old man and put his hand on the frail shoulder.

"Please come with me, Mr. Frost."

"But . . . there's something; something I should say."

"Please come with me."

Before Frost was even out of the office, the president was on the phone to the Pentagon, getting the latest update on the situation in Cuba. Frost was still protesting that there was something he needed to remember, to say, as the door shut behind him.

　　　　　•　　•　　•

The Russian freighter cut through the Atlantic, north of the Bahamas, bow pointed toward the south and Cuba. The American blockade was somewhere ahead, and the ship's crew was uncertain what reception they would receive, even though their new orders from Moscow were to help in the removal of the missiles.

The unusual fog appeared off the starboard bow, a small patch at first, but it grew at an alarming rate, spreading over the ocean. The freighter's captain ordered a course adjustment to the southeast to avoid the rapidly approaching swirl of gray and yellow, but the ship was too slow. The first tendrils of the mist swept over the decks, followed shortly by the screams of the terrified and dying.

Five minutes later, when the fog pulled back and faded, there was no sign of the freighter.

　　　　　•　　•　　•

The disappearance was noted both in Washington and Moscow five minutes later. The first missile lifted out of a silo outside of Moscow, heading toward NATO forces in Europe. The order to launch against the United States was transmitted to the sites in Cuba two minutes and twelve seconds later.

　　　　　•　　•　　•

The car carrying Robert Frost was pulling through the gates of the White House when the sirens began their wail. The old man leaned back in the seat and closed his eyes. In his mind's eye, he saw Miami, the mushroom cloud rising over what had once been a city.

"Stop here," he told the confused driver. He pushed open the door and got out. He stood on the sidewalk outside the White House, feeling the fear of the people around him running for the shelters. Beyond that, though, he felt another connection, one that had touched on him all his life. He realized what he had failed to say. He looked south, across the Mall, at the Jefferson Memorial. That was it, he realized, just as the first intercontinental ballistic missile from Cuba screamed down over the city.

The first bomb detonated over the Lincoln Memorial, less than a mile from where Frost stood. The blast came toward the poet, a racing wall of blazing death.

"Fire this time," Frost said a split second before the wave hit him.

* * *

Dane jerked upright in accompaniment to Chelsea's whine. His first action was to put a comforting hand on the golden retriever's head, fingers automatically scratching her forehead. He felt cold, even though a warm Pacific breeze came through the open porthole in the cabin. He became aware that his skin was wet. He was puzzled for a moment, and then he realized it was sweat.

He got out of the bunk and pulled on a black T-shirt with a Special Forces crest on the chest to complement the faded green jungle fatigue pants he wore. Barefoot, he silently padded out of the cabin, Chelsea right behind him. He went to the railing at the edge of the deck and halted. Chelsea sat next to him, waiting, then slid down to lay her belly against the cool metal, her nose just over the edge, nostrils flared, smelling the ocean.

He was on the deck of the FLIP, a unique research vessel over 200 meters long. Just behind him was the control section, and in front was the bulbous bow, which contained the muonic probe that had allowed Dane and the others to enter the gate and go through the portal inside. When in operation, tanks near the bow were flooded, and the long ship went from horizontal to vertical, the probe going down, while the decks in the control section pivoted to keep everything level.

Muons, formerly called mu-mesons, which the probe could detect, were subatomic particles with a negative charge and an incredibly short, mean lifetime; or at least muons that were generated by nature were like that. The muons that the gates generated were a different matter, lasting far longer than traditional physics said they should. Dane knew it had taken decades of research to discover the muon emission that occurred whenever the Shadow acted. He also knew that Professor Nagoya and his assistant Ahana had learned to manipulate muons enough to allow his entry into the Devil's Sea gate the previous day and that the two scientists were now in the control room, studying the data he had gathered and trying to make sense of it. He was also aware that Foreman, the CIA agent who had been studying the gates for decades, was in contact with Washington, trying to decide what the next move would be in this strange war mankind was raging with the Shadow, the malevolent, unknown power behind the gates.

"What's wrong?"

The voice startled Dane. He hadn't sensed Foreman's presence, which was unusual.

"I had a strange—" Dane paused as he realized he had been about to say *dream,* but he knew better. "Vision."

"Of?" Foreman asked. The old man was a silhouette in the dark, his sharp nose the most prominent feature, the starlight glinting off his silver hair.

Dane quickly related his vision, from the meeting of Frost and Kennedy in the Oval Office through the detonation of the atomic bomb over Washington. When he was done, Foreman made no immediate comment.

"It was sent to me," Dane finally said.

"It was a dream," Foreman differed.

Dane shook his head. "It was too detailed."

"But it didn't happen that way," Foreman said.

"So part of it is true?" Dane wasn't surprised.

Foreman nodded, remembering events almost forty years ago. "We picked up the Bermuda Triangle gate opening from a reconnaissance plane flying the blockade. I called Professor Kolkov in Moscow immediately on the CIA landline. He got hold of the Russian military, and they managed to change the freighter's course early enough. It avoided the gate. That was the last day of the crisis. That freighter picked up the first of the missiles from Cuba that night and removed them."

Dane ran a calloused hand over the metal railing, listening to the gentle lap of the sea against the ship. "I felt what Frost did. That's not a normal dream. And I saw the freighter get caught in the Bermuda Triangle gate."

"Why would you get a vision of something that didn't happen?" Foreman asked.

Dane had been thinking about that while he stood at the railing. "We're missing something important about these gates and the true nature of the Shadow. Something very important. I was given that vision for a reason."

"Get some sleep," Foreman said. "We've got a lot to do tomorrow." He nodded toward the pitch-black wall two miles to the west, the Devil's Sea gate that Dane had escaped out of the previous day.

The CIA agent wandered off into the dark. For the first time, Dane wondered why Foreman had been out in the middle of the night also. Then, unbidden, the thought struck him that maybe what he had seen *had* happened. How that could be, he had no idea, but he couldn't shake the feeling.

480 B.C., Greece

The king, one of the few kings who still ruled in Greece against the rising wave of democracy, was alone, a most strange occurrence for someone of his rank. Leonidas was also far from his kingdom. Sparta was 150 kilometers due south of his current location. He rode along a rocky trail that wound its way through the steep hills that constituted the northern shore of the Gulf of Corinth. He saw a temple on a mound to the right and knew he was close to his goal. It was dedicated to Apollo, who was worshiped here at Delphi.

He pulled back on the reins, eyes darting about in the shadow cast by the two cheek guards of his bronze helmet. His right hand went to the pommel of his sword, resting there, fingers lightly curled over it. There was no one about, which was most strange. Usually, the area was crowded with supplicants trying to see the oracle. Still, he felt a strong sense of threat, as if an enemy force lay in ambush. Decades of warring—and living to learn the lessons—had taught him to trust these feelings.

Then he noted the fog, a thick, unnatural mist, creeping up from the low ground to the south, out of the gulf. He spurred the horse forward, passing the necropolis that held the temple and the place where the oracle held formal meetings with supplicants. The sacred grove was ahead, but he edged the horse toward the Corycian Cave.

The fog was rising faster, covering all the land below and coming closer. Leonidas halted as a flame appeared in the mouth of the cave. An old woman, wrapped in a long, white cloak, held the torch.

"Quickly," she called out. "Enemies come."

Leonidas rode up to her and dismounted, drawing his sword as his feet touched the ground. He pulled his heavy shield off the saddle and hefted it with his off hand.

"You must attack the eyes," the oracle said. "It is the only place they are vulnerable to your weapon."

"Whose eyes?"

With her free hand, the oracle pointed toward the mist. "There."

Leonidas turned. A white figure floated in the front edge of the fog, less than forty feet away and approaching rapidly. At first, the king thought it was a ghost or a demon of the gods, as it was completely covered in white and its feet were six inches above the ground. It moved as if carried by the fog.

But when it raised its arms, hands extended, and he saw the six-inch-long blades on the end of each finger, he knew this thing was real. He went on guard, sword point toward the creature, shield covering the other half of his body, and waited. He felt a moment's shock as he saw that its face was featureless white, with only two red eyes, bulging like an insect's.

It swiped at him, and he ducked the blow, blocking the second swipe from the other hand with his sword. Then he struck, a lifetime of military training making the movement lightning quick.

The tip of the sword entered the creature's left eye, smashing through the crystal. The arm propelling the metal blade was well-muscled and covered with scars that rippled as the sword plunged deeper into the smooth, white face. Leonidas twisted the sword, the metal scraping along the rim of the socket, giving to the hard, white material. He jerked back, pulling his sword out as a terrible scream rent the night.

The creature struck at him once more, the blow so powerful that it dented his shield and knocked it from his left hand. He jabbed with the sword once more, the point hitting the open socket, and the creature screeched, pulling back. The creature floated backward into the thickening mist. The oracle was behind Leonidas's right shoulder.

"Wait," she whispered as the creature disappeared. "There's something else out there."

Leonidas checked his blade. The edge was ruined where it had caught on the creature's armor. The shield lay five feet away and slightly behind him, and he dared not turn his back on the fog to retrieve it.

"What was that?" he asked as he peered into the mist.

"A Valkyrie," the oracle said. "An emissary of the Shadow." She pointed once more. "There."

Something bounded through the fog, an animal, but like none the king had ever seen. It had the head of a serpent, the body of a lion, and the tail of a scorpion. Leonidas barely had time to register that image before he was on the defensive, slashing at the darting head and ducking to avoid the simultaneous jab by the barbed tail.

The snake head struck again, getting past the sword and slamming into Leonidas's chest, the strike blunted by the armor, venom spurting onto the metal. Before the head could pull back, Leonidas parted it from the body with one mighty downward stroke.

Breathing hard, he stood over the strange body, looking at the fog, waiting for the next opponent. But the mist was dissipating, pulling back, revealing the stars and quarter moon above.

"It is over," the oracle said.

Leonidas was aware that he was gasping and abruptly slowed his lungs to not appear tired or afraid in front of the old woman. There was a strange hissing noise, and he glanced down to note that the creature's venom was eating through the metal on his chest. Cursing, he quickly ripped off his breastplate and threw it to the ground.

"What was this?" With the tip of his sword, he prodded the body of the creature he had just killed.

"A demon creature from the other side," the oracle said.

"Other side of what?"

"Come into my cave and warm yourself by my fire." The oracle turned and disappeared into the cave, the torch reflecting off stone walls.

Leonidas checked his armor first. There was a four-inch-long by half-inch-wide hole in the breastplate, where the venom had eaten through. He touched the edge of the hole with the tip of his sword, but nothing happened. Carefully, he put the armor back on, and then he followed the woman inside. The oracle sat on a stone throne opposite a glowing blue stone set in the floor. Leonidas frowned, and as he watched, the glow disappeared. *Another strange thing in an evening of the bizarre,* he thought.

The oracle thrust the torch into a pile of kindling and started a small fire. "Sit," she instructed, pointing to a flat, black stone opposite her.

Leonidas hesitated, not wanting to be lower than her. Reluctantly, he settled down on the rock. "You sent for me," he said.

"You are a king." The old woman's voice held an edge that Leonidas didn't like.

"I am," he replied. He was uncomfortable sitting stiffly in front of the old woman. The journey to Delphi had been hard, not because of physical difficulties, but because of the constant reports brought to him by scouts about the invading Persian forces.

King Xerxes of Persia was leading his massive army forward out of Asia. He was near the Hellesponte—the waterway dividing Asia and Europe—and would be on Greek soil soon. The fools in Athens were too concerned with the *Carneia,* an annual festival, and the preparations for the Olympic Games, which were to be held soon. Or so they claimed, Leonidas thought. Cowardice took on many faces and many excuses. Athens and Sparta had been at each other's throats for generations, and he knew there was much debate among the leaders of Athens about which posed the greater threat: the Persians invading or allying with Sparta. It was one of the many failings he saw with democracy; the inability to take decisive action when time was short.

"You are a Spartan."

Leonidas knew that the rest of Greece viewed his home city as something of an enigma. The difference came not because Sparta still had a king but because of the focus in Spartan society on the military. In essence, the entire city-state was designed to support its army. Because of that, Sparta was the most powerful city-state in Peloponnisos, the southwestern part of Greece, connected to the rest of Greece by only a narrow isthmus. The city was located on the northern end of the central Laconian plain on the Eurotas River and commanded the major land routes in Laconia.

Even the Spartan heritage was somewhat different than the rest of Greece. They were descended from the Dorians, who had invaded that locale around 1000 B.C. That was the reality; the legend the Spartans preferred was that their city was founded by Lacedaemon, a son of Zeus.

The society had three classes: the Spartiates, who were the only ones allowed to vote; the perioeci, or freemen, who did not have the vote but were graciously allowed to fight and die for the state; and the helots, who, while technically not slaves, were only slightly better off than if they had been.

The old woman continued. "You are a warrior. There are times when warriors are needed, and this is one of them."

"You summoned me, old woman."

"You had a vision," she corrected.

"You summoned me," he repeated, unwilling to discuss the vivid dream he'd had a week ago, directing him to Delphi and to travel alone. Even though he was not a strong believer in dreams and visions, the dream had been so powerful, he'd known he had to follow the path it indicated. He had never been here before, but he had seen the woman before him in the dream, so he knew now it was a true vision. Of course, he had not seen the Valkyrie nor the strange creature in the dream, which might have been helpful. Such were the ways of the gods—to show one hand while keeping the other hidden.

The Delphic Oracle sighed. "Who are you loyal to?"

There was no hesitation in the answer. "Sparta."

"And Greece?"

Leonidas shrugged. "If the threat to Greece is a threat to Sparta, yes."

"You have called up your troops in response to the Persian threat," the oracle noted. "Yet Athens hasn't, and they would fall to King Xerxes's forces before Sparta."

"Why am I here?" Leonidas pressed.

"I, too, have seen a vision I could not ignore."

The Spartan waited.

"You will fight the Persians," the oracle said. "And you will gain much honor and fame. And you will die."

Leonidas's scarred and tanned face was smooth, no reaction apparent.

"But there is something you must do before you die," the oracle added.

"Besides kill Persians?"

"There is something you must take from the Gates of Fire."

"Thermopylae?" Leonidas frowned.

"Yes. It is where you will fight the Persians. You must get there first. And you must recover something and send it back to me safely."

"What is this thing?" Leonidas was already picturing the tight pass in his mind, realizing it was an excellent location to set up the defense against Xerxes's overwhelming numbers. However, defending there would leave northern Greece—the city-states of Thessalia—open to the ravages of the Persians, which had strong implications for various alliances. Still, if—

"Listen to me," the oracle snapped, as if knowing his mind was already drawn to the battle and tactics. He blinked, not used to being talked to in such a brusque manner.

"What you must save is a circle," she made a vague gesture with her hands in front of her. "A sphere," she amplified.

"Of?"

"I don't know."

"You're the Oracle of Delphi. How can you not know? And if you don't know, why should I do this?"

"It is important. Not just Greece but the entire world lies in the balance."

"What is this important sphere?"

"It is a kind of map."

"Of?" he asked once more.

"I don't know. But someone else will."

"Who?"

The oracle's eyes lost their focus as she looked inward. "Someone who is not yet alive, but is alive. One who is of this world, but not of this world. Another warrior, like you, but not like you."

"Riddles." Leonidas pulled off his helmet, revealing chiseled features and a lined face. White hair spilled out, tied in a ponytail that touched the back of his neck.

"No, the commands of the gods. Will you do it?"

"You promise me glory and honor and death in battle." He smiled, highlighting a scar on his left cheek. "What Spartan could refuse such an offer? I will do it."

1

The Present

A little old lady was walking across a flat, stony plain in Peru, an umbrella held in one hand to protect her from the sun, the other carrying a folding canvas seat. She had a faded leather backpack looped over one shoulder. Her skin was tanned and leathery, etched with lines from many years in the harsh sun.

Cresting a small hill in the middle of the plain, Dr. Leni Reizer opened the stool and sat down, giving a sigh of relief as she did so. She'd lived in the valley of the Nazca for over fifty years, and the combination of heat, sun, dryness, and age was beginning to wear on her.

She was in the exact center of a high plain between the Inca and Nazca valleys. The plain was almost fifty miles long and several miles in width. To the east, the high peaks of the Andes were visible, white-capped and wreathed with clouds. The ground was hard, littered with small stones.

She had walked every foot of that plain and knew every stone, and more importantly, every line cut into the surface of the plain where there were no stones. She was seated in the midst of what some called the world's largest work of art. For its size, covering almost 500 square miles, it was also the least visible work of art as the complex patterns cut into the surface of the plain could only be truly appreciated with an aerial view, an enigma given that the lines had been cut well before the birth of Christ.

Reizer knew all the designs by heart. She came to this spot, a small knoll where she had first realized the magnitude of the complex so many years earlier, for solitude. Several lines originated on the knoll, radiating outward at various lengths. Also, what she called the master line terminated here. The master line began with a huge wedge cut into the plain five miles due south of her position. The wedge was almost a mile long, and at the small end, a line extended that stretched five miles to this location.

The few tourists who visited, when they found out vehicles were forbidden to enter the plain, went to the nearest large town, Ica, and took the small plane tour, looking down on the site. The tour plane only flew once a week, as this site was very remote and difficult to get to. She'd camped for days in the middle of the complex and not seen another human being.

The Nazca Lines had first been noted in the 1930s when planes surveying for water had spotted them. A person walking on the ground might note a line when they crossed it—the ever-present small stones removed, a gouge cut in the hard earth—but the magnitude of the lines and the designs many of them formed would escape the person on the ground. The lines and geoglyphs were well preserved, given the dryness of the climate, the lack of rainfall—less than twenty minutes a year—and the remoteness of the site.

There were over 300 designs cut into the plain, and there were almost as many theories about why they were built and by whom. In 1969, Erich Von Daniken had proposed that they were ancient runways for extraterrestrials, but Reizer had never heard of a monkey-shaped runway. There were indeed quite a few large, wedge-shaped patterns besides the master line, some more than 2,500 feet long, with lines extending from them for over 5 miles, but the lines dwindled to less than a foot in width, hardly space for any decent-sized craft to land upon. And even the straight lines went over knolls such as this one, or into small gulleys, which precluded a level landing field, if they were just markers.

Others had postulated that the lines were astronomical designs, keyed to various stars. But a close examination of the designs, even regressing star fields to the time the lines were supposed to have been built, found that less than 20 percent had any connection to stars, certainly not a significant number, well within the range of statistical chance. Reizer had even projected out all the lines to see if they lined up with specific peaks in the mountains that surrounded the plain, but she had had little success. In her younger days, she had traveled to the few peaks that seemed to correlate but found nothing of significance on them.

Some said the lines were the work of an ancient cult. But where had the people who made up the cult come from? Reizer had questioned. Remains of pottery from the Nazcas and other people who had lived in the area held designs, but nothing similar to the Nazca Lines. Wouldn't it have made sense that there would be similarities? she had argued.

Another thing she took issue with was the dating of the lines. The best guesses had come from radiocarbon dating of ceramic and wood remains in the area. But that simply proved that the people who used those artifacts lived or passed across the plain at that time, not that those people made the lines. She felt that would be like dropping her backpack on the plain, and a thousand years from now, someone radiocarbon-dating it and announcing that the lines were made in the twentieth century.

Reizer felt the lines were much older than anyone realized. And she had always believed that their existence was the result of something no one had ever considered. Given the events of the last several months, with the proof of the reality of Atlantis and the existence of an ancient enemy, the Shadow, which attacked the world through gates, she had come to believe that the lines were somehow connected to these recent revelations. How, though, she wasn't quite sure. She had come here today to ponder possibilities.

She spent most of the day in quiet contemplation, occasionally pulling out a sketchbook and jotting down thoughts as they occurred to her. She shifted the umbrella to keep in the shade as the sun arced overhead. Having emigrated from the apocalypse of post–World War II Germany, she still savored the quiet and solitude of the plain.

As dusk approached, she saw a dust cloud to the west, near the edge of the plain. She reached into her backpack and pulled out a small set of binoculars and brought them to her eyes. Twisting the focus, she zoomed in on the solitary figure walking across the plain toward her, the truck that had brought him already heading back to the village.

He wore new khakis—she could still make out the store creases—and of all things a pith helmet. She had a good idea who he was. She'd had correspondence from an Englishman named Davon several times in the past year. She had always thought from what he wrote that he was, as the English would say, a bit daft. After recent events, though, she was viewing his theories in a different light. His last fax, yesterday, had indicated he was en route to Peru.

"Hello!" he called out when he came within fifty feet, his voice carried by the slight breeze.

Reizer simply waited. Years of walking these plains had given her immeasurable patience. The young man was perspiring when he finally arrived, even though the sun was almost down and it was at least ten degrees cooler in the past hour.

"Dr. Reizer, I presume?"

Reizer shifted her umbrella, keeping her face in the shadow. "You expected someone else?"

"I've sent you several queries, but you never responded. I'm Davon. From the Dragon Project." He was looking about. He could see the nearby lines, several of which extended to the horizon and beyond. "Amazing. To actually see them."

"To see what, exactly?"

"The lines. They're all over the world, you know. But here, you can see them on the surface."

Reizer had entertained many so-called experts over the years. "And you think they are?"

"Leng mei. That's Chinese for dragon paths. Lines of power." He raised his arms and turned slowly, while Reizer watched with an amused smile. "Can't you feel it?"

Reizer did grant him that. The first time she had come here so many years ago, she'd felt something, a power in the atmosphere. It was similar to the way the air felt before an approaching thunderstorm, but the power came not from above but from below, from the belly of the earth itself, she felt.

"Is it a good power, though?" she asked.

Davon shrugged. "It's power. That's neither good nor bad. It's who uses it and how they use it that determines good or bad."

"Tell me more about *leng mei,*" she said.

"I think the gates that are opening now are nodes for the dragon paths," Davon said. "Where major lines intersect." He frowned. "This, though"—he pointed at the nearest line, a two-foot-wide etch in the surface of the planet, the main channel—"is different in some way." He turned to her. "Is there a gate of the Shadow near here?"

"I've never seen one nor heard any reported anywhere close by."

"Strange. There's nothing like this anywhere else in the world. We have the cliff drawings in England, but that's not at all similar. I've been there. No sense of it like here. I've felt something like this at nodes near standing stones and megaliths. But lines, no, I've never seen lines, even though I knew they were there." The words were coming out of him like water rushing down a mountain stream.

"There's Avebury, the Rollright Stones, Carnac, and of course Stonehenge. Massive stones aligned in circles or lines. Along the leys of power. The ancients knew something, didn't they? Or did they even make them? Maybe the Shadow made them? Maybe the stones are something else?"

Reizer remained quiet, letting the words pour out of him.

"I was visited by a woman a couple of days ago. In England. She was American. Ariana Michelet. She wanted to know about the dragon paths. The nodes. The stones. She said they were connected to the gates, but I already knew that. I took her to the Rollright Stones. I camped in the center of the stones one night. A year ago. And I heard the screams of the damned. And saw the creatures come out of a dark circle in the center of the mist. White, hard skin. Red, glowing eyes. Others who have been in the circles have seen people from other times. Did you know that?"

Reizer listened to his manic litany and didn't interrupt or answer. Everyone had their cross to bear in life, and she realized his was his own mind, skittering between lucidity and mania, not completely under his control. His body mimicked his mind, moving about, unable to stay still, his arms flailing about.

"Tell me about this place."

Reizer was almost startled by the change in his voice and demeanor. His tone was level and rational, his body still.

She quickly related the various theories and why she didn't believe them.

"What do you believe?" Davon asked.

"There's something very important that most people don't take into account about the Nazca Lines," Reizer said. She paused, finding it strange to be talking here on the plain where she had spent so many years in solitude.

"Go on, please," Davon pressed.

"I think there are *two* sets of lines on the plain made at two different times. The geoglyphs, or forms—which are primarily animal forms—made at a very ancient time, and then the lines and wedges made after that.

"There are many places where the lines or wedges cross the various forms and take supercedence. I think ancient people who lived in this area and sensed the power made the forms. They drew the figures as a means of worship.

"And the lines and wedges? I don't think men—or women"—she added with a smile—"made them."

"Who then?"

"I think those came from below," Reizer said. "From the power inside the planet."

"Seems likely, given all that has happened recently." Davon looked around at the barren plain. "Why here?"

Reizer hesitated, and then answered. "I don't know."

Davon nodded. "Inside the planet—you know, scientists really don't know what's far inside, at the core."

"I know."

Davon looked at her oddly. "Why have you stayed here for so many years?"

For the first time, Reizer was uneasy.

"The driver of the truck I hired to bring me here," Davon continued, "said you were a witch."

Reizer laughed. "That is because of the brooms."

"'The brooms'?"

"When I first arrived here after the war, the lines weren't clean. Dust and small stones covered many of them. So I swept them."

Davon looked around. "All of them?"

"All of them. It took me four years. And many, many brooms. And brooms are linked with witches. The people didn't understand why I came into town every so often and bought more brooms." She laughed once more. "Perhaps they thought I was flying about."

"You've been here since just after the war, right?"

Reizer nodded.

"And you were born in Germany in 1903."

Reizer didn't immediately respond. She'd known there was always the chance someone would find out the truth. "That's not right. I was just twenty when I came here."

"Now I know you're lying."

Reizer sighed.

"I did some checking on you," Davon added. "You were born in 1903. To Maria and Klaus Reizer in Düsseldorf. You were married once; your husband was drafted and died on the Eastern Front. I believe his name was Eugen."

Reizer closed her eyes. She could still see her husband's face, peering out through a dirty, cracked window near the rear of the train, his hand raised in a farewell as he went back to the war from a short furlough. She had felt in her heart that she would never see him again. She had felt his despair and hopelessness throughout the short five days they'd had together. He'd wanted to leave her with child, but she had taken steps to avoid that. To bring a child into the future that Germany faced? It would have been insane.

Davon's voice intruded on her memories. "I am correct?"

"Yes."

"You don't look your age."

"The desert air is—" she began, but he cut her off.

"That's why you stay, isn't it?" Davon pressed. "The power of the lines. They keep you from aging as quickly, don't they? You hardly look fifty, yet you're twice that."

"I am not sure that is exactly it," Reizer said. "Rather, I think over a hundred years has passed in the rest of the world, but not here."

"What do you mean?"

Reizer was about to respond when the hairs on the back of her neck tingled, the sensation spreading into her body, racing along her nerve endings. She stood so suddenly the chair fell backward. It was dusk, the sun low on the western horizon, its rays almost horizontal.

"Oh, my," she murmured as a glow appeared due south of them, emanating up from the surface.

"What the hell is that?" Davon demanded, taking an unconscious step toward the glow, which was getting brighter.

"I think you should move," she said to Davon, who was now straddling the main line.

But either he didn't hear her, or he ignored her words. She could see that the glow was getting stronger because it was coming closer. She'd never seen the like before, but her heart pounded in anticipation. After all these years of waiting for something to happen!

Then she saw it, coming up the main channel line. A line of fire ten feet high from the earth itself. She turned to Davon, to warn him, but he saw the danger and began to move, but he was too slow, the fire too fast. It caught his right leg as he tried to jump free.

Davon screamed as he stared at the stump where his leg had cleanly been severed at midthigh. He collapsed to the ground, blood pulsing out.

Reizer was frozen, not by Davon's wound but by the sight of every line and wedge on the plain ablaze.

. . .

In Japan, three miles below the surface of the planet, in an abandoned mine, was a much larger version of the muonic transceiver mounted on the FLIP. The superkamiokande was a 50,000-ton ring-imaging water Cerenkov light detector. The tank holding the detector was forty meters in diameter by forty meters high. It was filled with purified water, and the walls were lined with over 13,000 photomultiplier tubes that were sensitive light detectors.

It worked under the principle that any charged particle traveling through water produced Cerenkov light, which was light generated by a particle moving faster than the speed of light in water, which was slower than the speed of light in a vacuum. The particle of light produced a shock wave similar to the sound wave set off by a supersonic aircraft. The wave hit the tubes and formed a ring, which when analyzed, could tell the type of wave, the strength, and to a certain extent the location.

The superkamiokande had been Professor Nagoya's brainchild, funded by both the Japanese and American governments, ostensibly to do pure research in physics but in reality to try to find a way to track the actions of the gates. The public had been told it was located this far underground to prevent interference from human sources on the surface, but while that was true, it was also oriented into the planet.

The control center for the SK was linked to Ahana on board the FLIP via real-time satellite feed. Thus those in Japan only had about half a second to consider the data that exploded across their screens before Professor Nagoya saw it aboard the FLIP.

. . .

"What is it?" Foreman was hovering over Professor Nagoya's shoulder, trying to make sense of the information being forwarded from the superkamiokande.

Nagoya turned to Ahana. "Put it on the main screen."

The young woman quickly typed the command into her keyboard. The Western Hemisphere appeared in outline form. And along the meeting lines of tectonic plates with which they had all grown so familiar in the past year, there were lines of extreme muonic activity, flowing, moving toward a spot in South America, as if a vortex had opened on the surface of the planet and was drawing everything into it.

"What does it mean?" Foreman asked.

Ahana answered. "The Shadow is drawing power from all the tectonic lines. There must be a gate in South America that it's being funneled into." She tapped the screen where there was a crimson red dot. "There."

"I'll get us satellite imagery of that spot," Foreman said. He pulled out his SATPhone to dial the National Reconnaissance Office, but he paused. "How much power is being drawn?"

"Off the scale."

"And?"

Nagoya knew what Foreman meant. "At this rate, the tectonic plates will become unstable soon."

Foreman seemed to have aged a decade in just a few seconds. "How much time do we have?"

"We'll have to run the numbers."

"Do it."

· · ·

The top edge of the sun creased above the horizon, sending horizontal rays just above the blue Pacific and cutting toward Dane. He looked to the west from the deck of the FLIP, at the black wall that delineated the edge of the Devil's Sea gate. It absorbed the rays of the sun as if eating them. He felt a chill ripple across his skin, the smell of death and destruction in his nostrils, although whether the odor was real or a figment of his sensitive brain, he couldn't really tell. He knew that smell was the strongest of the five senses, and any time he was near a gate, the odor was sickening.

He could sense something was happening in the control center, but he had no desire to go in there and find out. He knew bad news would be brought to him soon enough. And regardless of what it was, he would be going back into the Devils Sea gate at least once more.

His first foray into a gate had been done out of ignorance at the command of Foreman. Dane had been a member of MACV-SOG (Military Assistance Command Vietnam– Studies and Observation Group) a rather innocent-sounding name for teams of elite Special Forces soldiers and their indigenous counterparts that conducted clandestine missions into Cambodia, Laos, North Vietnam, and even into China during the Vietnam War.

Foreman had sent Dane's team—Recon Team Kansas— on a mission far into Cambodia to recover the black box of a downed U-2 spy plane. What Dane hadn't known was that the U-2 was part of an experiment Foreman had run to check if there was a connection between the Angkor gate and the Bermuda Triangle gate on the other side of the world, where he had sent the submarine *Scorpion.* The two had managed to make communication with each other before the *Scorpion* disappeared into the Bermuda Triangle and the U-2 went down in Cambodia. They had proven there was a connection that defied conventional physics, but at a high cost.

In the end, Dane was the only member of his team who made it back. Several members of the team had been killed outright, and his team leader, Flaherty, had disappeared. Dane had gone into other gates since, including a return into the Angkor gate thirty years later, where he briefly met Flaherty once more, the man appearing not to have aged at all since his disappearance and telling Dane of the battle between the Shadow and the Ones Before, the latter indirectly helping mankind against the darkness. Dane shivered as he felt the lurking presence of death and terror close by.

He looked down as a dorsal fin cut the water forty feet away. Dane stripped off his shirt, kicked off his shoes, and dove into the warm water. He swam forward, the Pacific water cleansing him of the oppressiveness given off by the gate.

He felt warm skin against his and rolled as Rachel swam by. The dolphin rose halfway out of the water and then flipped over, splashing Dane's face. He reached out and rested his right hand on the lower front edge of the dorsal fin. He felt a wave of emotion and thoughts flow over him from the dolphin. There was so much, he couldn't make sense of anything. He focused on the vision he had had the previous night, and sent that to Rachel in return.

He felt it come back to him like an echo, which confused him. Kennedy, Frost, Cuba, the freighter, Washington destroyed, jumbled and confused as if it had been taped by a faulty machine and was being played back.

Dane let go of the images and focused on the feel of Rachel's skin, her warmth, and the water sliding over his body. Rachel pushed him up above the surface, and he took a deep breath. Then she dived, pulling him down with her. Dane remembered Rachel's handler, Dr. Marsten, saying a dolphin could dive to 600 meters and stay down for over fifteen minutes, but he felt no panic, no worry as they descended. He swallowed, equalizing pressure on his ears as they went down, then relaxed as Rachel leveled off at about fifty feet.

Dane began to feel faint as the oxygen in his lungs was absorbed. Still, there was a feeling of panic. He realized he'd almost welcome the oblivion of death. The threat of death was all he had known from his time in Special Forces in Vietnam through battling the Shadow in the past year. The list of those who had gone before into darkness was long. His recon team in Cambodia in the Angkor gate; Sin Fen in the Bermuda Triangle gate; the Viking warrior he'd met inside the space between Earth and the Shadow's world, along with the Romans and Amelia Earhart; Ariana Michelet killed while trying to stop the detonation of Mount Erebus in Antarctica; and the destruction of the Pacific Rim by the Shadow. All gone. And the Shadow had been only halted once more, paused, not defeated. And the riddle of what was on the other side of the gates, beyond the wall, in the unknown place where the Shadow came from, was still as great. They'd only discovered that the portals led to a strange space—the space between—a staging area between Earth and the Shadow's world, where some humans who had disappeared into the gates, such as Amelia Earhart, eked out a timeless existence. There were also two graveyards deep under the Atlantic and Pacific at each ocean's deepest trench.

Starved for oxygen, stars flickered in Dane's eyes as the blood vessels constricted. His mind was fluttering between conscious and subconscious. Then in his mind he saw an object, a sphere, glittering as if made of gold and other precious metals, the surface uneven, covered with twisted cords that seemed to be moving and pulsing with power. The image was too faint for him to make out more detail. A man in armor was stepping up to the sphere, a staff in his hand. Dane recognized the weapon—a Naga staff—sharp blade on one end, the only thing that could cut the white skin of a Valkyrie, and seven-headed snake figure on the other. The man lifted the Naga staff above the sphere, prepared to bring it down. Dane felt a terrible sense of dread, and he tried to call out through the vision, but he knew it was another place, another time, and there was nothing he could do. But floating on the edge of his consciousness was an awareness that he knew what he was seeing, that he had heard or read of it, but he couldn't pin down exactly when or where.

Then he saw Ariana Michelet. She was standing on a white surface, ice-covered with drifting snow, and she was looking right at Dane. She was yelling something, but he could hear nothing, only see her mouth moving, trying to get a message to him. She moved her arms in a gesture, but Dane couldn't figure out what it was. Then behind her, the ice began buckling, cracking, a tidal wave of hard, white death. Dane reached forward, letting go of Rachel, trying to get to Ariana, but she faded as his brain slipped further into darkness.

Then Rachel turned her nose up and put her wide forehead under his back, pushing him upward. Dane broke the surface and gulped in a deep breath, letting go of Rachel and rolling onto his back, hacking and coughing to get water out of his lungs. The blue sky was cloudless, unmarked. Dane floated, rising and falling with the slight swell, regaining his breath and consciousness.

He'd "drowned" before. It had been a part of the training at the Special Forces scuba school at Key West, which he had gone to over three decades previously. The instructors kept students in the water, pushing them hard, until inevitably the body broke down and the student passed out. The instructors would haul the student out and resuscitate him and then tell him to get back in the water. It was brutal but effective training—as was all the training Dane had experienced in the Special Forces. He had truly only understood that when he was in his first firefight in Vietnam and he had reacted, his body and mind honed by the brutal repetition, keeping him alive while others with lesser training died. The bonds he had forged with those he had served with had been greater than anything he'd experienced before or since.

But his experience in the Angkor gate had broken him.
Upon his return to Vietnam, after months of barely surviving the long trek through the jungle from Cambodia, his account of what had happened to his team had been met by
disbelief. And he had had no desire to ever again be in a position where the orders of another man would put him in a
life-threatening situation. He had let his hitch run out and
then come back to the States.

He'd bought a Harley and ridden. For five years. All over
the country. Working when he needed money. Many times
making his living playing poker, his special sense of emotions and thoughts allowing him a definite advantage over
the others he played.

Then he'd found a puppy, a stray eating out of a Dump-
ster, and picked it up. He stayed in that town for two months,
feeding and taking care of the puppy, a mixed breed—
mostly German shepherd with something else mixed in—
until it had its strength back. Then he realized he didn't want
to ride anymore. He sold the Harley and took the puppy to a
training academy, where they both learned search and rescue. Twenty-five years of doing that and three dogs—
Chelsea being the most recent—later, here he was. Drawn
back into a role he didn't want, in a situation he hated. He
was no longer a rescuer but back to being a warrior.

Gradually, Dane became aware of someone calling him.
He looked to the right and saw Foreman on the deck of the
FLIP, indicating for him to come over. Reluctantly, Dane
began kicking with his legs until he reached the side of the
ship. He climbed up a rope onto the deck. He knew it was
bad news time.

"Enjoy yourself?" Foreman asked, the tone indicating his
disapproval.

"I had another vision," Dane said.

"Of?"

Dane quickly explained the sphere and the man in armor holding the Naga staff.

"These visions aren't very useful," Foreman said.

"A vision saved the world when I was in the Angkor gate," Dane reminded the CIA agent. "It showed me how to stop the Shadow's propagation. I think they're sent by the Ones Before to help us. And what I saw . . ." Dane paused, not sure how to continue. "I've seen that image of the man in armor before or something very much like it. Maybe in a book or a movie. I don't know."

"Maybe it was a vision of something that didn't happen," Foreman said, "like your vision of Robert Frost and Kennedy."

"I've been thinking about that, too," Dane said.

"And?" Foreman prompted.

"In the vision, Frost was saying that his poetry wasn't his but rather the voices of the gods, which Sin Fen first told me about. The same voice I heard in Angkor that showed me how to destroy the Shadow's power propagation."

Foreman's patience was running thin. "And?" he repeated.

"Maybe there are more messages in Frost's poetry," Dane said.

Foreman's face was tight. "Good. Real good. You go read some poetry." He slapped his hand on the railing. "In the meanwhile, would you mind sitting in on something that might actually be worthwhile?" He didn't wait for an answer. "Professor Nagoya has picked up high levels of muonic activity along the edges of all the tectonic plates terminating in South America."

"And?"

"The Shadow is attacking us once more. Nagoya and Ahana are crunching the numbers right now, but it doesn't look good."

Foreman led the way, and Dane followed. They entered

the control center, where Professor Nagoya and Ahana were seated in front of their computers. The elderly Japanese scientist turned in his seat and scooted over to a small conference table, Ahana following, her hands full of reports.

"What do you have?" Foreman demanded, taking the seat at the head of the table.

Nagoya's face was pale. "It is most serious."

Ahana passed out a series of pictures. "I have the satellite imagery of the site in South America being forwarded to us."

Dane looked at the picture and frowned. Lines, wedges, and animal outlines etched in fire spread over many miles. He handed it to the CIA man.

"What the hell is that?" Foreman demanded.

Ahana had the coordinates. "It is called the Nazca plain."

"What's happening there?" Dane asked. The name of the location seemed somewhat familiar to him, but he couldn't quite place why.

"We're not exactly sure," Ahana said. "But the muonic activity is worldwide, all the power being drawn toward that spot."

"Time," Foreman slapped a hand on the tabletop. "How much time do we have?"

"Two days, maybe three." Ahana said.

"That's a lot of variance," Foreman said. "I need a tighter prediction."

"No sooner than sixty hours, no later than seventy two," Ahana said firmly.

"And then?"

"When it reaches critical levels, everything we've seen so far—Iceland being destroyed, the tsunami in Puerto Rico, Mount Erebus erupting—will seem like child's play. There will be massive destruction all along the tectonic lines."

"The bottom line?" Foreman asked.

"The end of the world."

2

Whenever he was away from Sparta and in a situation where he felt there was a threat, Leonidas slept in his body armor, a habit he had acquired years ago. It wasn't physically comfortable, but for the king there was a certain degree of mental solace to be taken from the protection provided by the metal surrounding his vital organs. It also meant he could be ready for battle in a matter of seconds rather than minutes.

He slowly stood, his body aching from age and old wounds. He felt stiff and worn, wishing his squire Xarxon was here to work the muscles. Decades of scar tissue tended to harden during the night, producing stiffness. Without the aid of Xarxon, he began the most basic of the phobologic exercises that had been drilled into him as a youth in his agoge.

He spent fifteen minutes working his body until he felt prepared for what the day might offer. He picked up his sword from where it had lain near at hand on his right side. He noted the damage caused by the strange creature the or-

acle had called a Valkyrie. He would have an armorer work
on it as soon as he could. The same with his chest armor.
And his shield, he remembered as he picked it up.

He heard steps and turned, weapon at the ready. A woman
wrapped in a red cloak, similar to the scarlet cloak that Spartan knights wore, stood about fifteen feet away on the path.
The woman was almost as tall as he, with red hair shorn
tightly against her skull. In an age where few lived past
thirty, she was old, appearing to be about forty, given the
etched lines around her eyes, but she was in excellent shape,
as far as he could tell. He wondered how long she had been
within view and whether she had seen him doing his exercises.

Leonidas sheathed his sword and nodded a greeting to the
woman, uncertain who she was or her status here. He had
spent the night outside the Corycian Cave with just a thin
blanket underneath him and his cloak over him. It was what
he was used to in the field.

"Hail and well met, King," the woman said as she came
closer, halting a few paces away as he picked up his helmet.
There was no special ornamentation to his headgear, just the
stiff brush of hair indicating his rank. The metal was not as
highly polished as Leonidas would have liked, another disadvantage of not having Xarxon with him on this trip.

"You have the advantage," Leonidas said as he set the
helmet on his head, changing his appearance as his face disappeared in the shadows cast by the cheek guards—almost
a skull-like visage, the last thing many an enemy had seen.

She bowed ever so slightly at the waist. "I am Cyra,
Priestess of the oracle. I am to accompany you on this journey and task."

Leonidas grimaced slightly as if in pain. "I think not,
Priestess of the Oracle."

"I think so," a voice behind him interjected.

Leonidas turned and faced the oracle. "I go to war. It is

not a place for a woman." To him, it wasn't an argument, just a fact.

The oracle didn't agree. "You go to do more than slay other men. You go to fulfill a higher task. Cyra will help with that. She will bring the map back to me."

Leonidas had been wondering about that part of the oracle's plan, given that she'd said he would die in the coming battle. "An army on the march is no place for a woman."

"She is not just a woman," the oracle said. "She is a priestess."

"A priestess is not a warrior," Leonidas began. "I don't—"

"She is my daughter."

"I don't—"Leonidas tried once more, but the old woman cut him off.

"We are descended from Helen, who Agamemnon led a great fleet across the ocean to Troy to rescue. Even your ancestors fought at Troy, and many died. And our line goes back farther than that. To Thera and before that to Atlantis until it was destroyed. Our aid is a valuable thing. Our enmity a terrible curse."

Leonidas stiffened, not used to being threatened, especially by someone he could not draw his sword against. And the talk of this place Atlantis made him wonder. He had never heard of it. Thera he knew, having sailed past it. The island had obviously suffered a great disaster long ago. It seemed as if the oracle's people had lived with much misfortune over the years, which did not speak well of their forecasting abilities.

"What is this Atlantis?" he asked.

"A great land that once existed beyond the Pillars of Hercules."

"There is nothing beyond the Pillars," Leonidas said. The farthest west he had been was to Sicily, part of Magna Graecia, where both Athens and Sparta had founded colonies that constantly fought with each other. There he had heard Phoenician sailors tell of the waters to the west and how, many miles in that direction, the Great Sea was closed in on both sides, ending at the Pillars of Hercules. They had said there was a gap between the pillars, but that only death and darkness lay beyond. Of course, the Phoenicians were a strange people, often offering their services to the highest bidder, but he saw no reason why they would lie about that.

"There isn't anything there now," the oracle said. "Atlantis was completely destroyed by the Shadow, and the few survivors scattered. All that remains is a boundless ocean, much greater than that which you have sailed upon."

Leonidas found that hard to grasp. The journey to Magna Graecia had taken several weeks, as the galley had tacked with whatever wind could be found and been rowed when there was no wind, along the coastlines.

"This Shadow. Is it a god?" To Leonidas, gods were meddlesome creatures who seemed to delight in tormenting men.

"It is beyond what we know, so it might well be a god," the oracle said. "I only know its emissaries, the Valkyries. No one has ever seen one of the Shadow."

"Why do they seek to destroy us?" Leonidas asked.

"That is also beyond what we know, but we do know it tries. Isn't that enough?"

Leonidas almost answered in the negative. He knew that an enemy's motivation was critical in combat. Victory went not to the side that killed the most, but to the side that broke the other side's will. A man defending his home was always a greater threat than a man marching in a foreign land simply because his king had ordered him forth.

Most would have found the oracle vague, but Leonidas had experience with seers, and he actually thought she made more sense than many. Most spoke so vaguely that their words could be interpreted in a dozen different ways. At least she was specific in what needed to be accomplished.

"The other creature I killed—what was that?"

"It came from the Shadow's world," the oracle said.

"It must be a strange place," Leonidas said. "How far away is this Shadow's kingdom?"

"We do not know."

"Perhaps that is why you need the map," Leonidas said.

"The map is not for my use."

"I will send one of my men back with the map," he offered.

"Do you remember Croesus, last of the Lydian kings?" the oracle asked.

Leonidas nodded.

"He sent many gifts here," the oracle said. "To my great-great-grandmother. And she gave him a prophecy. He only listened to what he wanted to hear in the manner in which he wanted to understand. She told him that if he warred against the Persians, that he would destroy a great empire. That was what he wanted to hear, so he marched forth and entered into battle with Cyrus, king of Persia. And he was defeated. A great kingdom was indeed destroyed: his own.

"I have told you that you will have great honor on the battlefield," the oracle continued. "But that prophecy is contingent on Cyra traveling with you. Let me remind you, King, that the Valkyrie would have had your head last night if I had not told you its weakness. The paths of fate are very tenuous and easily swayed if one is not careful."

"And let me remind you, Oracle, that I would not have been here to lose my head if you had not sent a dream to me," Leonidas replied. "And if I had not honored that dream."

"The Persians are coming, regardless of whether you traveled here or not," the oracle said.

"Women," Leonidas muttered. The oracle didn't hear

him, but Cyra did. The priestess smiled slightly but said nothing. "Let us be going then." He slid his sword in the sheath and walked toward his hobbled horse.

. . .

"Master, remember the Greeks."

King Xerxes, son of Darius, grandson of Cyrus, king of Medea and Persia, ruler of Libya, Arabia, Egypt, Palestine, Ethiopia, Elam, Syria, Assyria, Cyprus, Babylonia, Chaldea, Cilicia, Thrace, and Cappadocia, and most blessed of God Ahura Mazda, had heard the same admonishment every evening for five years, whispered into his ear by the woman who stood to his right rear. Five years, from the first day he was king in 485, succeeding his father, Darius. Who, five years before his demise, in 490 B.C., had his army defeated on the Plain of Marathon by the Greeks. It had been a stunning defeat given that Darius's army had outnumbered their opponents by more than five to one. Xerxes was certain that his father's death, even though it was years after the battle, began that day. The defeat was like a cancer that had eaten away at his father's pride and life.

Time was indeed the enemy of all, kings and peasants alike, Xerxes ruminated, listening to the rain and wind batter at his imperial tent as he began eating his breakfast. His campaign throne was at the head of a long wooden table. Along each side sat his generals, and around the outer rim of the massive tent fifty of his Immortals stood guard.

There were 9,950 more Immortals encamped directly around the imperial tent to bring the total to 10,000. That number, like the rising of the sun each morning, was a certainty. Even if one of the Immortals were to be struck this very second by one of the bolts of lightning that were crackling about outside, there would be a man ready to take his place. Because the number was kept always at 10,000, the imperial guard had gained its name of the Immortals, since it appeared as if the unit could never be depleted or destroyed.

Outside of the ring of Immortals, another 200,000 troops were camped in varying degrees of discomfort. Most weren't even Persian but levies raised by vassal states to answer the call of Xerxes rather than face his wrath. There were even Greeks camped there, Ionians, who had chosen to side with the powerful ruler from their side of the Aegean. Their decision was understandable, given the reluctance of Athens and the other mainland Greek states to send troops or ships to their defense when the Persians came marching out of central Turkey.

There were also Babylonians, Arabs, Egyptians, Phrygians, Medes, Cissians, and dozens of other states represented. Such a mixture of weaponry, armor, and languages had not been seen in ten years, since Darius had set forth for Greece. There were soldiers from three continents, which encompassed the entire known world for the Persians.

The massive camp sprawled along the western edge of the Hellesponte, which separated Europe from Asia. Other than going around the Black Sea through southern Russia, this thin strip of water running from the Black Sea to the Aegean was the easiest place for an invading army to cross. At its narrowest, directly ahead of the army, the strait was only a mile and a quarter wide.

And on that water, even in the midst of the howling storm, engineers had been at work all night, adding boat after boat to the pontoon bridge they were constructing. It stretched almost a mile now, the far shore close enough to add impetus to the muscles laying the planks and stringing the ropes that connected the boats.

Each boat was a *penteknoters,* fifty-oar galley. They were set about ten feet apart, side to side, and secured to each other first with rope, then heavy planks that constituted what would be the roadway. The entire affair was at a critical stage, as water kicked up by the storm surged through the Hellesponte and the wind added its own fury. A cluster of galleys, oars manned by slaves, was tied off to the unanchored end, desperately trying to keep it in place as another boat was brought into line.

Disaster struck slowly but irrevocably. One by one, minor lines to the anchor boats began parting, the strain too great. The main control line, over a foot and a half thick, was soon the only thing holding the end of the bridge to the anchor boats. Men desperately tried throwing new lines to the boats, but the wind made the effort futile, whipping the ropes into the water with ease. A few intrepid engineers even tied lines to the bridge and the other end around their waists and attempted to swim out to the boats.

The six-foot swell and the weight of the rope took each of these men under. Then their dead weight added to that of the bridge, and their bodies, pulled by the current, added to the horizontal strain.

The main cable parted, the sound even louder than that of the thunder, the two ends whipping through the air, slicing men in half and cutting through wood like sand. The bridge gave way, curving, the road boards cracking and splitting, the remaining control ropes snapping easily.

Xerxes and his generals, alerted by the sound, ran out into the storm and watched futilely as the work of a week was destroyed in less than a minute.

What had never been bridged by man would not give in so easily.

• • •

Thermopylae. In Greek it means "hot gates." The name comes from numerous hot springs in the area. It is a pass southeast of Lamia, between Mount Oeta and the Malian Gulf. It is the primary passageway from Thessalia in northern Greece into Locris and the rest of southern Greece,

where the major city-states were. Other than by sea, it was
the main thoroughfare by which an invading army had to
travel to conquer the southern half of Greece, where Athens
and Sparta lay.

There were other passes to the west, but Thermopylae
was next to the sea, where a fleet could cover an invading
army's flank and also—something most who were not military men did not understand but was of utmost impor-
tance—resupply it. An army of a quarter million troops,
along with their beasts, consumed vast quantities of supplies
each day. Xerxes's generals counted on finding little food or
supplies as they marched into Greece, as it was customary
for retreating armies to scorch the earth, even if it were their
own land, as they fell back.

Of course, an army taking the pass had to practically go
through the proverbial eye of the needle, as the track narrowed to only fifty feet wide between the mountain and a
cliff overlooking the sea. Xerxes's generals had assured
him, though, that the pass would not be a place for defense,
as the heavy Greek infantry would not be able to deploy in
their beloved phalanxes to fight in such a tight space.

There were spas with hot springs in the area just to the
north of the pass that in more peaceful times were visited by
people from all over Greece. But with the storm cloud of
war to the east and north, the mountains were empty of people. The ruins of a defensive wall known as the Middle Gate,
built by an unknown people against an unknown enemy
some time in the far past, cut across the pass. In front of the
Middle Gate was a smooth, open area, about 200 meters
long by 80 wide.

The pass itself was used only by travelers who hastened
through, usually early in the morning after camping at the
springs to the north, or just before the pass to the south. No
one took extra time traversing the pass because there was a
strange feel about the place, and those who lived north or

south told strange tales of the mountains and pass. Animals would have to be forced through, then almost break their reins galloping down after getting through the Middle Gate. Dogs howled and snarled when they were in the narrowest part. There were rumors of demons and other strange creatures, and the place was avoided if at all possible.

This morning, as lightning cut through the sky and hit the mountain high above, and the strong wind churned up the water in the sea below, the pass was empty of travelers. Thus there was no one to witness as just to the north of the ruined wall a pure black circle appeared, consuming the scant light.

As another bolt of lightning illuminated the land, a hand, skin red and blistered, could be seen extending out of the black circle about five feet above the ground. The fingers were stretched wide, grasping, as if searching for a handhold out of the darkness. The hand disappeared back into the darkness for several moments, then reappeared, the skin peeling back. Still it groped and reached. And once more was gone.

The third time the hand appeared, the flesh was gone, and there was just the bone with the tendons stretched tight and burned raw. Still, the fingers moved, reaching bones clattering together as they closed on themselves empty-handed.

When the next bolt lit the scene, there was just the black circle and no hand. And with the third strike, the circle itself was gone.

3

The Present

Since the dramatic events of 26 April 1986, the Russians had monitored the remains of Reactor Four of the Chernobyl Nuclear Power Plant. Although encased in a thick layer of concrete and stone, the interior of Reactor Four had remained clear since the disaster, protected by a shield generated by the gate that had opened inside it and caused the tragic accident that evening.

The core of the reactor, the rods that provided the power, had been tapped by the Shadow. Above the core, a black triangle fifteen feet on each side and ten feet in height had appeared and remained through all the years, drawing energy from the decaying rods. It was a gate, not as large as the others, but a gate nonetheless. A probe, carried by a dying volunteer, had been sent through the gate just two days ago and helped provide information about the makeup of the gates and the connections among the portals that existed inside the gates. It had been discovered that the gates were like foyers established on Earth by the Shadow, and inside the gates were the actual doorways—portals—that led to other places.

The rods were down to less than 2 percent strength, and still the black triangle drew the remaining power. There was quite a bit of speculation among Russian scientists about what would happen when the rods were completely spent, but it was all conjecture, as most everything thought about the gates was.

It was just before midnight when the *Spetsnatz*—Russian special forces—soldiers manning the monitoring station built into the concrete wall surrounding the core jumped to their feet as alarms sounded. Looking at the video screens that were linked to cameras inside the core, they saw a black, cylindrical object with four tail fins fall out of the black triangle onto the floor of the core container. There was no doubt what the object was: a bomb, but one of old design. As they watched, a half-dozen similar objects hit the floor and came to rest.

The major in charge ordered a withdrawal before the last bomb appeared. The men unbolted the shield door leading to the outside world and dashed up the tunnel, the major taking the time to shut the door and slap one of the bolts in place before running after his men.

They exited the encasement and paused, bodies tensed, waiting for the explosion. But nothing happened

· · ·

The strap from Reizer's leather bag cut so deeply into the skin on Davon's upper thigh that she couldn't see most of it. Her hand was on the handle of the umbrella, which was attached to a knot on the strap. She had cranked the handle around several times to tighten the tourniquet, but Davon had lost a lot of blood.

She looked up at the wall of flame in front of her, feeling the heat coming off it but not as much as she expected,

being this close. It was as if the fire was contained between two invisible planes of glass extending up ten feet.
For the first time, she noted that the ground was trembling
slightly.

Reizer was startled as Davon grabbed her arm. She
leaned over the young man and ran a comforting hand
across his sweat-soaked, pale forehead. His lips moved as he
tried to speak. She leaned closer.

"What is it?" he finally managed to get out. His eyes
shifted over to the wall of fire to let her know what he was
talking about.

"Power into the planet," Reizer said. "Channeled somehow."

"The Shadow?"

Reizer shrugged, and then she realized he couldn't see
the movement. "I don't know."

"Lines of power," Davon said. He smiled, his lips almost
drained of color. "I knew I was right."

"You need to rest," Reizer said, although she knew that
he had scant seconds, if even a minute of life left.

A surprised look passed over Davon's face. "I've
seen . . ." He paused, and the next couple of words weren't
audible. ". . . before. The other . . ." His head slumped back,
and the eyes went vacant.

• • •

"We have to destroy the portal that's drawing the power
through Nazca," Foreman said. He and Dane were standing
on the deck of the FLIP.

Dane shook his head. "We don't have a priestess to go
into the gate and then the portal and stop it, like Kaia did in
the Devil's Sea. We don't even know exactly what's going
on there." He tapped the photo of the fiery images that he
had carried out of the control center. "We're not sure there's
a gate there, and even if there was, we might have trouble

finding the portal. We only managed to find the one here because of the Chernobyl probe."

"We know more than we did," Foreman said. "Nagoya
has analyzed the data you picked up from the last trip into
the gate." Foreman nodded his head, indicating the dark
wall two miles away. "He thinks there are numerous portals
inside this space between our worlds. Some lead to other
gates on our planet, but at least one has got to lead to the
other side. To the Shadow's world. Maybe we can stop this
at the source."

"And does he know which is which?" Dane asked.

"Not yet."

"So, what are we going to do?" Dane asked. "Try each
one?"

"Nagoya has mapped the one that leads to Chernobyl by
tracking the emissions from the probe the Russians sent
through that gate. He thinks we can map others doing the
same thing. Send probes in, then see where the emissions
come out in the space between."

"That could take a while," Dane said. "And we don't
have much time, according to Ahana's numbers."

"Do you have a better idea?"

"Not yet." Dane rubbed the stubble on his chin. "What
about the Ones Before? Flaherty said they were on our
side."

"If we could contact them, it would help," Foreman acknowledged. "But getting hold of them seems as hard as
fighting the Shadow."

"They sent Flaherty into the Angkor gate," Dane noted.

Foreman's SATPhone buzzed, and he flipped it open. He
listened for a half minute, then shut it. "There's another
problem."

"Great."

Foreman turned for the control center, Dane following,
waiting for the further bad news.

"A half-dozen World War II–era five-hundred-pound bombs were sent out of the Chernobyl gate into the remains of the reactor core," Foreman said over his shoulder.

"Did they explode?"

"No. The monitoring personnel evacuated, but when nothing happened, they went back in. The bombs are just sitting there."

They entered, and Ahana spoke before Foreman could. "The superkamiokande in Japan tracked a burst of muonic activity at Chernobyl."

Foreman told her and Nagoya about the bombs.

Dane had been considering this new development. "Do you think the Shadow could have backtracked the probe we sent through Chernobyl?"

"Possibly," Foreman allowed.

"Chekhov once wrote that a playwright shouldn't introduce a gun in act one unless it was fired by act three," Dane noted.

Foreman frowned at the arcane reference. "And?"

"The Shadow sent those bombs through for a reason," Dane said. "They will be detonated."

"We assume that also," Foreman said. "The Russians are rigging a remote-controlled robot to go in and remove the fuses."

"I've been in contact with Professor Kolkov," Nagoya said. "He has done some rough calculations, and he believes that the Tower Four containment wall will hold, even if all six bombs are detonated."

Dane turned to the old Japanese scientist. "And what about the gates?"

"We have learned much," Nagoya said. "We have a good idea now how the gates work on our planet. The gate that we see on the surface"—he nodded toward the bulkhead, beyond which lay the Devil's Sea gate—"is like a foothold established on our planet. It appears that all the gates lead to one place via portals inside of them. That place is where the two of you were," he said, looking at Foreman, then Ahana. "For lack of a better term, we will use what you say Amelia Earhart called it: the space between.

"Time here," Nagoya pointed down, indicating Earth, "is linear and relatively fixed. But as you know, there are people in the space between who are from many different time periods—Viking warriors, Roman legionnaires—people from varying times who appear to not have aged from the time they disappeared, such as you claim Ms. Amelia Earhart appeared."

Dane bristled at the word choice but said nothing, knowing Nagoya meant no insult but was simply speaking as a scientist who had not seen the famed aviatrix with his own eyes.

"Inside the space between," Nagoya continued, "time appears to be a variable. Indeed, it must be, because the space between is connected via portals to various times in our planet's history, as recent events have shown. Such as when the Roman legion came to your aid inside the space between and gave you time to escape."

Although he knew what Nagoya was saying was true, Dane found it confusing. As if sensing this, Ahana spoke. She was a young Japanese woman, a brilliant scientist who was Nagoya's primary assistant. She had accompanied Dane through the Devil's Sea gate and met Amelia Earhart, along with thirteenth-century samurai warriors who had accompanied the aviatrix.

"I think the best way to envision this," Ahana said, "is to view time like you view locations. You can travel five miles and you are in a different place. Via the portals, you can travel to a different time."

"Can we go forward in time?" Dane asked.

Nagoya frowned. "I have not thought about that."

"The crew of the *Scorpion* went forward from their time to our time," Dane noted. He was trying to think this through the current situation. "Maybe we could go forward and see what we should do, then come back and do it?"

"That makes no sense," Foreman said.

"None of this makes sense," Dane said. "Or maybe we could go back in time and do something different?" He felt a spark of excitement. "Perhaps we could save Ariana and others?"

Nagoya shook his head. "I think we are stuck with our present. If we go back and change something in our past, it would already be changed, and we would not have our present. There are the traditional paradoxes associated with time travel. I do no think the space between is time travel but rather a timeless place."

Dane found it all quite confusing, and he had a feeling that Nagoya was overwhelmed also by the implications but not willing to admit his lack of knowledge.

"Can we get to the Shadow's world and stop the power drain from our planet?" Foreman asked, bringing the conversation back to the beginning.

"At least one of the portals inside the space between must lead to the Shadow's world," Nagoya said. "That is the portal we must find if we are to be successful in taking the war to the other side. The power drain must also go through that portal."

"Why do you say that?" Dane asked.

"I think the major purpose of what is going on is to get power from our world, like the Shadow did from Chernobyl all those years," Ahana said. "The destruction of our world is just a by-product of that."

"And if we find it?" Dane asked. "What then?" When there was no immediate answer, he shifted in his seat so that he was facing Foreman. "I know you have a plan. Why not let me in on it beforehand this time?"

Foreman evaded a direct answer as was his wont. "We're working on several things."

"I assume you want me to go back in the Devil's Sea gate with Rachel to search for this portal." Dane didn't make it a question. "I'm not going unless you tell me what options you've worked up and what their implementation priority is."

Foreman steepled his fingers just below his chin. "I briefed the president via secure SATCOM link. The plan is simple. We find the Shadow portal. We send through a muonic transmitter. If we can lock in the portal to the other side—the Shadow's world—then our first option for attack is the first one readily available. We send through cruise missiles armed with nuclear weapons. Twenty-four missiles and warheads are being modified as we speak to survive the trip through the gate."

Dane saw a big problem with that plan. "So you're hoping the missiles will function once they get to the other side, even though nothing else electromagnetic has worked inside a gate?"

"We hope that electromagnetic devices can be shut down while traversing the gate and portals and then function on the other side. The Shadow has to have electromagnetic capability on their world."

"That could be a fatal assumption," Dane said. "And how will you get the cruise missiles through the portal when their rockets won't work in the gates?"

Foreman's answer was succinct. "By hand."

It was the answer Dane had known was coming.

• • •

The voice echoed in the small cabin, bouncing off the steel walls. "The mission of the United States Naval Academy is to develop midshipmen morally, mentally, and physically and to imbue them with the highest ideals of duty, honor, and loyalty in order to provide graduates who are dedicated to a career of naval service and have potential for future development in mind and character to assume the highest responsibilities of command, citizenship, and government."

Captain Tom Stokes hit the Mute button on the remote control, and the TV went silent. The video was a recruiting pitch from the Naval Academy. On the screen, a panoramic view of the Naval Academy at Annapolis was displayed. Seeing the granite buildings, Stokes felt the familiar ache in the pit of his stomach: part ingrained fear, part pride, part amazement, even after all these years.

Stokes had been assigned as an instructor to the Academy up until six months ago, when he'd received his new orders bringing him to this small room, the captain's quarters on board the Navy's most modern submarine, the USS *Connecticut*. It wasn't that recent assignment, though, that had caused him to pull the video out of his desk, but rather the report that lay open on his desk: the findings of the board that had been commissioned to examined the loss of the USS *Seawolf*, the *Connecticut*'s sister ship, and the first Seawolf-class submarine commissioned.

The Seawolf class was the Navy's most expensive and deadly submarine, the end result of over a billion dollars in research and development before the keel of the first boat was laid down. As an attack submarine, a Seawolf-class ship had one primary mission: Kill other submarines.

The *Seawolf* had indeed destroyed another submarine, but it had been destroyed in the process. It had been lost in the Bermuda Triangle gate stopping the captured USS *Wyoming* from launching the remainder of its missiles. The *Wyoming*'s first MIRV missile had destroyed Iceland, and the *Seawolf* had barely stopped a second launching, which would have split the meeting of the tectonic plates in the center of the Atlantic and devastated America's eastern seaboard and Europe's western coast.

It appeared from the report that the captain of the *Seawolf* had accomplished this mission in a most drastic way—by detonating one of his sub's own nuclear weapons while it was less than three miles from the *Wyoming,* destroying both subs in the process.

The report noted that it had been a rather extreme command decision by the *Seawolf's* captain, Joe McCallum, but surmised it had been his only choice, given the lack of time and the strange effects of the gates on electromagnetic systems, which had most likely negated using most of the *Seawolf's* weapons in their normal mode against the *Wyoming.*

Costing over two billion dollars to build, a Seawolf attack submarine incorporated every advance in underwater warfare ever developed. It had Mark-48 torpedoes, along with Tomahawk cruise missiles. And it packed that punch in a surprisingly small size, bucking the recent trend of making submarines larger. At 353 feet long, the *Seawolf* was not much longer than the first U.S. Navy sub given that name during World War II. However, its forty-foot beam was almost twice the diameter of those earlier vessels.

The rear two-thirds of the submarine were taken up with the nuclear power plant, engine room, and environmental control systems. Stokes's cabin and the rest of the living and working areas were in the forward third. Stokes commanded 13 other officers and 120 enlisted men.

At the present moment, the *Connecticut* was five miles due east of the Devil's Sea gate, so the report on the *Seawolf* encounter near the Bermuda Triangle gate held great interest for Stokes. More importantly, on a personal note, though, was the fact that the commander of the *Seawolf,* Captain McCallum, had been a classmate of Stokes's at the Academy. His eyes went back up to the view of the Academy. The camera was panning by the chapel, and he could visualize McCallum's wedding, two days after they had graduated twenty-one years ago. Stokes had been best man, and McCallum had returned the favor on the next day.

Over the years that followed, the two had crossed paths in their careers often, making their way up the ranks. McCallum getting command of the *Seawolf* had been considered a plum assignment, and Stokes had to admit he'd been jealous until the board had chosen him to take command of the second Seawolf-class submarine to be commissioned.

And now McCallum and his crew were gone. Stokes looked down, noting that the fingers of his right hand were twisting the large gold ring on his left. The setting was black hematite, the exact same that McCallum had gotten. On one side was their class crest and the year of graduation, and on the other was the Academy crest, a shield with a trident running behind it, two fasces on the side, and the motto: *Ex Scientia Tridens.* "Out of knowledge, sea power." But the report on the death of his friend gave Stokes little knowledge and raised more questions than it answered.

What the Shadow was, how the gates were formed, and most importantly *why* this strange force seemed bent on destroying the world, all were unknowns. Stokes's orders were to monitor this side of the gate. He knew that the destroyer USS *Thorn* was with the FLIP on the south. On the west side, a Los Angeles–class attack submarine held post, while on the north was the destroyer USS *Fife*.

They had the gate bracketed, but given what had happened to the *Wyoming* and the *Seawolf,* Stokes wondered what good it did. He was still pondering this when a sharp chime sounded, then a voice came out of the speaker bolted above his door.

"Captain to command and control. Captain to command and control."

Stokes was out of the door, through the connecting corridor, and in the operations center in less than five seconds. "Report?" he called out as he went to the center of the high-tech C and C, which was at the base of the sail.

"We've got activity on the edge of the gate," his executive officer (XO) informed him.

"Helm, back us off, two-thirds," Stokes immediately ordered. "Weapons, prepare targeting information." He turned to his XO. "What kind of activity?"

"Noise."

Stokes was irritated at the vague answer. "What kind of noise?"

The XO turned to the chief sonar man. "Tell him, Chief."

"Captain . . ." The petty officer held out an extra set of headphones. "You'd better listen yourself. I've never heard anything like it."

Stokes put the headset on, cutting off the sound of activity in the command and control center. He heard a faint, high-pitched, echoing sound that went up and down in volume. After a couple of moments, he pulled back one of the cups. "No idea, Chief?"

The petty officer shook his head. "It's coming from the gate."

"Almost sounds like whales," Stokes said.

"It's not whales." The petty officer sounded convinced.

"Porpoises?"

The chief considered that. "Maybe, but I've never heard that many mixed together. And there's something else in there. Some other source."

"Forward it to the FLIP. They've got that dolphin lady

there. Maybe she can make sense of it. Stand down from battle stations."

"Aye, aye, sir."

. . .

Reizer closed Davon's lifeless eyes and placed his jacket over his head. She had been raised a Catholic but had no idea what faith the young man had held. Her knees hurt from kneeling, but she remained at his side for several minutes, saying the few prayers she could remember from her childhood. When she could think of nothing further, she got to her feet and finally considered her predicament.

She could discern no diminishing in the walls of fire; indeed, if anything, they might even be higher. Decades of walking the plain and looking at aerial imagery had imprinted every single line in her mind's eye. She knew she was in the middle of an intricate maze with walls of death surrounding her.

Was there a way out without crossing a line? It was something she had never considered.

She considered it now.

. . .

Another half-dozen 500-pound bombs dropped out of the Chernobyl gate, clattering down on those that had already been deposited. The thirteenth one was indeed unlucky as it came out nose down, detonator armed.

It hit and exploded, setting off an instantaneous reaction that detonated the other twelve bombs. Kolkov's calculations had been for six bombs, not thirteen. The concrete containment wall buckled, bulged, and then collapsed. The vast majority of the explosion was used up in that effort, thus the immediate effects of the blast were minimal to the other three reactors and the nearby town.

It was fear of the other effect of the blast—the escape of

contaminated air billowing out of the destroyed shield—that had alarms blasting and every living soul scrambling to get out of the area.

• • •

Dane's reaction to Foreman's brilliant first assault option was forestalled as a crewman stuck his head through the open hatchway with a startling announcement.

"There's a ship coming out of the gate."

The words had just registered with those gathered around the table when one of the computers let out a soft chime.

"Muonic activity," Ahana said as she spun her chair about and checked the screen. "Here. And Chernobyl."

Foreman's SATPhone buzzed, and he snatched it off his belt. He listened for a few seconds and then hung up. "That was Kolkov. Tower Four has been breached. The bombs went off."

"I thought you said—" Dane began, but Foreman cut him off.

"More bombs came through just before the explosion. The other reactors are being shut down and the area evacuated."

Dane was already to the hatch and through, the others following. He went to the railing. He didn't need binoculars to see the ship, which was now clear of the gate and heading directly toward them. A vintage clipper ship, sails snapping in the light breeze, picking up speed. A ghost ship, as nothing was moving on the deck. The destroyer *Thorn,* which was the FLIP's escort, was already moving to intercept.

"I don't like this," Dane said.

"Maybe someone escaped," Foreman had binoculars to his eyes, scanning the empty decks.

Dane knew that the CIA man held some hope that his brother, who had disappeared inside the Devil's Sea gate in

1945, might still be alive, somewhere inside the space between.

"I recommend—" Dane began, but his words were cut off as the clipper ship disappeared in a massive explosion that engulfed the *Thorn*, which had drawn up less than 200 meters from it.

Dane reacted, grabbing Ahana and pulling her down to the deck as wood splinters streaked toward them and hit the FLIP with sharp cracks. He heard someone cry out in pain. He held tightly on to the slight Japanese woman as the warm breeze generated by the blast swept over them.

The silence that followed the explosion was unsettling. Dane let go of Ahana and got to his feet. There was no sign of the clipper ship. The *Thorn* was devastated, the side that had been toward the old ship gutted, with several fires blazing.

"That was meant for us," Dane said as he turned. "I think—" He stopped as he saw Ahana kneeling over Professor Nagoya, her hands trying to stanch the flow of blood around a foot-long splinter of wood that protruded from his stomach. Dane immediately knelt next to her.

"Exit wound," he said.

"What?" Ahana was in shock, her only focus trying futilely to stem the blood. Dane reached behind the old man and felt wetness—blood—then the tip of the splinter that had punched all the way through. From the amount of blood he felt pulsing through his fingers, he knew there was nothing that could be done.

Nagoya's face was pale, and he was trying to say something. Dane leaned close, but the old man was speaking in Japanese. "Listen," he snapped, grabbing Ahana by the arm and forcing her head close to Nagoya's lips.

"More . . . than . . ." Ahana translated, then paused, her voice shaken. "Time . . . place . . ." She waited for more, but

Dane saw the spark of life leave Nagoya's eyes, and the body slumped back.

"What did he mean?" Dane asked.

Ahana was staring at her bloodied hands.

"What did he mean?" Dane repeated gently.

"I don't know."

Dane could tell she was too shaken to make sense of anything. He carefully guided her to her feet. Foreman was on his SATPhone, yelling into it. Dane could see that there were survivors on the *Thorn,* fighting the fire. He looked past the devastated ship at the gate.

Their attempt at action through the Chernobyl and Devils Sea gates had not only failed, but they had just received a response.

The Space Between

The pencil was worn down to a nub, barely enough for Amelia Earhart to hold between two fingers. She was writing between the carefully scripted lines of her journal, using every possible white space. There was little free space left in the leather-bound book. She noted how much smaller the letters she used now were than the original entries she had made, during her attempt to fly around the world in 1937. When now was, she had no idea. How much time had passed since she'd come to this strange location, she also had no clue.

She had been flying on one of the last legs of her record flight when she'd encountered the Devil's Sea gate. A large fog had appeared in front of her Lockheed Electra, which she and her navigator, Fred Noonan, had been unable to fly around. She'd made an emergency landing on the Pacific, and then the fog had drifted over the plane. Noonan was killed by a strange sea creature, a kraken, while she had stayed on board the plane. A large black metal sphere had surfaced, encompassing the plane, with her in it. She'd been taken from the plane by a blue glow, and when she'd awoken, she'd been here, a place she called, for lack of a better term, the space between. She called it that because it appeared to be between the world she had known on the day she disappeared, 2 July 1937, and someplace else, where the Shadow came from.

The others she met here all told similar stories of a blue glow that had saved them. The small camp, of which she was the leader by default, consisted of fifty-two individuals. None of them knew how long they had been in this place, and they came from a variety of times and places, including a dozen samurai warriors from fourth-century Japan.

There were no mirrors in the space between, so Amelia Earhart didn't know what she looked like now. She had never been vain about her looks, adopting an almost mannish manner, which had led to her being called Lady Lindbergh. Her hair was short and curly, her body tall and lean. Among the many curious features of the space between was the fact that her hair had not grown, as far she could tell, in the time she had been here. Since there was only the steady glow from unseen light sources here, and watches didn't work, there was no telling exactly how long that was, even in terms of days.

She glanced down at her latest entry, a summary of recent events. A man named Dane had appeared, followed shortly by a Roman legion, which had fought a brutal battle with the Valkyries. Dane had claimed to be from her future, many decades in her future. The legion had been destroyed, the men turned into stone by a weapon of the Valkyries, but not before one of Dane's companions had shut one of the portals that ran through the space between. Dane had promised to return, but some time had passed since he had disappeared.

Earhart and the rest of her group had escaped to go back
to their miserable existence, barely eking a survival by raising food in a few patches of Earth soil they'd managed to
scavenge near the portals. Occasionally, they supplemented
their diet with either Earth or Shadow-side creatures that
wandered through an open portal.

She found it strange that these creatures could survive
travel in a portal. Not long after she had arrived in the space
between, one of the band had tried going into one, trying to
get back to Earth. The man had swum out to the dark cylinder, while the rest of the band had lined the shoreline. He
had disappeared into the blackness, only to reappear seconds
later, screaming in agony, his skin red and blistered. He'd
died within an hour, and no one had attempted to enter a portal since.

Earhart could only assume that the creatures, much like
she and the others here, had been caught in the large black
sphere that transversed the portals and dumped out here in
the space between. The portals, cylinders of black, usually
opened in the large, circular lake in the center of the space
between, but sometimes they opened on the land. There
were two forces on the Shadow side, of that Earhart had become convinced. A gold force, which bode ill and was from
the Shadow, and a blue force, that which had saved her. She
had no idea who was behind the blue, although Dane had referred to a group called the Ones Before.

A commotion near the edge of the camp drew her attention from the journal. A pair of samurai came over a ridge
made of the black, gritty sand that compromised the ground.
Between them they carried a man.

Earhart hurried over as the samurai laid the man down.
His clothes were singed and the skin burned and blistered,
reminding her of the man who had attempted to go through
the portal on his own. When she saw the man's face, she
froze, her heart pounding.

"It can't be." She didn't even realize she'd said the words out loud.

She knelt, cradling the man's head in her hands. "I saw you die," she whispered as Fred Noonan's eyes flickered open and he smiled at her.

4

480 B.C.

Xerxes's anger knew no bounds as he surveyed the tattered remains of the bridge. He had stood in the storm for hours as the debris from the bridge was blown away and his men desperately tried to salvage as many boats as possible. His cloak and robes were thoroughly soaked, clinging to his body.

The rising sun produced steam from the rain-soaked ground and the bodies and clothing of the thousands of men at work. It also revealed the extent of the disaster. All that was left of the bridge were the main anchor pylons on the near shore.

This invasion was five years in the planning and making. Four years earlier, Xerxes had dispatched a force ahead to the peninsula of Mount Athos in northern Greece, off of which his father's fleet had been destroyed in a storm. Rather than try the dangerous waters around the mount, he had ordered his engineers to cut a canal through the isthmus that attached the mount to the mainland. For four years, conscripted laborers had dug, and the canal was finally ready ahead of them so his fleet could shadow his ground movement.

But first there was the Hellesponte to be crossed by the mighty army while his fleet waited on the eastern side of the Aegean. Xerxes walked to the land's edge, between the two large tree trunks that were set ten feet into the ground and had served as anchors for the failed effort. Behind him were the chief engineers, cowering in the arms of Immortals.

"Time is short," was the whisper in his ear.

Xerxes looked at the woman who all in his court thought was a slave and perhaps a concubine, as she slept inside his imperial tent when the army was on the march. She was indeed worthy of the imperial bed, tall and willowy, with striking black hair that had a single streak of gray in it from above her left eye and flowing over her shoulder. However, Xerxes had never bedded her.

Her name, according to her, was Pandora. Xerxes had had one of his Greek scholars tell him the legend of Pandora and Prometheus and the box given to her by the gods. He thought it no coincidence that she bore the name of that character, and he was always wary of her advice, taking some of it when it made sense to him, discarding other suggestions that he felt uneasy with.

Where her homeland was, Xerxes did not know. She had appeared at his court in Persopolis, unable to even speak Persian at first, except the three words that were her mantra at every meal. Her beauty and a weapon she was carrying had spared her long enough for her to show one of the captains of the Immortals a box she carried. It did not contain the evils of the world. Instead, there was a map, drawn on paper the likes of which the most educated scholars of his court had never seen. Shiny, resistant to tear, and waterproof, the material was enough to amaze. But even more astonishing was the detail of the land from Persia to the west, with all of Greece drawn in exquisite detail.

She'd also carried a spear, a most fascinating weapon. A staff with a blade on one end made of metal the likes of which had also never been seen by anyone in his court. The edge was so sharp it could slice through an armor breastplate as if it were water. The other end of the staff was also fascinating, metal carved into the shape of seven snakes' heads. She'd called it a Naga staff but said little more about it.

The map had been useful in finding the correct spot to build this bridge and in helping his engineers in the digging of the Mount Athos canal. It was also helpful in keeping Xerxes from having the strange woman executed until she learned enough Persian to tell him why she was here: to help him defeat the Greeks and gain revenge. Her motivation for that she did not reveal, nor anything else about herself. The Naga staff he'd had taken from her and placed in the guard of his Immortals.

"Why is time short?" Xerxes asked without turning his head, as he continued to stare at the dark waters of the Hellesponte.

"I have shown you many true things," Pandora said. "You must trust me on this."

"Trust you?"

"I have seen the futures."

Xerxes was intrigued by her use of the plural. "Which futures?"

"The future if you move quickly and the future if you do not cross the Hellesponte in the next four days."

"And?"

"The first leads to victory, the latter to defeat."

Xerxes was a Zoroastrian, a belief begun 200 years previously by the prophet Zoroaster. Unlike the beliefs of the Greeks and other countries, which both he and his father,

Darius, had conquered, Zoroastrianism was a monotheistic religion, worshiping Ahura Mazda, the Lord Wisdom. The core of the faith was the battle between truth—*asha*—and lies. He felt that battle every time he consulted with Pandora, uncertain of her motivations, thus unclear about the veracity of what she said. It was true she had never directly misled him up to now, but as far as Xerxes was concerned, that only meant she might be waiting for a moment when the stakes were immense. And many of those moments would be coming in the pending campaign.

"There can only be one future," Xerxes said.

"Yes, My Lord, but your actions will determine which one it will be."

His magi—wise men—had consulted the heavens before he began this campaign and told him that the timing was fortuitous. The previous year, on the tenth of April, there had been an eclipse, the sun being blocked by the moon. His magi had said the moon represented the Persians, and the sun was the Greeks. Thus he would eclipse the enemy of his father and have his revenge.

Omens. Vague words and predictions. Faulty construction. Xerxes felt the anger rise once more in his chest. He raised his voice so those surrounding him could hear.

"Perhaps the Greek god of the water—" He turned to his adviser, who quickly supplied the name. "Poseidon, has seen fit to try to stop us. I will show him what I think of him and his fellow Greek gods and how they hold no power over my kingdom and the followers of Ahura Mazda."

Xerxes signaled to his master-at-arms. "Throw a set of shackles in the water to bind this god. Then three hundred lashes and a branding to follow to show who rules this strait and the water that flows through it!"

There was no hesitation on the master-of-arms' part. The shackles splashed into the water before the end of the second sentence. Then there was the crack of the whip and the

snap, as the leather tip hit the surface of the water. There was
no laughter among the thousands assembled watching, no
muttering in the ranks.

When the last lash was delivered, the master-at-arms was
covered with sweat, the muscles in his arm quivering. Despite his rage, Xerxes had been thinking throughout the
symbolic act, and he knew that given the multiplicity of nations represented in the forces surrounding him, more was
needed to show he had a firm grip on the mantle of command after this disaster.

He signaled for the chief engineers of the failed bridge to
be brought forward. The six men—Egyptians—cowered in
front of him, begging for mercy. He was considering various
means of execution when he sensed Pandora stirring just behind his right shoulder.

"There is little time for this, Lord. The Phoenicians have
a plan for a new bridge. Actually, two bridges, which will
allow a quicker crossing and when tied off to each other will
be stronger than one span."

Xerxes was tempted to draw his sword and lop the im-
pertinent woman's head off, but he held back. He turned and
could see two Phoenicians standing just behind her. Technically, Phoenicia was part of his realm, but many of the merchants of that realm went their own way, seeking out the
highest bidder for their services. They had sent the troops he
had dictated along with the proper tribute, so they followed
the letter of his law but little more.

"What is your plan?" he demanded of them.

The taller of the two stepped forward. "Lord, we feared
that the Egyptians would not succeed. And given the advice
of your . . ." He paused, searching for the correct word to
identify Pandora. "Assistant, we have made preparations."

So Pandora had talked with them and foresaw the destruction of the bridges? Xerxes pondered that as he spoke.
"What kind of preparations?"

"Most wonderful King, we have a convoy of ships and barges less than a day's sailing from here loaded with woven flax cables. They are stronger than the ropes the Egyptians used. And our fleet carries enough for two bridges."

For the Phoenicians to have ships and barges carrying that much cable close by meant this was long in the preparing, Xerxes knew. He glanced at Pandora, her beautiful face expressionless. Plots within plots. She had warned him about the Egyptian bridge, but he had dismissed her concerns. After all, what did a woman know of such things?

"How long will it take to build the bridge once your ships arrive?" Xerxes demanded.

"Three days, Lord."

Xerxes knew this was not a coincidence—just in time for Pandora's four-day prediction for the crossing.

"How much will it cost me?" Xerxes asked.

The sum the Phoenician quoted was outrageous, but Xerxes had no choice. Besides, he planned to take the cost of this entire expedition out of the city-states he captured in Greece. He ordered his paymaster to make the funds available. Then he turned back to the six Egyptians with a cruel smile. "You will live to see another dawn."

And he left them with that cryptic statement, heading toward the imperial tent, Pandora behind him.

. . .

Leonidas pressed the march hard. He knew it would ruin his horse, but there was the knowledge that the Persians would be moving forward, combined with the desire to cause Cyra to fall behind. But the priestess kept up, pushing her own horse just as hard, not complaining about the brutal pace or the many hours in the saddle.

They crested a pass, and he could see the rocky trail ahead of them stretching for miles along the coast. A ship would save them time, but he didn't trust the Athenians, and their ships patrolled the Sea of Corinth. Land was safer.

"Your mother," Leonidas said abruptly.

"Yes?"

"Why is she sending you on this dangerous journey? Aren't you to be the next oracle?"

"The journey is necessary," Cyra said. "And no, I am not to be the next oracle. My daughter is."

"You're married?" Leonidas knew priestesses of Delphi could marry, but he had not sensed that air about her. In Sparta, a woman married young and became the property of her husband. Spartan women were strong, but they carried themselves in a way that indicated they were property. For the briefest of moments, he thought of his own wife and realized he had not considered her or his children at all when he had heard the oracle's forecast of his death. He was more surprised at having this realization than at what it meant.

"No."

Cyra's one-word answer cut through his thoughts and was a greater surprise than the first.

"But you said you had a child—" he began.

"One does not need a husband to have a child," Cyra said.

Leonidas did not respond to that, riding in silence for several minutes. He'd spotted a small cloud of dust ahead when they crested the pass and knew they would shortly meet whoever was heading their way. From the size of the cloud, he estimated four or five riders. Since Sparta was not currently at war with any of the other city-states, he was not overly concerned but more interested in who he would encounter.

The woman bothered him. A child without a husband. A priestess who did not act like one, but rather rode as well as any of his warriors. Her directness, which was most unbecoming for a woman.

Leonidas pulled back on his reins, halting in a grove of olive trees. Cyra came up next to him and also stopped her horse. He waited for her to ask why they had halted, but the minutes passed, and she said nothing, waiting silently.

"There are riders coming this way," he finally said.

"I know. Two Spartans, an Athenian, and a Persian."

Leonidas twisted in the saddle in surprise. "How do you know that?"

"I sensed them coming a long time ago. They seek you."

Leonidas slid off his horse, his right knee almost buckling as he touched the ground. Only a firm grip on the horse's mane kept him from tumbling in the dirt. He shot a quick glance at Cyra, but she seemed not to have noticed. An old wound, the result of a spear thrust by an Athenian, the knee bothered him when it stiffened.

"Since you know so much, tell me what news they bring me." Leonidas tied off his horse on a sapling.

Cyra dismounted and tied her horse off. "Doublespeak, treachery, and manipulation."

Leonidas smiled. "You seem to know politics."

"I know the rules and means of power," Cyra said.

"Still, it is an easy answer for any meeting."

Cyra nodded, acknowledging that. "You want specifics? There is a traitor in the group."

"Traitor to whom?" Leonidas wasn't to be drawn in so easily. "Sparta? Athens? Or is it the Persian?"

"That you will have to determine. I can only sense the aura of betrayal as it comes."

Leonidas could hear the approaching riders. They came around the bend. The lead man wore the red cloak of a Spartiate, followed by a man in the armor of Athens, then a third with the strange attire of a Persian followed by another Spartan.

The two from his own land Leonidas immediately recognized: Eusibius and Loxias. From the finery on the Athen-

ian's armor, Leonidas knew the man to be high ranking. The
Persian was dressed in what Leonidas considered an out-
landish costume: purple, flowing pants; a white shirt with
billowing sleeves underneath his chest armor; his helmet
like a dome, open-faced, revealing dark skin and a pointed
nose, giving him a hatchetlike appearance, accentuated by,
of all things, rouge on the cheeks. The Persians dressed like
dandies, but Leonidas knew better than to judge the man's
fighting qualities by that.

"Hail, travelers!" Leonidas stepped onto the track, causing Eusibius to pull back on his reins in surprise.

"My Lord." Eusibius swung easily from the saddle.
Leonidas studied the young man. Just past twenty, he was
from a good family and had shown bravery in the few battles he had been in. Loxias was a different story. He was
older, in his midthirties, a hardened warrior but one who always seemed to be in the midst of any controversy, whether
it be as large as division of power between the two kings that
ruled Sparta or something as trivial as deciding the fate of an
insolent helot.

Eusibius had taken the Athenian's reins, allowing him to
dismount. "May I introduce Idas of Athens and—" He
paused as the Persian rode past him without allowing him to
take the reins and dismounted, facing the Greeks. "Lord
Jamsheed from the court of Xerxes."

"King Xerxes," Jamsheed corrected as he tied off his
horse.

"King to some," Leonidas said, "not to us."

"Then I suppose I need not address you as king, either,"
Jamsheed said, "since you are not my king."

"You haven't yet," Leonidas noted.

"Gentlemen," Idas's voice was rough, and Leonidas
noted a knotted scar across the front of his throat. "We come
here to talk, not argue."

"I do not argue with words," Leonidas said. He lightly tapped the pommel of his sword. "I argue with this."

"Who is this, My Lord?" Idas nodded toward Cyra, who stood silent in the shadows cast by the trees.

"She's from the oracle at Delphi," Leonidas said.

A cloud passed over Idas's face. "Why is she with you, Lord?"

"I thought I could use some advice," Leonidas said. "And I do not believe it is your place to question me, Idas. This is not Athens, where any can use their tongues with impertinence."

Idas bowed his head a half inch. "My apologies, King."

Leonidas turned to the Persian. "What do you want?"

Jamsheed sat on a log with a flourish of his gold-lined cloak. "I come to seek peace."

"With an army behind you," Leonidas said.

"My king's army comes, whatever you say," Jamsheed said. "It can come in peace or it can come in war. The Ionians have already made peace. Many have even joined us."

Leonidas noted that the Athenian Idas shifted his feet in the dirt. While Sparta was the land muscle of Greece, Athens provided the sea power. And Ionia was across the Aegean, much closer to the Persians than their fellow Greeks. The Ionians had asked for help from their Greek cousins, and Athens had spent months debating, while the Ionians watched Xerxes's massive army come closer, and they ultimately made the sane decision to side with the east over the west rather than be destroyed.

"And . . ." Jamsheed let the word hang in the air for several seconds. "The Thessalians are wavering. Although that might be too impartial a way of putting it. They know they will be the first to bear the brunt of our assault. Emissaries from my king are speaking to them now. We are confident they will listen to reason."

Leonidas was watching the others, noting their reactions.

Loxias's face was inscrutable, something the king was used to. He could see a vein pulsing on the side of Eusibius's face, anger barely kept in check. He knew the young man was like most of his comrades, ready to fight, bleed, and die, rather than submit to the Persians. And Idas, the Athenian, was the most interesting in that he was studying Leonidas rather than focusing on the Persian. Leonidas knew that Idas must have heard all this already from Jamsheed.

"Then why is your king sending his army?" Leonidas asked. "It sounds as if he has already conquered Greece."

Jamsheed laughed. "I have some excellent wine tied off on my saddle. Perhaps you would care to partake, King?"

Before Leonidas could reply, Loxias was at the Persian's horse, untying the strap and carrying a leather flask to the king.

Leonidas took it from Loxias and extended it to the Persian. "You first, my friend."

Jamsheed laughed. "You fear poison?"

"I fear bad wine," Leonidas replied. "It is well known that Persians drink swill from their goats."

Jamsheed flushed in anger. He said nothing. Taking a deep drink, he then offered it back to the king. Leonidas took a drink, then turned and offered it to Cyra, to the astonishment of all the other men. The priestess nodded her head in thanks and drank deeply before passing it on to Eusibius. The young warrior was confused, glanced at his king, then drank, before passing it on to Loxias.

"Not as good as what we produce in Sparta," Leonidas noted.

"We?" Jamsheed repeated. "With all due respect, King, you produce nothing. Your slaves produce everything. I understand there are five male slaves for every Spartiate male."

"We don't have slaves," Eusibius said.

"Your helots then," Jamsheed corrected, indicating he

knew something of the way things were in Sparta. "The ratio is five to one, is it not?"

Leonidas didn't rise to the bait. A helot rebellion was something every Spartiate feared and one of the major reasons for keeping such a fiercely trained standing army. It was hard sometimes to figure which had begot which: the helot power allowing the freeborn men to train all the time, or the need to train all the time to keep the helots in shackles. It was a precarious balance, unique in Greece.

"What do you offer us?" Loxias asked Jamsheed.

Leonidas didn't hesitate. He was on his feet in a flash, his sword drawn. He slammed it into Loxias's right side, where the armor was weakest at the joint, punching through. Leonidas couldn't tell if the shocked look on Loxias's face was from the steel piercing his vitals or the unexpected attack. It didn't matter, because the look was gone, replaced by the slackness of death as Loxias collapsed in the dirt, blood seeping out. Leonidas removed his sword, wiped the blade on the pale skin on Loxias's face, leaving broad red marks, a harsher imitation of the rouge on Jamsheed's cheeks. Then Leonidas removed the scarlet cloak from the body.

No one else had moved throughout the action. Jamsheed's face was inscrutable. Eusibius was surprised but motionless. Idas was shaking his head ever so slightly. And Leonidas felt Cyra's eyes on him as if a red-hot blaze were in the center of his back.

"I am king. I do not know what this"—he kicked Loxias's body with his sandal—"told you, or offered you, but he is food for worms now. He does not, did not ever, speak for Sparta."

Jamsheed took another draft of wine. "I knew that. But he got me here to speak to one who does speak for Sparta."

Leonidas's hand was tight on the pommel of the sword, knuckles white. He faced the Persian. Jamsheed slowly lowered the wine and stood. He took an unconscious step back. "I am an envoy."

"Then act like one." Leonidas finally sheathed his sword. "Do not try to manipulate my people against me."

Jamsheed sat back down. "I did not have to say much to him. What he did, he did on his own. I understand you are not the only Spartan king, that another rules along with you."

Even Leonidas wasn't certain when his ancestors had decided to go the unique route of having two kings instead of the more traditional one. It made sense, though, in two important aspects: The two kings acted as a check against each other; and it allowed one king to lead an army away from home, while leaving a king behind to rule.

Leonidas wanted some of the wine to take away the bad taste in his mouth, but he didn't want to ask the Persian for the flask. "Then why didn't you go see him?"

"Because I have been informed that if there is to be war, you will be the one leading the Spartans in the field while he remains in Sparta. Therefore, you have more at stake."

Leonidas wanted to laugh. "I have been told by the Delphic oracle that I am to die in battle soon. That gives you little leverage with whatever you think I might have at stake."

Jamsheed was quiet for a moment as he mulled this over, and Idas took the opportunity to speak. "Xerxes—King Xerxes"—he amended at Jamsheed's look—"has already had an advance force dig a canal through the Mount Athos peninsula, so there will be no repeat of the storm that saved Greece last time. And he is bridging the Hellesponte so his army can cross. He had been preparing this assault ever since taking the crown. His greatest desire is to avenge our victory at Marathon.

"The construction of the bridge," Idas continued, "is why we could not sally forth with our fleet and keep the Persians from entering Europe."

A new voice surprised the men. "The bridge was destroyed yesterday in a storm." Cyra took several steps forward.

"How do you know that?" Idas demanded.

"I saw it in a vision," she replied.

Jamsheed laughed. "Are you an oracle also?"

"I am the daughter of the Delphic oracle," Cyra said. "I have the gift of sight beyond what my eyes can see."

"The inner eye," Jamsheed nodded. "My king has someone like you."

"Pandora."

Cyra's mention of that name brought a start of surprise from the Persian. "How do you know your vision of the bridge being destroyed was a true one?" he asked, as he looked at the woman anew.

"It was true," Cyra said. "But do not fear; Pandora has already helped your king with a new plan to bridge the strait." She turned to Leonidas. "Xerxes's army will be across the Hellesponte in four days."

Leonidas knew the distances involved. The Persians still had a long way to march, even when they were across the strait. And an army as large as his would move slower than a smaller, more disciplined force. "What do you want to say to me?" he asked Jamsheed, tired of the politics, his mind already on the coming battles.

As if sensing his disinterest, Jamsheed was to the point. "I am here—and he—" he added, indicating Idas, "because my king does not wish to wait while your two cities play local games. The great and generous King Xerxes will spare both your cities if you agree not to raise arms against him. Both Athens and Sparta must agree, and they will be spared destruction."

"And the other cities?" Leonidas already knew the answer, but he asked anyway.

"They are my king's to do with as he will."

"And if one of us agrees, but the other doesn't?" Leonidas asked.

"Unacceptable. With all due respect, my king does not wish to be deceived or double-crossed. Both cities will be neutral, or both will be destroyed."

Leonidas didn't believe the Persian. He saw no reason why Xerxes would be willing to let Sparta, the leading ground power in Greece, and Athens, the leading naval power, remain intact. He saw this as a ploy to get both cities to remain neutral while he dispatched the rest of Greece with ease; then he would turn his full might against Athens and Sparta when they could gather no allies.

"Then I determine the fate not only of Sparta but Athens also?" Leonidas mused. He saw the real reason for this ploy: to drive a wedge between the two cities. Idas would not be here with the Persian if the elders of Athens were not seriously considering agreeing to Xerxes's truce. And knowing that Sparta would never agree to such a thing, Xerxes was making enemies of the two leading powers in Greece. It was a shrewd maneuver that cost the Persian nothing and could destroy any hope of a consolidated Greek front against him.

Leonidas turned to Idas. "You know Xerxes lies, don't you?"

"Perhaps we should talk privately," the Athenian suggested.

"No. I will soon have Persian blood on my sword, so I do not care what he hears or thinks. Sparta will never accept this proposal. So this meeting is over."

Idas's face grew red, and he began to say something, but he was interrupted by Cyra. "The east versus the west." She looked from Leonidas to Jamsheed as she spoke. "The entire future of the world lies in balance. In more ways than any of you can imagine." She walked up to the Persian and put her hands on his shoulders, peering deep into his dark eyes. "Go back to your king. Tell him to weigh carefully the words of

Pandora. Very carefully. Tell him she does not speak for Persia, nor for Greece. He must try to find out where her true allegiance lies."

Leonidas was already in the saddle. He leaned over close to the Persian as he passed. "The next time we meet, I won't be so friendly. Tell your king that he will not conquer Greece unless he does so over the body of every single Spartan."

"So be it," Jamsheed said.

Leonidas rode off. He heard a horse behind him and glanced over his shoulder. Cyra was there. And he noted Eusibius and Idas hurrying to catch up. There was no sign of the Persian. Leonidas was surprised that the Athenian had left the emissary, and he slowed his horse.

"My Lord," Idas was breathing hard.

"Yes?"

"It is more than just losing Ionia and Thessalia," Idas said.

Leonidas rode in silence, waiting.

"There is a threat from the rear," Idas said.

"Antirhon," Leonidas said. It was a city on the western end of the Gulf of Corinth, commanding the northern end of the narrow entrance to the inner sea.

Idas was surprised. "Yes, My Lord."

Leonidas gave a short laugh. "They have been looking for an opportunity to cross the Gulf and take Rhion." The latter was a city across the Gulf from Antirhon on a southern spur and an ally of Sparta. The two cities had been enemies as long as anyone could remember, engaged in a standoff across the narrow strait. As long as Sparta was allied with Rhion, there was little that Antirhon could do.

"If Rhion falls to the Antirhonians," Idas continued, "then the Gulf will be open to the Persian fleet."

Leonidas resented the Athenian telling him something even a twelve-year-old Spartan knew. Holding Thermopylae to the north would be worthless if Xerxes could swing around and attack from the west.

"Will your city send its fleet to stop the Antirhonians?" Leonidas asked, although he knew what answer to expect.

"If we do that, we would be open to the sea from the east," Idas said.

"So, once more, Sparta must take the lead," Leonidas said.

"Unless we negotiate with the Persians," Idas said.

"You have had my answer on that." Leonidas spurred his horse and galloped away, leaving the Athenian in a cloud of dust as Cyra and Eusibius hurried to keep up with him.

5

The Present

"We're not ready to go into the space between via the Devil's Sea gate," Dane said. "We'd be stumbling around without a clue where to go or what to do if we do figure out where to go."

"We don't have much time," Foreman argued. The two were sitting at the conference table in the control center. The Navy had wanted to pull the FLIP back away from the gate, given the recent attack, but Foreman had overridden them.

"We're ignoring too many things," Dane said.

"Like what?" Foreman demanded. He was looking at new pictures of the Nazca plain just downlinked from a KH-14 spy satellite.

"The crystal skulls that Ariana collected. They're still in Antarctica with her gear. And there's Sin Fen's skull in the Bermuda Triangle gate on top of the pyramid, along with the Naga staff. The skulls channel power, and the staff is the most effective weapon we have against the Valkyries, given that our modern weapons won't work in the space between."

Dane pointed at the imagery of the power being drawn to the Nazca plain. "And I think we need to figure out what that's about before we go forward. We can't tell from the imagery if there is a gate there. Nagoya thought there is and that it's underground. But if I were on the ground, I could feel a gate.

"The Shadow is taking action, and we need to cover our rear before we try going forward. We have a couple of days before the situation goes critical. I think a day or two of preparation is better than going into the Devil's Sea gate half-assed." He had a thermal image and was impressed with the sharply defined lines, as if the heat were contained. Then his eyes noted something. He passed the image to Foreman, tapping a small red dot with his finger. "There's someone on the plain. Right in the middle of all the activity."

• • •

Just thirty feet away in her cabin, Dr. Martsen was unaware of Ahana's dire pronouncement and calculations for the end of the known world.

Dr. Renee Martsen had worked with dolphins for over twenty years, ever since her time as a grad student at the University of Hawaii. She found in them the acceptance she had never realized among humans. The fact that her research into dolphin linguistics for the past fifteen years had been funded by the U.S. Navy she viewed as a necessary evil.

She sat in her cabin playing the recording that had been forwarded from the *Connecticut* over and over. Foreman had given it to her with the vague instruction to "make something of this" and then hurried back to his control center and his muonic monitors. Since arriving at the Devil's Sea, Martsen had noted how there was much more focus on machines than mammals.

Martsen had loaded the sound into her laptop, then

played it. She had no doubt that there were dolphin voices, but there were other noises in the background. She had sophisticated acoustic software loaded into her hard drive, as her primary focus of research was trying to decipher how dolphins communicated. There were many who said there was no logic or sense to the sounds that dolphins made, but Martsen was convinced otherwise.

Her primary argument had been simple; she could send and receive messages to and from Rachel, a bottle-nosed dolphin she had been working with for over seven years. However, recent events had caused her some doubt. Dane had claimed to have a telepathic connection with Rachel, which meant that perhaps the sounds did indeed mean nothing and Rachel was simply picking up and sending messages in a form that couldn't be recorded but could be felt.

The computer beeped, the latest program having finished running. It had separated the different tracks, which took quite a while, since she had determined there were over sixty different sound emitters on the tape. She hit the Enter key, and the first one began playing—definitely a dolphin.

She shifted that track to her translator, no longer certain that her minuscule dolphin vocabulary was actually that. She moved on to the second track and continued the process until she hit the ninth track. At first she had no idea what the noise was; then her blood froze as she realized what she was listening to.

A human throat producing a scream of unimaginable agony.

She was so shocked by the scream that she simply sat there for several minutes. Then she regrouped and checked the computer. The first dolphin track had played through. The result was disappointing. Just a few potential words among hundreds.

Then it occurred to her; whether she was right or wrong about there being a dolphin language, there was no doubt that Rachel could communicate. She grabbed the recording and her translator. She left her cabin, heading for the deck.

She climbed down a ladder to the small docking bay on the side of the FLIP and dropped the waterproof mike and speaker into the water. She hit the button on her controller to send the message that summoned Rachel. In less than thirty seconds, she saw the dolphin's dorsal fin cutting through the water, heading toward the ship.

"Good girl," Martsen whispered as Rachel's nose poked above the surface of the water, the dark eyes regarding her.

Martsen hit the Start button, and the dolphin tracks began playing. Within seconds, Rachel began to show agitation, her powerful tail propelling her up, out of the water. She arched back, slamming into the surface, showering Martsen with water.

Martsen had to pull the headphones off as Rachel shot a powerful series of clicks from her blowhole, radiated through her forehead into the water. Martsen's fingers shook as she accessed the database and a series of words scrolled across the screen:

> END—THIS—WORLD—NOW—
> ONLY—CHANCE—
> CHANGE—PATH—POWER—
> GET—MAP

Then Rachel dove out of sight.

• • •

Foreman finally tore his gaze from the picture of the Nazca plain. "What do you suggest?"

Dane felt as if he were playing a game of chess, but much of the board was blocked off from his sight. He could only see a move or two ahead at best, and he had no idea what reaction would come from those moves. He also knew that—

despite what Foreman believed—there were other pieces on the board on his side and that he just hadn't met them yet. "I think at the very least, we need to recover Sin Fen's skull and the Naga staff and get the skulls that Ariana collected."

Foreman seemed relieved to be able to order something within his capabilities. "All right. I can arrange that." He pulled out his phone, then paused. "There's something I should have given you."

Dane waited, but Foreman didn't continue. Dane sensed confusion and embarrassment from the CIA man, something that he had never picked up from him before.

"Sin Fen," Foreman finally said.

There was sorrow coming off Foreman, a thin layer covering a deep pool of a lifetime of pain.

"Yes?" Dane asked quietly.

"She left you something. A tape." Foreman opened a drawer and pulled out a bulky, sealed manila envelope and handed it to Dane.

He ripped it open, and a videocassette fell out into his hands. "You didn't watch it?" Dane asked.

A flash of anger crossed Foreman's face. "I know what you think of me. Yes, I thought about it. I've been thinking about it ever since we lost her, and I found it in her gear. It's been there"—he slapped the desk hard, drawing unwanted attention from others in the control room—"all this time."

"Why didn't you give it to me before?" Dane asked. "It could hold important information."

"Sin Fen wouldn't have held back information that could have helped us," Foreman said.

"Then why not—" Dane paused as he realized why the old man hadn't handed it over: jealousy, something Foreman would never admit to. Sin Fen had been like a daughter to him, and she had left a tape for Dane, a newcomer in her life, rather than Foreman, who had rescued her from the streets of Phnom Penh. Dane nodded. "It took you a while to come clean."

Foreman's reply was interrupted by Dr. Marsten's excited entry into the control center. She bounded over to the table and slapped down a single piece of paper with eleven words written on it in front of Dane. "That's the translation of part of the dolphin message that the *Connecticut* picked up."

Dane read it, then passed it to Foreman. "We know we have to stop the power drain, but what is this map?" he asked.

Ahana came over and read over the CIA man's shoulder.

"I don't know," Marsten said. "There's more to the tape, but that's the first thing Rachel translated."

"Nazca's the key," Dane said. "Maybe those designs on the plain are a map of something. We need to get this person," he tapped the small dot.

"That person," Ahana said, "is probably Dr. Leni Reizer, a German woman who is considered the expert on the Nazca plain. I did an Internet search, and her name was constantly mentioned. And she lives right next to it."

"I need to go there," Dane said.

Foreman nodded. "All right. I'll arrange transportation."

He turned on his SATPhone. Dane handed the translation back to Marsten. "You get any more done, please forward it to me."

"I'll do that."

Dane left the control room and went to his bunk room. Chelsea was waiting inside. Her tail thumped against the wall as she greeted him.

"Hey, big girl." Dane leaned over and scratched behind her ears. He felt the comfort that the golden retriever always projected, but the tape was heavy in his hands.

A small TV with a built-in VCR was bolted above the desk. Dane slid the video into the machine and pushed Play.

The screen went blue, then Sin Fen's exotic Eurasian face

appeared. Dane took a step back, remembering the last time he had seen her, her head changing into crystal, focusing the power of the pyramid in the Bermuda Triangle and shutting the gate there.

"Eric," she said. "I never called you by your first name, and I imagine I haven't since I made this. I am sorry I lied to you about some things, but it was necessary." She held up a hand in front of the camera as if forestalling a response. "Yes, that is the excuse Foreman uses, isn't it?" The hand lowered. "If you are watching this, then I am no longer with you. But do not think I am gone. If you are watching this, it means I succeeded. And you—and the world—are safe for the moment. But my role—the role of the oracles and priestesses—is defensive. And that can only work so long."

Dane realized he had stopped breathing and that there were tears flowing down his cheeks. Chelsea whined, her tail smacking against his legs. "Easy," Dane whispered. "Easy, girl."

Sin Fen continued. "You are the one who has to change things. From Atlantis forward, the oracles and priestesses— the Defenders, of which I was one—have always been women. We have used warriors to help us in the fight and to keep the line alive.

"But from the first, the very beginning, there was a prophecy that there would be a man who would be a warrior and an oracle. A Defender who will be more than that. Who would be the one to bring many paths together. I believe you are that man."

Dane took another step back, hitting the bunk with his legs and dropping to a sitting position.

Sin Fen tapped her head. "I told you some of how your mind is different. Left brain, right brain. Redundant. Except for the areas of speech. Broca's area, which in ninety-seven percent of all humans is controlled by the left side of the brain. And Broca's area on the right side? Dormant. Unused.

And smaller. Except in a small percentage of the population again. So combine the two exceptions, and you have less than a thousandth of one percent of the human population. People like you and me."

"Why are we different?" Dane whispered.

"I was only told so much," Sin Fen said. "That is wrong. I know that now." Her face shifted, a perplexed look crossing it, something Dane had never seen in the short time he knew her. "Or maybe I am wrong. Maybe there is a valid reason why I was not told things. But I have told you all I know. I believe you are the one who is to take the fight to the Shadow. I don't know how. I don't know what you are to do. But you do.

"There is something else. The mind is powerful, more powerful than we ever realized. And your mind, and mine, they are different. But if enough normal minds are gathered together at a certain mental and emotional pitch, it can also affect the world around us."

She closed her eyes. "I wish I was with you to help. I truly do. Trust the voice. It is from the gods." Her eyes opened. "I think there are other oracles like me in the world. You might find help where you least expect it."

The tape froze with the image of Sin Fen on it.

Dane stood and reached forward, touching the screen. "Who are we?" He was startled by the sound of a light knock on his cabin door. "Who is it?"

"Ahana."

Dane opened the door, his mind still on Sin Fen. The Japanese woman entered the cabin, glancing at the image on the screen. "A friend?"

"Yes."

Ahana clasped her hands in front of her. "I do not wish to disturb you." She edged toward the door.

"It's OK," Dane said. He indicated the chair in front of the desk. "Please. Sit."

"I do not wish to disturb—" Ahana stopped herself and gave an embarrassed laugh.

Dane reached over and turned off the TV. "What is it?"

"Mr. Foreman," Ahana began, then seemed to search for words. "He is a—" She said something in Japanese, then tried to clarify. "A man who works in an office for the government."

"A bureaucrat?"

She nodded. "Yes, that is the word. You, on the other hand, are a soldier."

"I was a soldier."

"Once you have served, it is always part of you. My father was a bureaucrat. My grandfather a soldier. I know."

Dane waited.

"The Shadow," she finally said, her head lowered.

"Yes?"

"It is our enemy."

Dane wasn't sure whether it was a question or statement. "Yes."

"I told you my grandfather was a soldier. In the Second World War." She lifted her head, and her dark eyes met his. "He followed orders. He fought the Chinese. He was at Nanking and followed orders."

Dane remained still. He knew of the Rape of Nanking. The winter of 1937–1938, when the Japanese sacked the Chinese city. Almost 400,000 Chinese were slaughtered after the city surrendered. Women and children raped and murdered. And the Japanese government to this day had never acknowledged that it occurred.

"He never spoke of what happened in China. I never knew until I found his journal. What he wrote about what he saw there in China. How he knew he—and Japan—were doomed from then forward. How they would never win the war. Yet he still fought. It was his duty and his honor bound him. But his heart was never in it. His spirit was wounded, crippled in China and never recovered.

"I have never spoken of this to anyone, not even Professor Nagoya—" She paused, tears welling in her eyes.

Dane took her hands in his. He wasn't sure what to say.

"Reading my grandfather's words, I came to know him. More than I ever knew my father, who was so ashamed of his own father."

Dane, who had never known his parents and had grown up in orphanages, squeezed her hands, feeling the smallness of them inside his own.

"My grandfather never turned on his duty as a soldier. On the oaths he swore. But—" Again, she seemed to search for the correct English. "He realized the choice of enemies, the war, was wrong. The Chinese, the Australians, the Americans, posed no real threat to his home, to his country, that he had sworn to defend."

Dane nodded. "I fought in Vietnam."

Ahana squeezed his hands in return. "So you understand what he felt?"

"Yes."

"What I am trying to say is that the Shadow is different. It is a threat to mankind. To all nations. I sometimes see the way you respond to Foreman, and I can tell your heart is not in this, in the things we do. But it must be. This is a good war, if there ever was a good war."

There was a rap on the cabin door, and Foreman stuck his head in. "Chopper's here to take you to the carrier. From there you'll go by F-16 to Bogota, where you'll be transferred to a Combat Talon." The CIA man's eyes were shifting between Dane and Ahana as if he were trying to interpret what had been talked about.

Dane stood. He put a hand on the slight Japanese woman's shoulder. "Take care of Chelsea for me, would you?"

Ahana nodded.

A good war, Dane mused as he threw his rucksack over his shoulder and left the cabin, following Foreman. For the first time since he had been contacted by Foreman's agent to go into the Angkor gate, there was a slight bounce in Dane's stride as he headed toward the waiting helicopter.

The Space Between

Amelia Earhart held the water bottle to Fred Noonan's parched lips and impatiently waited while he drank. He'd regained consciousness just a few moments ago and tried to speak, but he only managed an unintelligible rasp. Water poured down the sides of his face over blistered skin unnoticed as he drained the bottle. While she waited, Earhart thought back to the forced landing she'd made in the Pacific. There was no doubt that she had seen him killed, a tentacle from a kraken punching through his body from front to rear, lifting him off the wing of the Electra and down into the water. Without thinking, her hand strayed to his chest, feeling for some sort of wound, but the skin was smooth and unmarked. Perhaps by some miracle he had survived the attack. She halted that thinking. She had seen what she had seen.

She pulled the bottle from his lips. "Fred."

Noonan nodded. "I was hoping to find you here."

"I don't understand. Where did you come from? How did you survive? I saw you—"

He weakly held up a hand, stopping the onslaught of questions. "I don't have much time. I'm dying. I came unprotected through a hot portal."

"Why did—"

He waved the hand slightly. "Listen. There is something you must do. A task." He stopped speaking as he began a terrible, deep coughing.

Earhart glanced up at Taki, the leader of the samurai. She had been here long enough to learn enough of their language to communicate. *"Where did you find him?"*

Taki pointed back over his shoulder. *"The shore."*

Earhart had expected that. It was where they found most of the castaways. *"Any debris?"* It was how they got their scant supplies, and even though she knew that Taki and his men would have brought anything they found back, she found she couldn't help asking. There might even have been something from the plane.

"Nothing. The black—" He gestured with his hands, indicating a cylinder, and Earhart knew he was talking about a portal—*"is still there. Close to shore. A new one that was not there last time we looked."*

Noonan stopped coughing. Earhart tenderly wiped a trickle of blood from his chin and was surprised when he smiled. "You've changed," he said.

"What is this task?" Earhart was surprised by his comment.

"You must capture a Valkyrie. And remove its suit."

"And?"

"And someone will come for it. Someone—" Noonan began coughing, his body wracked with pain. Earhart could feel the strength of the coughs, as if he were trying to expel something from his body.

She leaned close. "Fred. Where did you come from?"

"A place like this," he said. "The space between. That's what we call it. I volunteered to come. When they told me." His eyelids slid down, and he appeared to be unconscious.

Earhart shook him slightly. "Fred. Who? Who told you? What did they tell you?"

His eyes flickered open. "The Ones Before. They're trying to save your world." He coughed several times. "Get the suit. And wait."

"How do we kill a Valkyrie?" Earhart asked. "We don't have a Naga staff."

"The eyes are weak."

Earhart knew that. "Even disabling the eyes doesn't stop them. They just retreat."

"A Naga staff will come. Watch for it. Then use it."

"How do you know this?"

Noonan's voice had dropped to a whisper. "The Ones Before. They will try. Have tried." His eyes closed. His lips moved, and his voice was so low, Earhart had to put her ear next to his mouth to hear his next words. "They have been trying for a long, long time to save the world."

Noonan was so still that for a moment Earhart thought him dead. But she felt a slight exhale on her cheek as she held her head close to his. She straightened and slid a blanket over Noonan's chest.

"What now?" Taki asked.

"The Valkyries are still in their lab?" Earhart asked.

Taki shrugged. *"The last time we looked they were."*

She pointed down at her navigator. *"He said we must get the armor suit from one of them."*

Taki nodded as if that made perfect sense. *"We can go look."*

6

480 B.C.

The Phoenician ships and barges were beached just south of the bridging point. Soldiers and slaves worked together to off-load the lengths of intricately woven plant material. The first length was tied off the near anchor point and the first ship position. A second length of flax reinforced the first. A second anchor point had been dug during the night while they waited for the barges, and two large trees were already in place.

As a second boat was moved into position and planks were laid from the first, Xerxes raised his hand, halting work. He signaled to his master-at-arms, and the six Egyptian engineers whose bridge had been destroyed were brought forward. The master-at-arms and several Immortals hustled the confused engineers onto the planks. The confusion changed to terror as each man was tied in place between the first two lengths of flax roping, one across their back, one across their chests.

Xerxes then signaled for work to continue, savoring the

desperate cries of the trapped men. More ropes were tied in to the anchor point until only the Egyptians' feet and heads were visible, the rest of their body cocooned with strands of flax extending outward from the shore pylons. As more boats were added, and additional lengths were tied in to the end, the pressure increased.

The screams of the trapped men became muted as the ropes across their chests restricted their breathing to the point where they couldn't cry out. Every man working on the bridge had to walk past the trapped engineers, which was exactly what Xerxes had in mind. It certainly gave them a focus on their tasks.

With a crackling noise clearly heard even above the chants of the slaves hauling on ropes, the first engineer's chest gave way, and blood poured out of his mouth, covering the ropes across his front. One by one, the rest died, dyeing the flax red and leaving their heads dangling over the top of the cable.

Boat by boat, the two bridges began extending across the strait. And on the eastern shoreline, Xerxes sat on his throne and watched. And behind him, just to the right, stood Pandora.

• • •

"I do not approve," Leonidas said.

"Of?" Cyra asked.

Dusk was falling, and Leonidas was still pressing the pace, wanting to get some more miles behind them before halting for the night. He had sent Eusibius ahead as a scout. He had not seen Idas nor the Persian Jamsheed since his last conversation with both. He assumed the Athenian was headed for the coast to take a ship back to his city. As far as the Persian, Leonidas figured he would be heading north to link up with his king's army.

"Having a child without a husband."

Cyra laughed, causing a flush of blood to the king's face. "What is so funny?"

"That I would care about your approval."

They rode in silence for several minutes. "I suppose things are different in Delphi," the king finally allowed.

"Most open-minded of you, Lord."

Leonidas gritted his teeth, and they rode for another mile. "Do you have family?" Cyra asked.

"I have a son," Leonidas said proudly.

"His name?"

"Amphion."

"And your wife?"

Leonidas smiled. "Thetis."

"Just one child?"

"We have a daughter also."

"I am not surprised you only mentioned your son. Spartans do not think much of girls, do they?"

"They are necessary," Leonidas allowed.

"Your mother was a girl once. Aren't you fortunate she was valued?"

"Women . . ." Leonidas began.

"Yes?"

"They are good for some things. To keep the home. To bring forth the children. And, yes, to be priestesses and oracles, although we do not have such things in Sparta."

"Do you think Spartan women think like that?"

"Of course."

"You may be a very smart commander of men, My Lord," Cyra said, "but you know nothing of a woman's heart or mind."

Leonidas pulled back on his reins and came to a halt. "What are you talking about?"

Cyra also stopped. She pulled a dagger out from somewhere in the folds of her robes. She held it against the wrist of the other hand. "If I am cut, do I bleed the same as you?"

Leonidas's forehead wrinkled. "Yes."

She leaped off her horse, throwing her long cloak to the side. She was dressed in leather pants and a sleeveless jerkin. She spread her legs shoulder width apart, left forward. The point of the dagger was toward the king.

"What are you doing?" Leonidas leaned back in the saddle, amused.

"Fight me."

"I would not fight a woman."

"You are old," Cyra said. "An old man who has to hold on to his saddle to get off his horse or his leg will not hold him."

The smile was gone from Leonidas's face.

Cyra slapped her chest. "I wear no armor. I don't even have that pig-sticker you carry at your waist, your sword that is so feared. All I have is this leather and a puny dagger. And . . ." She drew the word out. "You are a Spartan. The king of the Spartans. The most feared warriors in the world. I am just a priestess."

Leonidas shook his head. "I will not be provoked."

"I'm not trying to provoke you," Cyra said. "I am trying to teach you something. You have trained for warfare almost all your life. Do you think you know everything? That you cannot learn something new? You will soon be in the battle of your life. Perhaps I could teach you a thing or two that might help."

Leonidas slowly got off the horse, his hands clear of the saddle. He turned toward Cyra. "What can you teach me, Priestess?"

"I can only show. What is learned depends on the student."

Leonidas cocked his head. "My first teacher in the agoge told me that. Polynices. He was a fine warrior."

"So you should not fear me," Cyra said. She moved forward and slashed. Leonidas jumped back, her blade missing by a few inches, his hand instinctively drawing his sword. He was moving forward, a jab with the point, followed immediately by the second strike he had been drilled in, an upper thrust toward her solar plexus.

But she wasn't there, spinning gracefully out of the way. She clamped down on his sword arm, pinning it against her side. Leonidas was surprised at the unexpected move and pulled back when he felt steel against his throat, between chest armor and helmet. His eyes rotated down. Her knife was against his skin.

Very, very slowly, Cyra pulled back the knife and released his sword arm. She sheathed the blade and picked up her cloak. She threw it over her shoulders. Leonidas had not moved, standing as if carved in stone. Cyra mounted her horse and rode off, leaving the king standing alone.

• • •

The weather on either side of the pass was fine, but storm clouds hovered unnaturally on Mount Oeta, extending down to the Gates of Fire. Lightning split the air, and peals of thunder echoed out over the Aegean.

The sphere of black appeared, hovering a foot above the ground. A lightning bolt hit it, and the darkness absorbed the strike, sucking in the power, conquering the force of nature in a blink.

Several seconds later, a man staggered out of the sphere, his skin red and blistered, whatever he had been wearing seared away. His head turned back and forth, as if he were searching, but his eyes had been burned and were blind. In his right hand he held a curved, thin sword, the metal bright and unmarked by whatever had destroyed his body. Two arrows poked out of his back, the wood blackened.

He yelled, the sound unintelligible, and swung the blade as if he were surrounded by enemies. His movements showed training and skill, despite his agony. His feet moved as he backed up. He jabbed with the sword, slashed, and backed up further.

Then his rear foot went over the edge of the cliff. He tried to regain his balance to no avail. He fell over, tumbling down toward the sea-ravaged rocks below, all without a cry issuing from his lips.

The body slammed into a rock, rolled down into the surf, and disappeared.

In the Gates of Fire, the black sphere coalesced on itself until it was a dot and then disappeared.

7

The Present

Reizer had never been so tired. She'd rationed her water bottle, but it was empty now. She knew dawn wasn't far off, but it was hard to tell, as her eyes were numbed from the fierce red glow of the fire walls that surrounded her. She was so tired that she worried she would make a wrong turn. As near as she could figure, she was halfway out of the plain, but it had been a circuitous journey, going along lines, circling around flaming figures. Twice she had chosen wrong and ended up at a dead end, her way barred by high walls of fire. She'd noted that the wall was higher along the straight lines and wedges, lower on the figure lines.

She passed around the end of the tail of the monkey and saw a straight line of fire in front of her. She felt despair, realizing that although she had walked almost the entire night, she had moved just slightly over a mile from where she had started. She estimated she had walked over seven times that.

She turned about in a circle, confirming her location,

knowing she didn't have the energy to continue on after another mistake. Her eyes widened as she realized where she was: near the base of the main line, where it met the wedge. And the flame was different here, darker in color, a scarlet red. Higher. Three times as high. And there was a blackness in the center of the flame in the wedge, a dark circle that ate the light and drew in the nearby flame, consuming it.

Reizer staggered as her eyes were mesmerized, trapped by the darkness. She felt as if her soul were being ripped out of her body. She had no idea what was in that darkness, but she feared as she had feared nothing before, not even when she'd been in Berlin when the Russians overran it. She had always thought that had been hell on Earth, but looking at the black sphere, she sensed an evil inside of it that transcended even that nightmare.

She took another step backward, unknowingly closer to the wall of fire behind her. Then another. Her subconscious could feel the heat, but her aware mind could only be repelled by the sheer evil of that dark hole.

She stopped, then took a step forward. And another. She was being drawn against her will toward the darkness.

• • •

"There," Dane pointed at the small, glowing dot on the thermal imager of the Combat Talon, almost lost among the overwhelming glow of the fiery images.

"What?" The targeting officer was mesmerized by the numerous patterns displayed on a scale never before seen.

"There she is," Dane said.

"We need to save her."

"Who?" the targeting officer repeated. The dot had disappeared, and Dane wondered for a moment if he'd really seen it.

Dane had flown from the Devil's Sea to Hawaii in the

backseat of a Navy F-16. Then he'd been transferred to one of the few remaining SR-71 Blackbirds and crammed in behind the pilot on a supersonic flight to Lima. He'd been met there by the Combat Talon, which had been sent from antidrug missions in Colombia to meet him there on landing.

The MG-130 Talon is based on the airframe of the venerable Hercules C-130 cargo plane. It has four engines and a wide, stubby body like the C-130, but it has been extensively upgraded. Four Allison T56-A-15 turboprop engines power the plane with each producing almost 5,000 horsepower of thrust. The true key to the plane is the sophisticated electronics, which allow it to fly in all weather at low altitude. The pilots can use terrain-following and terrain-avoidance radar, allowing it to fly "on the deck" at high speeds, avoiding both obstacles and enemy radar.

The plane also has a contraption called the Fulton Recovery System. Two steel whiskers extend out from the bottom of the nose of the plane. Their purpose is to snatch a steel cable attached to a balloon on one end and a person on the ground on the other. The cable is snagged, then reeled in, recovering the person from the ground.

Right now, the Talon was at 5,000 feet and had just gone "feet dry" over the coast of Peru. As Dane had crossed the Pacific eastward, he'd felt both pulled and repulsed. He knew there was evil ahead, but he also sensed inside the evil a person in need. It reminded him of all the search and rescue missions he and Chelsea had been on. When disaster, usually the result of human stupidity, occurred, he and Chelsea had been called in to find those who had survived.

Dane clicked the Transmit button on the headset he wore. "Do another flyover of Nazca. Thermal imaging. I'm sure there's somebody down there."

He made his way to the cockpit, climbing up the few

steps and looking over the shoulder of the navigator at his display. They'd all seen the satellite imagery of the burning lines, so it was no surprise as the imaging screen showed them once more, bright red lines and shapes covering the plain 5,000 feet below.

"Hard to find a person's image among all that," the navigator said. He fine-tuned the display as he spoke. "Funny thing is, those flame lines are very hot, but they're not giving off much sideways heat. Almost as if they're being contained. I've never seen anything like it."

Dane still felt strongly that there was a survivor below, even though he had no idea what the lines of fire displayed represented.

"Any image at body temp?" he asked.

"I'm going to fade out the temperature range for the lines," the navigator said.

Dane clutched the handrail, and the plane banked. The pilots were now settling into a racetrack, circling the Nazca plain.

The lines slowly disappeared, and all that was left was one tiny orange dot. "There's your person."

Dane took another step up into the cockpit to get the attention of the pilot in command. "Here's the plan."

• • •

Reizer focused the small percentage of her brain she still had conscious control of into stopping her slow movement forward. For a moment, her body came to a halt. But then, like an alcoholic who'd been dry for days and was offered a drink, her left foot shuffled forward toward the darkness.

There was a strange noise above her, one she couldn't immediately place; then she realized it was a plane.

But then her right foot moved forward.

• • •

Dane stood, pressing a hand against the headset. "Open the back ramp."

"You're crazy!" was the response from the loadmaster.

Dane tugged on both leg straps, making sure the parachute was tight to his body as he headed toward the rear of the plane. "Open the goddamn ramp."

Dane threw the headset to the floor and waited. He was rewarded with a swirl of air coming into the cargo bay as a crack opened between the back ramp and the top of the rear as it began to recess into the tail section.

The crew chief was maneuvering a bundle in a torpedo-shaped plastic case onto the ramp, attached to a steel cable with a static line. Dane attached his own static line just behind the bundle's. The ramp locked down level. The night sky, strange looking with the red glow from below, beckoned. They were low now, just below 500 feet, to insure better accuracy. Dane didn't have a reserve, because if the main didn't open, there wouldn't be time to deploy a second.

Dane didn't want to jump. He'd done hundreds of parachute jumps in the Special Forces. That wasn't the issue. The danger and evil below was what repelled him.

But he could feel the old woman, lost, drawn into the darkness.

The light turned green, and he followed the bundle off the ramp. His feet met air, and he free-fell for three seconds, then the static line deployed the chute, jerking him abruptly. He caught a glimpse of the bundle's chute ahead and below, then saw he was headed toward one of the lines of fire. His hands grappled with the toggles on the front risers, trying to turn. The chute gave way reluctantly.

Three seconds after the chute opened, Dane was less than fifty feet up, descending rapidly, less then thirty horizontal feet from a twenty-foot-high wall of fire. He pulled both toggles, dumping air.

His feet touched down less than ten feet from the flame, the leading edge of the parachute hitting it, being incinerated in the process. Dane stumbled forward, the chute caught in a breeze, tugging him forward toward oblivion. His hands scrambled at the quick releases located on the front of his shoulders. He flipped open the metal plate, fingers searching for the small metal loops he had to pull to release the chute from the body harness.

He stuttered another step toward the fire, feeling the heat on his face. One finger caught the loop and pulled. The other was still searching as he took another forced step forward. The chute was half incinerated as it collapsed into the fire, and that was what saved Dane from the flame, the chute losing form and power as it was destroyed. He jerked backward with all his strength, falling onto his back, still feeling a pull on the one shoulder, until he popped the second quick release.

He lay on his back, breathing hard for several moments. The first thing he noticed was that there was no sound. The flames were eerily silent. He lifted his head slightly. The wall was as if a blast furnace was caught between two panes of glass. The fire swirled, but he noted that it was overall moving from left to right, as if there was a destination for it.

Dane got to his feet. He didn't take off the parachute harness. He looked about for the bundle, hoping it hadn't been caught in the flame. Instead of the bundle, he saw an old woman about forty feet away to the right, standing absolutely still. Looking past her, he spotted what had her mesmerized: the black hole into which the flames were swirling.

"Hello!" Dane called. He'd read the data on the Nazca Lines on the flight across the Pacific. "Dr. Reizer?"

She didn't appear to hear him, and Dane was startled as she took a step toward the black hole. He broke into a jog, heading toward her. "Dr. Reizer?"

Still no acknowledgment. She took another step toward the darkness.

Dane reached her and laid his hand on her shoulder. She started and turned in surprise.

"Dr. Reizer?"

She blinked, her eyes regaining focus, then she nodded. "Yes. Who are you?"

"Eric Dane. I'm here to get you out."

"How?"

"Come with me." Dane gently took her elbow with his hand and led her back toward where he had landed, knowing the bundle would be in that area. He pulled a small black box out of his pants side pocket and turned it on, activating the receiver. It immediately began beeping, and the small screen showed an arrow pointing to the left.

Dane and Reizer went down a small incline and then he saw the bundle lying among the rocks and stone. He knelt and opened it.

"Who are you?" Reizer asked as Dane worked.

"I'm an American. I've been . . ." Dane paused; he'd never quite explained his strange role to anyone. "I've been fighting the force inside the gates."

Reizer looked over her shoulder at the dark sphere drawing in the flame. "It is evil, isn't it?"

"I don't know much about good or evil," Dane said. "I just know that whatever is behind that doesn't give a damn about us. And it appears we are in the way of whatever it is trying to do." He laid out a steel canister, then heaved a large nylon bundle out on the ground, unfolding it. "Do you have any idea what is causing these lines of fire or what they are?"

"The old ones—the lines and wedges—are more powerful than the newer ones, the animal images. I've always picked up a sense of power about this place. Something I've never experienced anywhere else."

Power. Dane thought about that. *The Shadow always seems eager for power.* He attached a hose from the canister to a valve on the bottom of the nylon. Then he made sure the looped steel cable inside the container was attached to the bottom of the deflated balloon. He took the loop at the free end of the cable and, using double-locking snap links, attached it to the center point on the front of his harness.

"What are you doing?" Reizer asked.

"Getting us out of here."

"I think there is a way to walk out," Reizer said. She pointed. "If we go around the tail of the monkey and then go south . . ." Her voice trailed off.

"I've seen the images from the sky," Dane said. "There's no way out of here except that way." He pointed up.

"How—" Reizer began, but Dane shushed her as the small earpiece crackled.

"Dane, this is Talon Six. Status?"

"Inflating," Dane said.

"Don't forget to turn the beacon on," the pilot reminded him.

He'd almost forgotten. Dane cursed to himself as he went over to the balloon and switched on a small electronic beacon. He went back to the helium canister and twisted a knob. "Inflating," he repeated.

The balloon began to inflate, growing in size.

"Where's the basket?" Reizer asked.

"There isn't."

Her eyes followed the thin steel cable at the base of the balloon into the canister and then the end to Dane's vest. "You're joking."

"Afraid not." The balloon was half full and lifting off the ground. Dane pulled another harness out of the bundle and held it up. "Turn around and put your arms out."

"Oh my, this is not good for an old woman," Reizer complained, even as she did as he asked.

Dane slipped the harness over her shoulders, then squatted. He ran one of the straps through, between her legs from behind. "Hold this in your left hand." He grabbed the other strap. "This in your right."

The balloon was full and lifting, uncoiling the cable. Dane went around to Reizer's front and quickly connected the leg straps, pulling them tight, hearing Reizer grunt as he did so. There was no time for niceties.

The earpiece came alive. "We have the beacon. Are you ready? Over."

Dane grabbed a small piece of nylon webbing that had double-snap links at both ends. He hooked one set into his chest connection point. "Ready," he said as he attached the other end to the connection point on Reizer's harness.

"Are you sure this will work?" Reizer asked. They both could hear the airplane inbound.

Dane had been pulled out of exfiltration points during his time in Vietnam this way, usually by helicopter instead of the Fulton, but one time he had actually done the Fulton. "Yes."

"Will it hurt?"

"It'll be a fun ride."

The pilot's voice intruded. "Ten seconds out. Are you green? Over."

"We're green," Dane said. He reached forward and gathered the tiny old lady in his arms. The sound of the plane was growing louder.

Two hundred feet above them, the pilot of the Talon had the beacon centered on the low-light-vision television screen he was using to fly. "Five seconds," he announced. "Four. Three. Two. One."

On the ground, Dane felt nothing for about two seconds

as the slack was pulled out of the cable. Then he was jerked straight up into the sky, almost losing his grip on Reizer.

The force vector on the cable was vertical for about three seconds, lifting them over a hundred feet up. Then they were pulled horizontally, behind and below the Talon.

"We have a lock on the cable," the pilot announced. "Cutting balloon free."

A set of metal shears closed on the cable, just above where clamps held tight between the whiskers. They snapped shut, and the balloon was released. The cable below the plane slowly went from vertical to horizontal until Dane and Reizer were bouncing about in the air almost 150 feet directly behind the plane.

The loadmaster in the rear of the Talon had locked down a small crane and winch onto the open rear platform as soon as Dane had jumped, and he was ready. He lowered the crane, then reeled out a small length of cable with a hook on the end. As the plane with its two human attachments roared through the sky at 150 miles an hour, he fished for the Fulton cable.

"Are you all right?" Dane had to scream to be heard above the air whistling by and the roar of the plane just ahead of them.

There was no verbal reply, just Reizer's head nodding into his chest. Dane tried to look at the open back ramp, but the wind was too strong, causing his eyes to tear up.

The loadmaster snagged the cable on the fourth try. He slowly lifted until the Fulton cable slipped into the crane's mouth. Then he clamped down on the cable with the teeth of the winch. For insurance, just in case something went wrong, he also secured the Fulton cable with a loop of cable fixed to the plane.

"I've got it," he announced. "Disengage the nose lock."

The pilot flipped a switch.

Dane felt his stomach lurch as they both free-fell for a second, then were jerked forward once more.

The loadmaster hit the control for the winch, and the cable was slowly reeled in. As the two got closer to the ramp, he had the crane lift up so that they would clear the edge.

Dane saw the tail of the plane above his head as he and Reizer were slowly drawn into the cargo bay. The wind decreased as the plane enveloped them. He bumped against the floor and tried to gain his feet but was unable to. Hands were on him, holding him steady, pulling Reizer out of his arms.

"We've got them," the loadmaster announced. The back ramp slowly went up, sealing them off from the outside world.

Dane allowed the men inside to unhook him and strip the harness off. He turned to Reizer to see what kind of shape the old woman was in, hoping the trip hadn't killed her.

She was smiling, thanking the Air Force crew members. She saw Dane looking at her. "I'll have to do that again sometime. Most fun I've had in decades."

Dane slumped back on the cargo web seating, exhausted. The Talon banked and headed for the nearest landing strip at Ica. Behind and below it, the Nazca plain burned fiercely in the night. Then, in an instant, the flames roared up into the sky over a thousand feet high, still narrowly caught in their channels.

·   ·   ·

Chernobyl was a ghost town for the second time. A light breeze blew down the empty streets and over Cooling Tower Number Four, pushing death with it. Nothing lived within twenty miles in an elongated teardrop that was spreading to the northwest.

Thus there was no one to see when the black triangle

reappeared in the center of the ruined tower. Two Valkyries floated up out of the top of the triangle, their white forms slowly appearing. Between them, they held a black cylinder about five feet long and two feet in diameter. The front end tapered to a point, while the rear ended in a flat surface.

When they were completely clear of the triangle, they hovered in place, slowly turning until the point of the cylinder was pointing at Tower Number Three, a quarter mile away. The cylinder began to change at the rear, the black shifting to gold. When it reached the point, a golden ball began to form, growing to five feet in diameter. The golden ball remained still at that size for several seconds, then it suddenly shot forward.

The ball hit Tower Number Three and seemed to be slowly absorbed into the cement at the same rate the cylinder had changed. Then the tower imploded, releasing a cloud of radioactive gas into the air.

The two Valkyries didn't notice; they were already pointing the weapon at Tower Number Two.

• • •

Alarms were ringing as Foreman ran into the control center. "What's happening?"

"Activity at Chernobyl," Ahana reported.

"What kind?"

"The Russians don't know, but their monitoring equipment has picked up a large spike in radioactivity."

"I thought Tower Four was almost depleted." Foreman slid into a chair at the conference table.

"It is. There seems to be—" Ahana paused as her computer chimed, and she checked the report. "The other towers seem to have been destroyed." She held up a hand, anticipating Foreman's next question. "It will be bad, Mr. Foreman. The Russians fear they will have to evacuate Moscow.

If they can accomplish such a task before the radioactivity reaches their capital."

Foreman didn't seem too concerned. "Radioactivity or tectonic action, the clock's ticking."

The captain of the FLIP entered and went straight to the CIA agent. "We've been ordered by the Navy to evacuate the area."

Foreman didn't even acknowledge him with a glance. "Any muonic activity in our gate?" he asked Ahana.

She checked her screen. "Nothing."

"We hold in place," he told the captain.

The captain had already seen Foreman ignore the Navy once. "Sir, I must protest. The Navy is responsible for our—" He never finished, as a loud chime sounded from Ahana's computer. She spun in her chair to face the screen.

"Activity. Here."

Foreman jumped to his feet. "Get us out of here!" he yelled at the ship's captain.

· · ·

"Back us off, all weapons systems at ready." Captain Stokes remained in his leather command chair, issuing the orders in a calm voice. "Sonar?" he asked.

"No contact, just the warning from the FLIP of muonic activity."

The operations center of the *Connecticut* was bathed in a low red light, allowing crewmen to more clearly see their computer screens. It was a long way from the days of World War II submarines with cramped conditions and water dripping from pipes, looking more like a high-tech computer lab than the nerve center of a submarine.

"Range?" Stokes called out.

"Four thousand," the executive officer replied. "Speed fifteen knots and increasing."

"Contact, contact," the sonar man called out. "At the edge of the gate. Coming out. Large."

Stokes forced himself to stay seated, although he was tempted to walk over and grab a set of headphones.

"Range?" he asked.

"Four thousand."

"Speed?"

"Not clear yet."

Stokes turned his seat slightly. "XO?"

"We're four thousand five hundred meters from the gate. Speed twenty knots and accelerating."

He turned in another direction. "Radar?"

"I have the contact, sir. It's big. Very big. Range four thousand and holding steady."

Stokes knew that meant the contact was coming toward his ship at the same speed. "Helm, ahead full."

The *Connecticut*'s true top speed was classified. Stokes had gotten the submarine up to over forty miles an hour.

"Target still maintaining distance," the radar man reported.

Stokes had read the intelligence on encounters near the gates. He knew that if this was the large sphere—and it appeared to be so—then he would shortly lose all his electromagnetic power. He was prepared for this encounter.

"Helm, zigzag course. XO, launch mines on schedule."

The submarine began cutting hard turns, left and then back to right. From the rear deck of the *Connecticut,* a dozen MK-40 mines were released one by one, the zigzag pattern spreading them in an arc behind the ship. The disadvantage of this tactic was that he wasn't getting away from the pursuing craft as quickly as possible. But the reports had indicated that the sphere was able to travel at speeds in excess of fifty miles an hour, which meant it could easily overtake his ship. The mines had no electromagnetic parts and had been specially designed to explode on contact.

"Three thousand five hundred meters and closing," radar reported.

"Time to impact?" Stokes asked.

His XO had a stopwatch out, an anachronism in the high-tech center but one Stokes had insisted on, given the possibility that they might lose their high-tech gear any second.

"Thirty seconds."

Stokes looked about the control center, proud of the professionalism of his crew as they went about their tasks.

"Twenty seconds," his XO reported.

"Range three thousand and closing," the radar man called out. "Target speed is forty-five knots and accelerating."

"Ten seconds."

Stokes noted that his sonar man had taken off his headset in precaution.

"Five. Four. Three. Two. One."

Stokes's fingers dug into the arms of his command chair as he tensed. Nothing.

"Past one," the XO reported, looking at the stopwatch.

"Radar, is the target still coming?" Stokes asked.

"Yes, sir."

"Approaching two. At two and—" the XO's next words were cut off as an explosive wave swept over the *Connecticut*, immediately followed by another. A cacophony of sound hit the submarine as the final eleven mines went off one after another. A cheer broke out in the control center.

"Radar?" Stokes yelled, his voice cutting through the celebration.

Before the radar man could reply, the control center became pitch black, the cheers cut off as abruptly as the light.

"Battery power," Stokes ordered.

Dim red lights came on, bathing the room in a much darker light. Stokes could tell by the feel of the ship that the engines had stopped.

"Contact is closing," the radar man reported as soon as his system was back on-line.

Dead in the water: a phrase no captain, whether he is on board a surface ship or submarine, wanted to hear. Stokes stood.

"XO, take the center."

He could see the blood drain from his executive officer's face. He was the only other man on board who was privy to their last-ditch plan. There was no time for Stokes to comfort the man. He made his way forward, toward the cruise missile storage area. He could feel the eyes of crew members on him as he passed through compartments. They all knew the submarine was stopped and had heard the explosions. Stokes entered the storage area, where a half-dozen Tomahawk cruise missiles rested in their bins.

"All systems are off-line, sir," the chief petty officer in charge of the missiles reported as Stokes entered.

"Clear the area, Chief," Spokes ordered.

"Sir?"

"Clear the area."

"Aye, aye, sir." The petty officer hustled his men out of the compartment. Stokes swung shut the hatch behind himself and dogged it closed.

He then went to a plastic case secured to the middle of the floor. He pulled a key from around his neck and unlocked the case. He paused as the ship shuddered, then canted to the left twenty degrees before halting. He'd seen the video of what had happened to the *Revelle*, the research ship taken in by the sphere, and he knew his ship was now sharing the same fate.

He flipped open the lid, revealing a powerful array of batteries along with a laptop computer that was off. He pushed the On button for the computer, then took a lead from the case and went to the nearest missile. He attached the lead to a port on the side of the cruise missile, then went back to the laptop.

Stokes cursed when he saw that the computer hadn't booted. All he had was a screen full of unintelligible lines of numbers and letters. He unhooked the computer and grabbed a clacker, similar to the one used for claymore mines. He quickly screwed the wire into the clacker.

Stokes paused as he heard the sound of metal tearing, then screams coming from the center of the ship. He took a deep breath, then squeezed the clacker, sending a burst of power to the cruise missile.

He cursed when nothing happened.

Then a golden glow suffused the compartment, and he collapsed.

8

480 B.C.

It took the Phoenicians three and a half days to complete
both bridges. It was an engineering feat the world had never
seen before and would not see again for many hundreds of
years. Despite that, Xerxes spared no thanks to the engineers
and laborers. Even before the last plank was in place, he ordered his army forward, the lead scouts passing the engineers as they finished.

Thousands and thousands of troops moved forward,
crossing from Asia into Europe. To the south, the hundreds
of ships in the Persian navy set sail, covering the seaward
flank of the massive army. The holds of the ships were full
of supplies to keep the army fed and armed. It was the
largest army and navy movement the Earth had ever
known.

Xerxes remained perched on his throne on the eastern
shore, watching his forces move. All the reports he had received were favorable. His emissaries had been well received in Thessalia. There would be no battle at Marathon

unless the Athenians and Spartans moved north, and even then, his spies reported the city-states of Thessalia would remain neutral. His spies from Athens reported the city was locked in debate about what response to bring to bear against the Persians. Such debating had cost the Greeks Ionia, and now it was to cost them half of their homeland. Many gods, many city-states—Xerxes found it hard to believe that Greece had managed to fend off Persian assaults for so long.

It appeared that his ploy of playing Sparta against Athens with the promise of peace was working. If all went well, Xerxes pondered, he might—

"Their heavy infantry."

Xerxes turned in surprise toward Pandora. "What did you say?"

"Your generals, those who fought the Greeks at Marathon, they have been afraid to tell you the truth." She waved a graceful hand, taking in the tens of thousands of troops visible to them. "You will outnumber the Greeks. But they will choose the place of battle."

"You believe then that Sparta and Athens will not accept my offer?"

"Athens has considered it and continues to debate. Sparta will never consider it."

"And if they choose the place of battle?"

"They will pick a place where their heavy infantry will have an advantage, and your cavalry, archers, and light auxiliaries will be largely ineffective."

Pandora had never ceased to amaze Xerxes since she came to his court five years ago, and this brief discourse on tactics was something none of his generals had bothered to discuss with him. The common opinion, as far as Xerxes had been able to determine, was that this war against the Greeks would be no different than the dozens of other wars they had fought in the past five years and won. Numbers would carry the day, and victory would be his. Xerxes was aware enough to know that was what the generals had advised his father up until the debacle at Marathon.

"How do you know this?"

"I walk the camps at night, cloaked in a robe so no one can recognize me or tell I am a woman. I've listened to the Ionians and other Greeks, along with those of our allies who have fought the Greeks before. They fear the Spartans."

Xerxes slammed a fist into the arm of his throne. "They will fear me first, or I will have their heads decorating poles."

"If you would take the time, My Lord, to understand their fear, you will understand the Spartans."

Xerxes spat. "The Spartans. The Spartans. I hear so many say the word with such reverence for such a little city. What can they field? Ten thousand men in arms at best? And half of that auxiliaries? No Greek army ever defeated us before. Marathon was a fluke."

Pandora moved around until she was in front of Xerxes, between him and the vision of his magnificent army crossing the Hellesponte. Her words were like the beat of a ship's rowing drum, hammering at him. "Listen to me, Great King, and learn about your enemy. At birth, a Spartan male child is judged by a committee of elders. Any who seem sickly are taken to a hillside and left there. Female children are judged only in terms of their value to bear warriors.

"When a boy turns seven, he is taken from his family to live in a barracks called an agoge, where he will spend all of his time until he turns thirty. The training begins then and never ends. Even after they pass thirty, a Spartan considers his agoge his home much more than the place where his wife and children reside.

"As part of their rites of passage, each male Spartan

teenager is sent into the woods to live, with only their wits to guide them, for two weeks. They are required to kill a helot—one of the near slaves who work for Spartan—with their bare hands or whatever weapon they can forge from the wild before they can return to the barracks. It is felt that no matter how severe their training, they must have the experience of taking a life with their own hands to move on."

Xerxes's hands were gripping the arms of his throne. He had watched the sack and rape of cities, the massacre of the inhabitants, the execution of those who he decided needed to die. But he had grown up in a palace, his every wish taken care of, any discomfort immediately resolved. What Pandora spoke of, he could not conceive. It was, for lack of a better way for him to view it, barbaric.

Pandora continued. "At age twenty, a Spartan male becomes a citizen, and even if he marries, he must remain in the barracks. When going off to battle, Spartan wives and mothers admonish those men closest to them with the phrase: 'On your shield or with it.' They are either to come back carrying their heavy shield or be carried on it. Note that they do not say this about their sword or their spears. Do you know why the shield is so important?"

Xerxes said nothing.

"A Spartan who abandons his spear or sword only quits on himself. A Spartan who drops his shield exposes the man to his left to danger. That is the greatest disgrace and punishable by death."

Xerxes tried not to be impressed. "Cold metal in the bowels kills everyone, including Spartans."

Pandora moved forward slightly, so that she was even with the king, her eyes boring into his. "You have fought many battles, have you not, Lord?"

"Yes."

"But, My Lord, have you ever fought in the front line,

face-to-face with the sharp points of the enemy's weapons? That is where a Spartan king fights, from the front."

Xerxes stood so abruptly, the closest Immortals started forward, weapons at the ready, believing their king to have been struck by a missile. He pulled a dagger from his belt and slashed. Pandora moved but not quickly enough, as the blade sliced flesh along the left side of her face.

She took a step back as he advanced. Two Immortals reached Pandora, grabbing her arms and holding them out from her sides, leaving her open for whatever fatal blow the king wished to deliver. Xerxes pressed the blade against her throat.

"Who are you?"

Pandora was trying hard not to swallow; it felt as if even the smallest movement would sink the blade into her throat. "I've told you my name, Lord."

"Where are you from?" Xerxes pressed harder, bringing forth blood.

"I am Persian."

"You lie. You didn't even know our language when you arrived at my palace."

"I do not lie!" she protested as she saw her pending death in his eyes. "It is not so much an issue of where I am from, My Lord, but *when.*"

"You speak in riddles."

Pandora spoke rapidly to forestall her death. "Think of the map I brought. Have you or your advisers ever seen the like? Where—when—do you think that came from?"

Xerxes could see the two Immortals holding her exchange glances. First the bridge being destroyed, now the king's strange woman saying even stranger things. He was tempted to slit her throat and be done with it. He fought back his anger. She had forewarned the Phoenicians about the need for more bridges. She had been right about that.

With a twitch of his hand, Xerxes indicated for the Immortals to let her go. He went back to his throne and sat down.

"So tell me where and when you are from," he ordered.

"I am from Gordium."

Xerxes had heard of the place but never been there. It had been the capital of Phrygia, which had been conquered by Croesus of Lydia, who in turn was conquered by Xerxes's ancestors. Before he could dwell on this long, Pandora continued.

"I am descended from one of the Sibyls."

Xerxes had also heard of the Sibyls. Oracles. Ten of them, who lived in caves and made predications. The Erythraean Herophile, a Sibyl, had predicted the Trojan War. The beginning of the war between east and west.

Because of his religion, Xerxes did not believe in Sibyls or oracles. He consulted the magi, priests of his religion, but even their advice he viewed with suspicion. They were, after all, only men.

"Which Sibyl?"

Pandora smiled. "The Hellespontine, of course."

"Why did you not tell me this?" Xerxes asked. "I might have taken your warning on the bridge more seriously."

"No, King, you wouldn't have. You don't trust anyone."

"I am a king," he said as if that explained everything. Xerxes pointed across the Hellesponte toward Europe. "And once we are there? What help can you give me?"

"That remains to be seen," Pandora said.

"You said *when* was more important than *where.*"

"Sibyls live . . ." Pandora hesitated, then continued—"a timeless existence."

"How can that be?"

"I cannot explain it to you, Lord."

Xerxes shook his head. He could hear the clatter of thousands of hooves on wood as his main body of cavalry began crossing. He got off his throne and signaled for his men to begin breaking it down for travel.

"We cross. Now."

• • •

"We march west."

Leonidas's announcement was greeted with momentary silence by the assembled Spartan knights. It was considered bad form for someone to speak out immediately after the king spoke, an insult indicating the person was not taking the king's words seriously enough to contemplate them for at least a little while.

Finally an old gray-beard rose to his feet. Polynices was a veteran of many wars and a general who had planned many campaigns. "And what of the Persians, My Lord? They come from the north and east."

Leonidas had expected the question and could have been more verbose in his stated plan, but he had found it best to allow questions to be asked, to make the knights feel as if their input was essential for the plan that was to be followed. They were gathered outside the temple, the knights arrayed on the grassy slope looking down on their king. Leonidas had left Cyra at his home. Even a priestess could not attend this assembly; it was for warriors only.

"I will lead six *lochoi* to Rhion. They will provide shipping for us to cross the Gulf, and we will assault and destroy Antirhon. The Rhionians will then garrison the city, which will seal the Gulf of Corinth for us.

"We will then reboard the ships, go east along the Gulf, disembark at Delphi, and force-march to the north to meet the Persians at Thermopylae. The Persians are crossing the Hellesponte as we speak here. It will take them some time to march along the coast, across Thessalia, and get to the pass. There should be some opposition to the Persians in Thessalia, enough to give us time to accomplish what we

need to defend the west at Antirhon and march to the Hot
Gates."

A *lochoi* was a division of Spartan soldiers. There were
twelve altogether, and that naturally prompted Polynices to
ask the next question.

"And the other six *lochoi*, Lord?"

"Will defend our homes," Leonidas answered.

Polynices stroked his beard, and there was muttering
among the knights as they discussed this plan. It had been a
hard decision for Leonidas to make, to leave half his fighting force behind.

"Forgive my impertinence, My King," Polynices pressed,
"but would it not be best to bring all of your force to bear on
the Persians? It is reported their numbers are vast."

"I agree it would be best," Leonidas said. "But there are
other factors." He held up one long finger. "First, I plan to
battle the Persians in the Hot Gates. There is barely enough
room there for one *lochoi* to fight at a time. I do not wish to
disappoint so many of you having to watch only a few kill
our enemy."

That brought forth a deep chorus of laughter from the
gathered men.

"Second." Leonidas raised another finger. "We are not
sure of Athens's intent."

That statement brought forth a rumble of disgust.

"We must be loyal to Greece, but we must take care to
preserve our own city," Leonidas continued. "Even when we
succeed at the Hot Gates, the Persian navy will still be free
to maneuver. If the Athenians do not challenge them, they
could land forces near here to the east."

Leonidas hesitated before bringing up the third point, but
the Persian Jamsheed had been blunt about it, and the king
felt a need for his fellows to accept the reality of the situation. "Third." His middle three forgers were in the air. "The
helots."

A knight jumped to his feet as a clamor arose. "The boys of the agoges could handle the helots!"

"Not if the Persians arm them," Leonidas said, his voice cutting through the noise. "There is no purpose to going off to war if there is nothing for us to return to after our victory."

Polynices turned toward the knights, raising his old, gnarled hands, quieting them. "The king is right. We have piled the tinder high underneath our own homes, and any spark will have dire consequences." He turned back toward Leonidas. "If I might make a suggestion My Lord?"

Leonidas nodded.

Polynices hooked his thumbs in folds on his tunic. "Any campaign is fraught with uncertainties. The pace of the Persian' march can be calculated, but your assault on Antirhon is a different matter. If the city stands alone, then there are two issues: Will they issue forth to fight you or make you lay siege to their city? If it is the former, then things should proceed quickly."

This brought a chorus of laughter from the warriors.

"But if it is the latter, it might take more time. Then there is the factor that they may gain allies from other jackal states who see the Persian invasion as an opportunity."

Leonidas waited, beginning to get an idea of what Polynices was leading to.

"Because of these uncertainties," the old man continued, "I recommend that the best knights of the six *lochoi* who remain to guard our homes be culled from the ranks and sent directly to Thermopylae to prepare the defense. As our king has noted," he nodded his head toward Leonidas, "the pass is narrow. A small contingent of brave men, allied with those forces from other cities along the way, could hold the pass for a while. This would allow for any unexpected delay in the Antirhon campaign." Polynices smiled, revealing a black gap where several teeth had been smashed by an enemy sword years ago. "And it would allow those selected knights of the six remaining *lochoi* their opportunity for honor."

The old man had cut the heart of the matter as usual, Leonidas realized. The knights cared more for glory in battle than all the other issues. He raised his hand. "A force of three hundred of the best from the remaining *lochoi* will march at the same time my force marches to the west. They will go to the Gates of Fire, and they will prepare the defense."

9

The Present

Dane and Reizer were seated side by side at a computer console in the forward half of the cargo bay of the Combat Talon. The interior of the plane pulsated with the sound of the four turboprop engines as they headed north toward Lima to link up with the SR-71. Dane knew he had the length of the flight to decide on his next move. On the computer screen he showed Reizer the imagery Ahana had forwarded to the Combat Talon of the Nazca plain.

"What does it mean?" Reizer asked as she examined the photos.

Dane had already read Ahana's initial estimate. "We believe it's draining power from all the tectonic lines. The black hole you saw is a gate or portal. The power is going into it. When enough power has been taken, the fault lines between the plates will become unstable."

Reizer ran her fingers along the lines of power on the screen. "Why now? The Nazca Lines have been there for

millennia. Even among the native people, I have never heard
of them being on fire like this."

Dane had been thinking about that. "The Shadow destroyed Chernobyl, from which it has been drawing power
for quite a while. The rods in Tower Four were about out of
power, anyway. We thought they were tapping the tectonic
lines, but maybe they were just checking them out, preparing for this as a replacement for what they were taking from
Chernobyl."

"But the scale . . ." Reizer shook her head. "While I am
not a nuclear engineer, I am a geologist, and I doubt that
whatever power level they were taking from Chernobyl
comes close to what we are seeing now."

"Why the Nazca plain?" Dane asked.

Reizer tore her attention from the lines of fire on the
screen. "There has always been a strange force at work on
the plain,"

"What kind of force?"

Reizer held up her aged hands. "How old do you think I
am?"

In other situations, it was a question no man would want
to be asked by a woman. "Seventy?"

"I celebrated my hundredth birthday a few years back."
She pulled her sleeves back, revealing her wrists. "Notice I
do not wear a watch. They don't work on the plain, something most people don't know."

Dane glanced at his watch, then at a time display on the
console. His watch was off by over forty minutes, the
amount of time he had spent in the vicinity of the plain.

"I've gone onto the plain," Reizer continued, "and stayed
for what I thought was three days—at least I saw three sun-
sets—but when I came off, I found a month had passed in
the world around the plain, and people thought I was dead.
So few people travel there, and none other than me spend
the night, so most don't notice the time anomalies."

"It might be over a hundred years since you were born," Dane said, "but you have not lived for over a hundred years."

Reizer frowned. "What?"

"We know time is a variable inside the space between." Dane quickly explained the concepts of gates, portals, and the space between. "I think that time variable has extended onto the Nazca plain somehow. That means there is something different about it, if you've never seen a gate active before."

Reizer nodded. "While I was walking, trying to find my way out, I thought about it. And about what Davon told me." She had filled Dane in on the ill-fated Englishman who had shown up just before the lines came alive. Dane remembered Ariana talking about meeting him in England.

She pointed down. "He talked about people seeing things from different times inside of places where lines of power crossed. And that there were usually standing stones at such junctures.

"He also said the power for the lines went deep inside the planet. What if at Nazca it is closer to the surface than anyplace else? And that is why the lines were dug by the ancients? Like those who divine for water, maybe their priests or shamans or whatever could sense that. And they drew the geoglyphs in an attempt to channel it?"

"And the lines and wedges?" Dane asked.

"I think they were made by someone else."

"Who?"

"I don't know, but maybe they were preparation."

"For?"

"For what's happening now."

He had hoped Reizer would be more informative. The time disruptions on the Nazca plain were interesting but didn't say anything definitive about what was happening. Dane was still uncertain what the next step would be. The crystal skulls that Ariana had collected were en route from Antarctica. He had ordered that they be sent toward the Bermuda Triangle gate, as that had been his best guess as to the next stop in order to recover Sin Fen's skull and the Naga staff.

"Davon also said that the core of the planet was important," Reizer added.

"Why?"

"I don't know."

Dane leaned back in the hard seat and closed his eyes. The roar of the engines reminded him of Basic Airborne School so many years previously at Fort Benning, Georgia. The major purpose of the school had not been particularly to train men to jump out of airplanes, although if they were going to an airborne unit, that was indeed important, but to teach them to conquer their fear. To stand in the open doorway of a plane traveling at 140 miles an hour, 1,200 feet above a Georgia field, and step out.

At the moment, Dane felt as if he were free-falling. He thought back to when he'd been in the Angkor gate, and the solution to destroying the deadly ray of power there had just come to him, whispered by the "voices of the gods," as Sin Fen had called them. Dane took a deep breath and mentally stood in the door of the plane. He stepped out, spreading his arms and legs, floating.

There was the same man in armor with the Naga staff in his hand. Swinging it at the sphere whose surface appeared to be made of writhing golden snakes. Dane felt fear and knew what he was seeing couldn't be allowed to happen. Just as quickly, the vision shifted, and he saw a portal inside the space between. Then another portal and another and another, until they were flashing by his mind's eye at a dizzying speed, an infinite number.

Dane sat upright and opened his eyes, overwhelmed by the vision. He was saved from his inner eye by the computer screen changing from imagery to Ahana's face. For a moment, Dane was confused to see her face on the screen and hear her words coming out of the speakers.

"I do not mean to interrupt, but more has happened." She quickly related the loss of the *Connecticut* and the furthering disaster at Chernobyl.

"So we've given the Shadow a Seawolf-class submarine," was Dane's summation when she was done.

Ahana ignored the comment. "What has happened there?"

Before she went any further, Dane introduced Reizer and summarized what had happened on the Nazca plain as far as they knew.

Foreman appeared behind Ahana when he was done. "So there is definitely a gate there?"

"Yes, but there's so much power going through it, no one would survive going into it."

"We are linked live via satellite," Ahana said. She nodded over her left shoulder. "As you can see, Mr. Foreman is here, and we are also connected to Professor Kolkov in Russia."

Ahana looked down and typed something, then Dane's screen split, and an old man with pale skin and thinning white hair appeared. "Professor Kolkov, meet Eric Dane."

Kolkov nodded. "I thank you for your efforts so far in our cause."

Ahana didn't wait on the exchange of pleasantries. "This theory of Mr. Davon's regarding the interior of the planet is interesting. It is in line with what I believe the Shadow has been—and is—doing to our planet. Some of what I am going to discuss may sound very basic, but I think we all need to understand this."

Ahana's face disappeared, and a diagram replaced it. The diagram showed the planet, with several circles of varying size inside.

"This is the basic makeup of our planet," Ahana said.

"While most think the planet is solid, it is far from that. Originally, Earth was simply an accretion of small fragments of solid rock that came together about four point six billion years ago. Long after that, around four billion years in the past, this fledgling planet was subjected to an intense asteroid and meteorite bombardment lasting millions of years. The immense amount of heat energy released by this bombardment melted the entire planet and it is still cooling off today, four billion years later.

"Denser material from the bombardment, such as iron from the meteors, sank to the center, while lighter elements, such as silicates and oxygen compounds and water, rose to the surface. This was the beginning of the formation of Earth as we know it now."

Dane felt a pang of loss and realized Ahana's lecture on the formation of the planet was something that Ariana Michelet would have done. Ariana had been a geologist, and her expertise on tectonic plates had set the framework for whatever it was Ahana had come up with.

The Japanese scientist continued. "As you can see from the diagram, the interior of the Earth is divided into four major layers. The inner core, outer core, mantle, and crust. These have many subdivisions in them, but for our purposes, those four will do for now. As we travel from the outside in, we come across a strange phenomenon." Ahana paused in thought, then resumed. "Let me back up a little bit. It is important that you understand something, and that is that most of what I am talking about concerning the interior of the planet has been determined indirectly. After all, the deepest any shaft has ever been drilled is barely a scratch on the surface.

"Geologists use recordings of seismic waves from earthquakes to try to determine what the interior of the Earth consists of. There are two different types of seismic waves: P waves and S waves. P waves will travel through both fluids and solids. S waves, on the other hand, cannot travel through fluid.

"What was noted was that as one got farther away from the epicenter of an earthquake, there was a drastic change in readings of these waves at a certain distance, at an angle of approximately one hundred five degrees between the earthquake and seismograph. At this angle, S waves disappeared, while P waves eventually made their way around the surface. What this meant was that the direct S waves must have hit liquid and been stopped. Thus, extending this angle through the planet"—on the screen, a line appeared—"one has to deduce that there is a molten layer of material inside the planet and beneath the mantle. This is the outer core.

"On top of this, the fact that the planet has a magnetic field also indicates there is a molten layer inside that is in flux. The Moon and Mars have no magnetic field because both are cold planets and are solid inside. And the Earth cannot be magnetic in stasis, because magnetic minerals lose their magnetism once they are heated above five hundred degrees Celsius. The only way to explain the Earth's magnetic field is if there is a circulating electric current inside the planet. Thus, convection of molten iron in the Earth's outer core must be the source for our planet's magnetic field." Ahana's voice sharpened. "Please keep this associated electric field in mind as I continue.

"Few people know that the magnetic field to which our compasses point is not a constant. Indeed, it is strongly believed that it has switched directions many times over the course of time. As recently as twenty thousand years ago, compasses probably would have pointed to the South Pole rather than north. Think of the immense changes in power given off by such a planetwide switch.

"The convection in the outer core affects the mantle, which in turn affects the crust and causes the movement of the crustal or tectonic plates. You all remember learning about Pangaea and how the seven continents started out as one and how they rest on plates that have been moving for a very long time. The Earth's crust is only a thin skin that constitutes less than point two percent of the planet's mass. And there is a difference between the crust underneath the continents and that under the ocean. The crust under land averages about five times more thickness than that beneath the ocean.

"Except"—the word hung in the air for several seconds—"at Nazca. The crust is less than two kilometers in thickness at that point, and below it there appears to be lines of conductivity that lead deep into the Earth."

"That is Dr. Reizer's suspicion," Dane said.

Reizer leaned forward and spoke at the computer screen. "How have you confirmed this?"

Ahana was in her lecture mode, which Dane had seen before. "Geologists can use P and S wave scans of the planet to map it, much like a CAT scan of the brain does a similar thing. The boundary between the crust and the mantle is called the Mohorovicic discontinuity or Moho for short. At Nazca, the Moho has a hole in it, and extending down from that hole is a channel that leads to the molten outer core."

"How come no one has noticed this before?" Dane asked.

"It has been noticed," Ahana said. "No one thought it was important before."

"I'm confused," Dane said. "If the crust is so thin and there is a channel to the outer core, wouldn't that be like a perfect setup for a volcano?"

Ahana nodded. "Yes. Exactly. Except there aren't any."

"Why not?" Dane asked.

"I am not certain," Ahana said. "Looking at the data from satellite overflights and various imaging, it appears as if the crust at Nazca is thin but very dense, almost like a cap placed on top of this channel. I do have a theory on how this cap was formed, but please wait while I explain something else.

"Moving to the center of the planet, beneath the molten outer core, we come to the inner core. The inner core has a radius of only thirty-five hundred kilometers, but it contains a good percentage of the planet's mass, given its small size. And unlike the outer core, the inner is solid."

That didn't make sense to Dane. "Shouldn't it be even hotter at the inner core?"

"Yes, and it is," Ahana said. "The temperature of the inner core is estimated to be around four thousand degrees Celsius."

"Then shouldn't the rock be melted?" Dane pressed.

"It should be, except for the fact that it is under such extreme pressure that the rock remains solid."

Something was bothering Dane, something Ariana had said. "What kind of rock is there in the inner core?"

"Good question," Ahana said. "That is exactly what I have been researching. Because, while it appears that the lines of power are flowing along the lines of convection and plate boundaries, we have discovered that the strongest line, the most powerful thread of power, so to speak, is going into the inner core of the planet itself.

"It has been speculated, based on the available data, that the core consists of iron, but I think that is only an outer surface. I believe that the densest and hardest material on Earth has been collected at the very center of the planet under extreme temperature and pressure."

"Diamonds," Dane said.

Ahana nodded. "Yes. Diamonds are a mineral form of carbon and the hardest material known to man, rating a ten on the Mohs' scale. There are four known types of diamonds: a diamond proper, bort, ballas, and carbonado. A diamond proper is one that is a crystallized gemstone. Bort is an imperfectly crystallized diamond that is dark in color.

Ballas is a cluster of tiny diamond crystals of great hardness. Carbonado, which some call a black diamond, has no cleavage, which means it can't split along a definite plane. What if there were a fifth form of diamond, one that humans have never seen?

"I think there is a crystalline object at the center of the Earth. A diamond or cluster of diamonds on an unimaginable scale. And crystallized in a structure we have never seen or even postulated."

Dane was beginning to see a connection: the crystal skulls that were used to channel power from the pyramids to stop the gates. *Did the pyramids draw power from deep inside the Earth? But how could living tissue turn into crystal?* he wondered.

Foreman's voice cut into his thoughts. "If there is something like this in the center of the planet, what does it mean?"

"Diamonds are excellent conductors of heat," Ahana said, "but poor conductors of electricity and become highly positively charged when exposed to electromagnetic forces. I think there is a conductive layer between this center crystal and the inner core, which has a dynamo effect when combined with the Earth's rotation, the magnetic field of the outer core, and the convection of plate tectonics. Since the core crystal will absorb the heat but not the electromagnetic forces being generated, there is a mind-boggling amount of energy there, just waiting to be exploited. This is the ultimate power the Shadow is now beginning to tap through Nazca."

There were several moments of silence as each absorbed this summation; then it was Kolkov who broke the silence. "We are aware of the effects of the disasters that will happen because of the tectonic plate energy being drained by the Shadow. What will be the effect of this inner core crystal being tapped?"

"I am not certain," Ahana said. "I have been running several simulations on the computers. You do have to understand there are numerous variables and forces involved."

Dane leaned forward toward the computer. "Your best guess. Worst-case scenario," he added.

"Worst-case scenario is that the intrinsic structure of the planet becomes unstable," Ahana said.

"Which means?" Dane asked.

"The planet will break apart. Earth will become the collection of fragments it was in the beginning."

Dane summed it up. "So, one way or the other—tectonics or core crystal—we're doomed."

"Unless we can stop the tap," Ahana said.

"Which means we have the same problem," Dane said. "Which is we have to stop the portal the tap is running through."

"And do you have a plan to do that?" Kolkov's voice was harsh.

A long silence reigned.

"My government," Kolkov continued, "is in the process of evacuating Moscow. There is little patience."

"I think . . ." Dane began but fell silent.

"What?" Foreman pressed.

Dane chose his words carefully. "The path we must follow is not clear, but I know I must get Sin Fen's skull and then the Naga staff. I haven't been shown the step after that."

"I can't go to my superiors with that," Kolkov said. "I am sorry." The half of the screen he had been on went blank.

The Space Between

Amelia Earhart looked at the smooth skin on Fred Noonan's chest and frowned. Even if he had survived the kraken—and enough time had passed for the wound to heal—there should still be some scarring. Her navigator's condition was worsening, and he had not regained consciousness.

She looked up and saw Taki watching her closely. She had explained Noonan's message as clearly as she could to him, and the samurai had made no comment. She'd found the lack of dialogue with the samurai to be disconcerting at first, but she had quickly grown used to it.

She found it an ironic twist, given that a secondary mission of her around-the-world flight had been to spy on Japanese installations in the Pacific and forward that information to the U.S. Navy. She had even learned a smattering of Japanese in preparation for the flight, which had stood her in good stead when she ran into the samurai here in the space between. They had latched onto her as their new lord and would do what she said, no questions asked.

"He will die."

Earhart couldn't tell if Taki's words were a statement or question, but she nodded anyway. *"Yes."*

"The Naga staff will not come to us. We must go to it."

Earhart stood and signaled to Taki, circling her hand over her head and then pointing toward the center of the space between. He nodded and yelled commands to his men. They gathered round as Earhart grabbed her sword. She paused, looking down on Noonan's blistered face, then she set out.

They traveled through a low area between two ridges of black. Amelia Earhart had no idea how large the space between was. There was the surrounding wall that curved out of sight overhead, and once, she had followed it in one direction as long as she could before having to head back to her base camp for food. While on that journey, she'd had the eerie sensation that the ground was extending in front of her and that she could go forever and never come back to her starting point, even though her best guess was that she was traveling in a circle around the central lake.

The temperature was mild and unvarying, about sixty de-

grees Fahrenheit, as near as she could guess. The air was
tainted with a distasteful odor that she couldn't identify and
that, despite all her time here, she hadn't quite gotten used
to.

After several miles, Earhart raised her hand, and her
small band came to a halt. She got on her belly and edged
her way up the slope to the right, ignoring the gritty sand
that rubbed against her and slid into her flight suit. She
moved more slowly as she reached the top and edged up
enough to see over. They were near the lake that filled the
center of the space between.

The first thing she saw was a wide pillar of black that extended toward the roof far overhead—a portal. She slithered
up further to get a better view. She could see the surface of
the water: flat, black, extending out as far as she could see.
To the left and in the distance she could see another portal.

She scanned the shoreline. She sensed someone crawling
up next to her and spared a glance. Taki, sword drawn, was
at her side. She turned back to the shore.

She reached out and grabbed Taki's shoulder, pointing
with her other hand. *"There."*

There were five limp forms scattered along the shore.
Earhart began to stand when an abrupt jerk on her right arm
pulled her down into the black sand. She turned angrily toward Taki, but the samurai's focus was to the left. Earhart
followed his gaze. A half-dozen white figures were floating
above the black ground. Their faces were featureless except
for ruby-red eyes.

Earhart bit down, grinding her teeth, feeling the futility of
her position. Five of the Valkyries scooped up bodies. The
sixth stood by. With the bodies secured, the Valkyries began
heading back the way they had come. The sixth followed,
then paused. It turned, facing the ridge behind which Earhart
hid. She stopped breathing. She heard a sharp intake of

breath from Taki, and it was her turn to grab his arm, keeping him from doing something foolish.

After several minutes, which seemed like hours, the Valkyrie finally turned and followed its mates, sliding along the beach. Earhart watched until it disappeared. Then she stood.

"Come," she said to Taki as she headed down the slope in pursuit. When she looked over her shoulder, she saw Taki and the rest of his samurai following.

The Present

Since its launch in 1986, *Mir* had circled the planet over 85,000 times. Astronauts from dozens of nations lived and worked in the station. Since the end of the Cold War, eleven American shuttle missions had rendezvoused with the space station. Both NASA and the Russian Space Agency had touted the station as a sign of international cooperation. It was all a lie.

Launched while Ronald Reagan was still president, *Mir* had been Moscow's reply to Star Wars. If Reagan wanted to throw down the gauntlet and develop space weapons, Moscow, in its basic, working-class way, had picked up the challenge. Heavy booster rockets lifted the components of *Mir* into space, and hardy cosmonauts bolted them together, including a section that contained a half-dozen multiple warhead nuclear rockets.

There was little the United States administration could protest about, given Star Wars, so the entire matter was kept classified. When the Cold War ended, the rockets were still up there, along with their warheads, and it became the thing no one talked about among those in the know. The danger of bringing the warheads back to Earth was considered too great, so that section of *Mir* was sealed off. The United States invested considerable time and money into making sure *Mir* stayed operational and in orbit while the Russian Space Agency deteriorated and was unable to provide the maintenance required.

Mir's current crew consisted of three Russians and one American. Upon receipt of a highly classified and secure communication from Moscow, the senior Russian had the American locked in a storage area, and then the three began unsealing the missile compartment.

Three hundred fifty-five kilometers below the space station lay the blue of the Pacific Ocean with the western coast of South America rotating into view.

10

480 B.C.

Leonidas entered his home to be greeted with the sight of
Cyra holding his daughter on her lap, bouncing the squeal-
ing girl up and down. His mind was swirling with all the
preparations to be made for the march-out in the morning,
and for a moment, he was taken aback.

"Husband." A hand was on the small of his back, just
below where the armor ended.

Leonidas turned. His wife, Thetis, stood in the shadows
of the entryway. Her hair was pinned up, and she wore a
white robe fringed with gold, a gift he had brought her from
the sack of a neighboring town many years previously. He
recognized it for more than that though; it was what she
wore the night their son Amphion had been conceived. Or
had been wearing, he realized as a flush spread across his
tanned cheeks. Her hand was still on his back, and he
glanced at Cyra in embarrassment, but the priestess was focused on Briseis.

Leonidas took Thetis's hand in his, removing it from his

back. "Wife," he acknowledged. He could see the smile on her face and the sadness in her eyes. Word of the assembly's decision and the morning muster would have made it here, even though he had left the assembly and headed straight home. It was the way it always was, and Leonidas had never figured out how the women knew such things as quickly as they did.

"Xarxon has prepared your equipment for travel." Leonidas had not had time to tell his squire to get things ready, so he was grateful for his wife's intervention.

"Greetings, King." Cyra had finally acknowledged his presence. She stood, holding Briseis in her arms.

"Priestess." Leonidas felt uncomfortable. He suddenly realized that if the oracle's prophecy were true, tonight would be his last with Thetis. He turned to her. "We march in the morning."

"I know." Thetis was a slight woman, her hair prematurely gray as befit one who had waited out so many campaigns. She reached down and picked up a wicker basket that Leonidas had not noticed. "I want to go up the mountain. To our meadow."

Leonidas frowned. "It is late and—"

"I know it is late." There was a sharp edge to Thetis's voice. "Cyra will watch Briseis. Amphion is at his agoge and will see you in the morning on the field. Tonight, I want you to myself. Under the stars. On the mountain." Her hands were on the clasps that held his armor, unfastening it.

Leonidas looked at Cyra. The priestess gave the slightest of nods, and for some strange reason, he stood still and allowed Thetis to remove the metal from his body until he was clad only in his short tunic.

"King?" Cyra seemed reluctant to interject herself between husband and wife.

"Yes?"

"What was the decision of the council?"

"We march on Antirhon to secure our west, then to Thermopylae."

Cyra put Briseis down in her cradle. "How long will this campaign against Antirhon take?"

"That is something no one can predict."

"How far away is this city?"

When Leonidas told her, Cyra shook her head. "There is not time. Xerxes is marching quickly. He has already crossed the Hellesponte. He will reach the Gates and be through them before you arrive."

"We are sending three hundred troops directly to the Gates of Fire to prepare the defenses and hold the pass."

"Three hundred? What can three hundred men do?"

"Three hundred Spartans," Leonidas corrected her. He held up a weary hand as Cyra started to say something. "We may indeed be too late, but the council has spoken, and it is law. I must obey."

Thetis took his raised hand and led him to the door. "We will be back at dawn," she called over her shoulder to Cyra as she pulled Leonidas through the door. Once outside, she continued to lead the way, heading toward the mountainside where they had spent the first night of their marriage so many years previously.

Cyra stood in the doorway, watching the couple disappear into the darkness.

•   •   •

King Xerxes looked down from the mountain at the glow of lights ahead. It was a small town, the easternmost outpost of Macedonia, a kingdom that was in search of an identity. North of Greece proper, Macedonia was the invasion route for both the Persians from the east and the barbarians from the north. He thought so little of the small kingdom that Xerxes had not even bothered to send emissaries to the Macedonians to smooth his passage through this land.

"My Lord?" The commander of the Immortals awaited for his orders.

"Destroy the town. Kill everyone."

A female voice cut in. "That is not wise, King."

Xerxes was tired. The army was marching hard, and despite all the comforts he was provided, it was taking its toll on the king's body. "Why?" he asked wearily.

"There is no need to destroy the town, King," Pandora said.

"There is no need," Xerxes acknowledged, "only my desire that it be so, which supersedes need."

"Yes, Lord." Pandora remained quiet, which irritated Xerxes even more.

"You have a reason beyond that it isn't necessary, don't you?" he demanded.

"Yes, Lord."

Just as Xerxes was about to explode in anger, Pandora continued. "Time is like the ocean. It ebbs and flows. Much like kingdoms. Today one is powerful and can destroy. In a generation, the power goes the other way."

Xerxes nodded as if he understood. "True. But today"— he jabbed his finger down at his throne—"I am the one with the power." He turned to the commander of the Immortals. "Do as I order."

"May I go with him, Lord?" Pandora asked, which surprised Xerxes.

The king waved his hand. He could care less.

Pandora followed the commander down the slope, where a battalion of the Immortals waited. She was ignored as the troops moved forward. The rest of the Persian army had halted for the night, the glow of the thousands of campfires lighting up the eastern horizon like a false dawn.

The gates to the city were open, the inhabitants clearly aware of what approached. A cluster of men stood in the open gates, waiting. As the Immortals approached, they held their hands up and called out entreaties. Pandora began moving her way up in the column of troops. There were screams as the Immortals cut down the men.

Belatedly, the soldiers in the town jumped into action. They tried to shut the gates, but it was too late. The Immortals surged through, overpowering the defense. Men, women, children, and animals were cut down wherever they were found. Pandora stepped over bodies, pushing her way toward the vanguard of the Immortals. She saw merchants, hands full of offered gold, have their heads lopped off.

Unerringly, Pandora stalked through the streets. Immortals continued to ignore her, knowing her as the right hand of the king. Of course, none of them seemed concerned about her safety, either.

Screams of agony and fear echoed through the air, both human and animal. A red glow was lighting the sky as the town was being put to the torch. Near the center of town, Pandora shoved open the door to an elegant house. She walked in and then up a set of stairs. She threw open a door at the top of the stairs and entered a room where a woman huddled in the corner, a baby in her arms.

"Please," the woman pleaded.

Pandora walked over and took the child out of the frightened woman's arms. "His name?"

"Philip."

Pandora nodded. "Philip the First."

"What?" The woman was confused.

Pandora heard footsteps thundering up the steps. Two Immortals stormed into the room, blades drawn. Pandora put the child under her cloak. The soldiers looked at her briefly, then one stepped forward and separated the woman's head from her body with an expert stroke.

Pandora went down the stairs, keeping the child hidden. The streets of the city ran with blood, and the flames were spreading, leaping from building to building. Pandora kept her eyes straight ahead as she strode out of the gate and into the darkness. She turned to the left, heading toward a cluster of hills. She paused for a second, and her head swiveled back and forth, almost like an animal searching for prey; then she moved forward.

In front of the hills was a streambed, and she went down into it. "Come out," she called.

Nothing moved.

Pandora removed the child from under her cloak and held it up. "Come out."

Bushes moved; then a woman stepped out. She stood tall, her jaw set. "You took your time."

Pandora ignored the comment and held the child out to the woman. "His name is Philip."

The woman remained as still as a rock.

"He will be your king."

"We have a king."

"You saw what Xerxes did to your city?" Pandora didn't wait for an answer. "What he does to your capital will be worse. Your king will die as will every member of his family. This"—she indicated the child she held—"is a relative. A distant one, but the only one who will survive Xerxes's march. He will be your king."

The woman finally moved, coming forward. She held out her arms and took the child into them. She looked down at the child's face, then up at Pandora. "His name again?"

"Listen closely. He is Philip. Philip the First. He will have a son who will take the same name. Then his son will have a son. His name will be Alexander. To those who follow, he will be known as Alexander the Great. He will conquer all the world."

"How do you know this?"

Pandora reached out and grabbed the woman by the shoulders, her fingers sinking in. "Trust me that I do. You are brave. You came out while the men still cower in the bushes. You will raise him to be king."

Pandora turned and walked off into the dark, leaving the woman holding the child.

•   •   •

Leonidas woke, and the first thing he realized was that he wasn't wearing his armor. Indeed, he became aware that he was naked, and a warm breeze slid over his body. It did not bother him. He felt at peace, most strange for a man who was to march off to war shortly, toward a battle in which his death had been foretold. Turning his head, Leonidas saw the rising sun, highlighting Thetis's left breast. Leonidas leaned over, kissing it lightly.

Thetis's eyes opened, and she smiled, her face relaxed. In less than a second, the calm look was gone.

"No," Leonidas placed his fingers on her lips. "Let us have now like we had last night." He rolled over, placing his body on top of hers.

Later, the sun was clear of the horizon, and the king held his wife tightly in both his arms. He felt the pressure of duty. He could hear distant yells and knew his troops were marshaling.

"Thetis."

His wife buried her head into his scarred chest. "Yes?"

"I know I have not been there for you as I should have been."

"You were there as you should have been as king."

"But not as a husband who loves you. For that I am sorry."

•   •   •

The Persian army moved past the smoldering ruins of the city. Pandora walked alongside the imperial litter, which was carried by a dozen burly slaves. Immortals surrounded the king, a moving wall of humanity.

"I understand you went into the city," Xerxes's voice carried through the curtains enclosing the litter.

"I told you I was going, My Lord," Pandora answered.

"I also have been told you carried a child out of the city." Pandora remained quiet.

"My orders were that all should die. You heard them."

"Yes, My Lord."

"Yes, you carried a child out, or yes you heard my orders?"

"Both, My Lord."

"Disobeying my orders is punishable by death."

Pandora noted that two Immortals had edged closer to her, their hands on the pommels of their swords.

"Who was the child?" Xerxes asked. "I do not see you moved by pity, so there must be another reason for your actions."

"None that needs concern you, My Lord."

The curtain twitched open, and Pandora could see Xerxes now. He had a goblet in one hand and reclined on a pile of pillows. The slaves were specially chosen and trained as the litter moved smoothly, despite the unevenness of the road.

"I decide what is my concern."

"Yes, Lord. The grandson of the child I saved could be very important in his time, long after you and I are gone."

"A prophecy?"

"Yes, Lord."

"Interesting." Xerxes drank deeply, then stuck the goblet out of the litter. A slave grabbed it, quickly refilled it while keeping pace, and handed it back to the king in one smooth motion. "I do not trust you."

"I know, My Lord."

"This important grandson," Xerxes said. "Will what he does depend on what we do now?"

"Yes, My Lord."

"You did this in case I fail?"

Pandora hesitated, then told the truth. "Yes, Lord."

"Fail in what, particularly?" Xerxes was holding out the cup for more wine. Pandora wondered if the wine or the smell of burning corpses accounted for his benign mood this morning.

"Defeating the Greeks."

"I doubt that is your goal. I doubt also that you will tell me what you are really doing unless I let my master-at-arms loose on you. And that is something you might not recover from. If you violate another of my decrees, I will have your head decorate the front of my litter." The curtain closed.

•   •   •

Leonidas's heart felt as heavy as his shield. The six lochoi were lined up in battle formation in front of the Hellenion, the squires and battle train already on the road before dawn and out of the city. Cyra had been gone when he and Thetis arrived home, a neighbor woman watching Briseis. The woman said the strange priestess had told her that she had gone off to consult with the gods and that she would meet the king on the march.

Wives and daughters were in the shade of the temple. The boys of the agoge were gathered in their own ranks to watch their fathers march off. A low sound, almost inaudible at first, came from the women. It grew in strength until the words of the hymn to the battle god could clearly be heard by all. The ranks stood still, their spear points aligned neatly.

When the hymn died out and silence covered the field, Leonidas turned to the western road. Without issuing a command, he strode forth. The first rank of the first lochoi turned in step and followed. Row after row of Spartans trod onto the dirt road and headed to the west, casting long shadows before them. When Leonidas reached a rise in the road where he knew he would disappear from view after crossing, he paused and stepped to the side. His eyes were on the men, noting their deportment. It was only after the last rank had filed past and he was covered in dust did he turn and look back at his city. Stepping out from the shadow of the temple he saw Thetis. He raised his shield. She raised Amphion in her arms.

Tears coursed down the king's face, cutting into the dust caked on it as he turned to the west and followed his army. It was a while before he sped up his pace to catch up with the column.

11

The Present

Dane was slammed back in the seat as the SR-71 accelerated down the runway and leaped into the air. The nose of the jet was pointed almost vertical as they gained altitude. Dane pulled out an E-book that he had borrowed from one of the crew members on the FLIP. He'd downloaded all of Frost's books of poetry into it. He accessed the first book and clicked through to the preface, which had a brief summary of Frost's life.

As the SR-71 leveled off at 60,000 feet, Dane quickly read the bio to get a feeling for the man he had seen in his vision. Frost was born in San Francisco in 1874 and was named after General Robert E. Lee. His father was the editor of the *San Francisco Daily Evening Post*. Dane paused as he read the next entry in the bio: When he was nine, Frost told his mother he heard voices when he was alone and that he shared her gift for "second hearing and sight." So history agreed with the vision he'd had to a certain extent, Dane thought.

Frost's first poem was professionally published in 1894, and he was desperately in love with a woman named Elinor White. Frost took the first two bound copies of his collection of poems and went to her, begging her to marry him. She declined, and he burned his copy of the collection and returned home dejected. He then decided to leave Massachusetts and travel to the Dismal Swamp on the Virginia–North Carolina border. Dane found that strange. Why was the poet drawn to that location?

After some time in the swamp, Frost finally returned home, and White agreed to marry him. It was at that point, it appeared from what Dane was reading, that the poet's life entered an even darker phase. He had a son who died of cholera, and then his mother was diagnosed with cancer and died later the same year. Several years later, he had a daughter who died three days after her birth. Throughout these tragedies, Frost made his living teaching, but he also continued to write poetry.

His sister was sent to a mental institution for the rest of her life. Dane wondered if she, too, heard the voices and couldn't handle it. In 1938, Frost's wife died, and he suffered an emotional collapse. What Dane found interesting was that almost all of Frost's children suffered various ailments, with several deaths and at least one suicide and numerous commitments to mental hospitals.

Dane was surprised to see that Frost visited the White House in 1958 and met with President Eisenhower. He wondered what that meeting was about. Dane's eyes widened slightly as he read about Frost in 1959 predicting Kennedy's election in 1960. And then, in 1962, Frost did indeed travel to Russia. He was sick during the trip, but Khrushchev went to where the poet was laid up and visited him, and the two talked for ninety minutes.

Upon arriving back in the United States, Frost caused a minor furor when he said that Khrushchev had told him that

Americans were too liberal to fight. And, during the Cuban
Missile Crisis, Frost admitted that Khrushchev had not said
that. The poet died three months later.

Dane paused as he got to the end of the short biography.
It validated several things from his vision, and he was cer-
tain he had never read or heard these things about Robert
Frost before, so it wasn't coming from some old memory.

He began reading the poems, searching. He paused as he
read the last lines on one stanza from "Storm Fear," where
Frost doubted humans had the heart to save themselves.

Dane felt the connection of his own fear to those lines; he
also wondered if it was a reference to the Ones Before, who
seemed to be very chancy with their aid. He hit the Forward
button and stopped at the next poem, "In Equal Sacrifice,"
which appeared to be about Robert of Bruce, and the sacri-
fices he made, but seemed relevant to recent events Dane
had experienced.

Dane scanned down, searching for the words that rang of
the voice to him, skipping several stanzas till he got near the
bottom where Frost wrote about giving all to the hopeless
fight.

The lines echoed in Dane's mind. Was that his task? To
give all to a hopeless fight? And if so, why?

The next poems were from *North of Boston*, and Dane
immediately noticed a reference to seeing a figure in darkness with a face "as plain as a white plate." Had Frost seen
a Valkyrie? It was a very unusual way, even for a poet, to describe a face, but a perfect way to describe a Valkyrie.

Dane clicked on Frost's most famous poem about two
roads diverging in the woods. But he read it now with a different sense of what the poet might have been saying, sensing something deeper under the words. He remembered the
feeling he'd had about his vision, that he had seen something that had really happened. What if he had seen another
road, one that hadn't been taken in Dane's own life, but

maybe it had been taken in some other way? Dane felt as if he were very close to understanding something fundamental about the gates and the Shadow.

The next poem was the one Frost had recited to Kennedy: "Fire and Ice." Dane continued on. The title of another poem caught his eye: "The Trial by Existence." Dane found he was nodding, the rhythm of the words almost a mantra in his mind. When he had started reading the poems, he had wished that Frost had simply said what the voices told him, but Dane was realizing that perhaps Frost had had visions just like he did, and he had been forced to use the written word, the only means he had, to try to get those visions out of his head. Reading the lines, Dane knew he was picking up more than he was consciously realizing.

One poem even focused on quartz, which Dane found strange: quartz? Dane saw the crystal skulls in his mind and remembered watching Sin Fen's head transform into one. He could feel his body pressed against the shoulder harness as the SR-71 banked and began descending. Quickly, he punched the button, turning the page. A long poem, "The Generations of Men," lit up the screen. Dane began scanning it, searching it for lines that triggered a reaction, and he found them. It mentioned oracles, voices, visions

Dane could see the aircraft carrier directly ahead. The plane vibrated as the pilot decelerated, slowing the supersonic craft to just above its stall speed. At the end of the poem it mentioned meeting elsewhere.

Dane looked up as the nose of the plane lifted as the pilot tried to eke every square inch of drag out of the delta-shaped wings. With a heavy *thump*, the plane hit the deck of the carrier, raced down the deck, and then was snagged by red nylon webbing stretched across its path. Dane was just about to tuck the E-book away in his pack when he saw a footnote the editor of the last collection had made, listing a quote Frost made during an interview:

One thing I care about, and wish young people could care about, is taking poetry as the first form of understanding. If poetry isn't understanding all, the whole world, then it isn't worth anything. Young poets forget that poetry must include the mind as well as the emotions. Too many poets delude themselves by thinking the mind is dangerous and must be left out. Well, the mind is dangerous and must be left in.

• • •

The calculations were rudimentary: The two Russians on board *Mir* simply had to figure in their altitude above the target, terminal velocity once the MIRV rockets entered the atmosphere, cross-checked by the rotation of the Earth and the speed of the space station.

They programmed the data into the computer and waited while the result was tabulated. It didn't take long; about four seconds. A small flashing X appeared on the projected flight path of the space station and a digital countdown, currently at three minutes thirty seconds, also lit up. The senior cosmonaut sat in the command seat, his finger over the launch button. The fact that what he was about to do was an act of war with Peru concerned him little. What had happened at Chernobyl was also an act of war and on a scale that it threatened the capital of his country. What was happening at Nazca was a threat to the entire world, Peru included.

"Two minutes," his fellow cosmonaut unnecessarily announced.

• • •

The death zone around Chernobyl was a teardrop shape over ninety miles long by forty at its widest. Although it might be reasonably assumed that the Shadow had caused all the damage it possibly could by destroying Towers One, Two, and Three, and the leadership in Moscow was not focused on reason.

A single rocket lifted off from a silo just outside of Moscow and quickly accelerated to supersonic speed as it arced up into the sky toward the southeast. When it reached its apex, the engine flamed out, and the rocket followed the laws of physics at it headed back toward Earth, directly toward Tower Four at Chernobyl.

Nestled in the nose cone was a single nuclear warhead, specially adapted to detonate when an eight-foot prod that extended from the tip hit the ground and ignited a manual detonator, which would then ignite the conventional explosives that were the first step of exploding the bomb.

* * *

The lead cosmonaut hushed his companion, who had begun counting down from ten. Even though it was cool inside *Mir*—the heating elements had been operating below par for quite a while—a small bead of sweat made its way down his forehead. It was exactly between his eyes when the number went to zero, and his hand slammed down on the release button.

The rocket ignited and exited the launch tube, nose pointing straight down toward Earth. It gathered speed from both the engine and gravity.

* * *

The strikes had been coordinated so that the missiles would hit their targets simultaneously. The timing was close but not perfect. The Chernobyl missile touched down, probe first, into Tower Four about two seconds before the *Mir* missile hit Nazca.

The aim of the Chernobyl missile was perfect, though, as it struck the black triangle exactly and disappeared.

• • •

The *Mir* missile had been launched with a time-delay detonator set to go off at an altitude of 4,000 feet above the
Nazca plain. The scientists in Moscow had determined this
to be the best height for maximum effect, although they had
reluctantly admitted they weren't exactly sure what the
composition of the target was, other than walls of fire.

The warhead exploded.

And as fast as the blast, radiation, and light expanded
from the bomb, the lines of fire on the Nazca plain leaped up
and devoured it all. Within two seconds, all signs of the blast
were gone from the surface.

The Space Between

Amelia Earhart staggered as the ground hiccuped. She
turned to Taki with a questioning look.

The samurai simply shrugged and pointed. Earhart noted
the golden glow ahead. While blue seemed to be friendly,
she knew that gold was a sign of the Shadow. Because the
Valkyries floated above the black sand, following them had
been difficult. It had been a process of occasionally spotting
them ahead, then waiting as they moved away, then hurrying in the direction they had gone. Taki had cautioned her
that they might run into an ambush, but Earhart felt that the
Valkyries were more concerned with getting their captives
back than worrying about someone following them. Besides, she had a good idea where they were heading.

The wall appeared ahead, and the glow was coming from
the base of it. Once more, Earhart edged her way up a dune,
Taki at her side. Just before the top, she halted and peered
over. A large, open cavern had been cut into the wall. Her
mouth went dry as she saw what was inside the cavern: hundreds of upright metal tables, on which humans were

strapped down. She could see that much of the skin on the ones closest to the outside had been removed and replaced with a clear covering. Muscles, internal organs, all glistened underneath the wrapping. Some of the people were missing limbs. Most had the top of their skulls removed and numerous needles poking up with small, glowing bulbs on the top.

She ducked her head as a white figure floated along the lines toward the opening of the cavern. A Valkyrie. Collecting herself, Earhart lifted up once more and looked. The Valkyrie had stopped in front of one of the bodies. It was one of the five that had just been recovered, the skin still intact, clothes piled at the base of the table.

The Valkyrie raised its right arm, claws extended. With precise moves, the creature sliced into the man's chest. Two seconds later, it pulled back the arm, a heart dripping blood cradled carefully in the claws. It floated back the way it had come, the gory trophy in hand.

Taki tapped her on the arm, pointing. There were other new abductees in the Valkyrie labs, a half-dozen men whose skin and bodies were still intact and who were wearing khaki uniforms.

"Come," Earhart said.

Taki was at her side as she headed down the slope, the other warriors spreading out instinctively in a wedge formation. Earhart went straight to the newcomers and with her sword cut one free as the samurai did the same with the others. She grunted as she slipped the unconscious man over her shoulders in a fireman's carry and headed back the way she'd come.

The Present

"Slow down," Dane said into his SATPhone. "Start over." He was looking into the clear, blue water of the Caribbean. He was on board a launch from the carrier, cutting through the sea. Dane knew that not far below was the top of the pyramid on which Sin Fen had given her life.

Ahana's voice was still rushed as she repeated herself: "The Russians fired nuclear weapons at both Nazca and Chernobyl. The Nazca one detonated, but all effects were absorbed into the walls of fire. The Chernobyl one simply disappeared."

"So, in other words," Dane said, "all they did was add power to Nazca?"

"Correct. Our readings spiked right after the detonation."

"And sent a nuke, God knows where, into the space between via Chernobyl?"

"Apparently."

Dane wondered what a nuke would do inside a gate, if it went off at all, which he doubted, given the effect gates had on electromagnetic devices. Of course, he realized Kolkov and the Russians knew about that effect, so they had probably rigged some other means to detonate the device.

"The drain through Nazca is the same?" he asked.

"Yes," Ahana replied. "Actually, it might be a little faster. The nuclear explosion might have accelerated things."

"How long do we have?" Dane asked.

"Seventy hours."

"Tell Foreman it might be a good idea to get Washington to put a leash on the Russians," Dane said. He flipped the phone shut and handed it to one of the crewmen standing nearby. Stupidity. He'd seen it in Vietnam, in the places where he and Chelsea had been called to do search and rescue, and again in this battle against the Shadow. He knew it was the bane of mankind's existence.

He reached down and picked up a set of scuba tanks and slipped them on. With practiced ease, he prepared the diving gear, making all the necessary checks just as he'd been trained at Key West so many years earlier. He forgot about Nazca, Foreman, the Shadow, Ariana's death, Frost's poetry, and everything that had been rattling about his brain. His focus was totally on the task at hand, another trait the military had honed.

In scuba school, as in airborne training, one tenet that had constantly been stressed was that the trainee was entering a naturally hostile environment. One survived neither a parachute jump nor a dive without the proper equipment working perfectly. The slightest mistake in such an environment could easily be fatal. Because of that, concentration on the mission at hand had to be total.

Dane sat on the edge of the launch and, with one hand holding his mask in place, fell backward into the warm water. He paused and checked, making sure everything was working correctly. He wished Rachel was here, but he knew the dolphin's place was the Devil's Sea gate. He looked down and slowly descended.

As he passed through 100 feet, he could see the top of the pyramid. The little light that made it this deep reflected off the smooth, black stone. Dane knew the Navy had been all over this area, using all the scientific techniques they had to get an idea of the composition of the pyramid. And he had been briefed on the way over from the carrier that the black stone had defeated all those attempts.

None had disturbed what was on the flat top of the pyramid, though. Dane didn't know if Foreman had ordered that out of respect for Sin Fen's remains or because the CIA man feared that such an action would cause a reappearance of the Bermuda Triangle gate. Dane shook his head as he descended. Foreman wouldn't have given a damn about Sin Fen.

Dane slowed, then came to a halt standing on the top of the pyramid, several feet from a large, four-foot-high slab that was in the center. A Naga staff was upright next to the slab. Dane hesitated.

He could feel Sin Fen, her essence. Part of her. And hanging around the essence was a sense of power coming out of the pyramid.

Dane remembered his last view of Sin Fen as she lay in a human-shaped depression on the slab as her skull changed form, from flesh, bone, and blood to crystal, channeling the power of the pyramid against the blackness of the Bermuda Triangle gate. Blue lightning streaking from the skull, penetrating and dissipating the gate.

Dane took a step forward, the fins on his feet almost tripping him. He realized he was overbreathing, sucking in too much air. He stopped.

Mission. He focused on that one word. Years of harsh training pushed aside the emotions.

Mission.

Dane stepped forward. He could see down into the depression in the center of the slab, a pure crystal skull lying at the top. Dane reached out and put his hand on the top of the Naga staff. His fingers curled among the snake heads. His eyes peering through the mask at the skull, Dane twisted the staff.

With a solid click, it turned.

Dane's hand was tight on the Naga staff, his body tense, but nothing happened. He pulled the staff out of the slot it was in, careful to keep the razor-sharp edge away from his body. Then he leaned over and placed his free hand on the skull, fingers spread. A shock ran up his arm, but he didn't let go.

Dane closed his eyes, and visions flashed through his mind: a dirty street in Cambodia; monks praying in stone ruins; the mist of the Angkor gate covering the jungle; the towers of Angkor Wat.

Dane tucked the crystal skull in the crook of his arm and pushed off, heading for the surface.

12

480 B.C.

"There is someone we must meet." Cyra spoke the words softly, the slight breeze coming off the water carrying them away so that only the king heard her.

Leonidas was standing on the high bank, peering out at the Gulf of Corinth. The army had stopped for the night, and the air was full of the sound of an army encamping. They had made good time on the march so far, and spirits were high at the prospect of pending action.

"Who?"

"An oracle."

"Why?"

"To find the right path."

Leonidas laughed. "We know where we're going. And this is the quickest track to Rhion."

"It is not Rhion or Antirhon that concern me," Cyra said. "I do not think we will have enough time to get to the Gates of Fire if we follow the"—she searched for the right words—"conventional path."

"And this oracle will know a better way?"

"Yes."

"And where is this oracle?"

Cyra pointed to the sea. "She is coming this evening. We must go out to meet her. She never sets foot on the mainland."

Leonidas didn't seem very enthused by the idea. "How do you know she will be out there?"

"I have had a vision."

"Splendid."

"I have arranged for a boat." She nodded to the left, and Leonidas saw a small craft with a man standing by.

"Couldn't you have arranged for something larger?"

"You do not like the water?"

"You are an excellent seer," Leonidas said. He tapped the armor on his chest "One cannot swim well with this. I do not understand those who make their living plying the water. A man must have firm ground under his feet."

Cyra wrapped her cloak more tightly around her body. "Come, Lord. I think we will both want to hear what the oracle has to say."

"Which oracle is this?"

"She comes from Thera."

Leonidas knew of that shattered island south of Greece. He had heard tales from the few Spartans he knew who sailed. "It is said that island was smitten by the gods, that only a fraction of what was once there remains."

"It was once home to my people," Cyra said as they negotiated the rocky track down to the shore.

"What happened?"

"The Shadow tried to destroy it."

"This Shadow seems to be very powerful."

"It is."

They arrived at the boat. Leonidas offered his arm, but Cyra ignored it and climbed on board. The king followed, and the man shoved the boat into the water. He then jumped on board, sitting between two oars. Without a word, he began pulling. Leonidas watched the gap between boat and shore widen.

"Left," Cyra said softly, and the oarsman shifted their direction.

Leonidas turned his attention to the water and noted a fine mist ahead. "How do you know where she is?"

"I sense her."

They entered the mist, and visibility was reduced to less than a thousand meters. Leonidas could no longer see the shore, and he wondered how they would make it back.

"Hold here," Cyra ordered, and the oarsman pulled his blades out of the water. The boat slowly came to a halt. The surface of the water was perfectly smooth, undisturbed. Leonidas frowned, remembering the breeze on the shore.

There was no sound other than the slow drip of water from the oars, and even that ceased shortly.

Leonidas sat stiffly on the wooden seat. He wanted to stretch his legs out, but there was little room, and Cyra was so still, her head cocked to the side as if listening, that he didn't want to disturb her.

Cyra's head straightened. "She comes."

Leonidas looked into the mist, which, if anything, was growing thicker. He felt uneasy and at first attributed that to being on the water, but then he realized it was more than that. This fog reminded him of that which had been at Delphi.

"There is danger here," he whispered to Cyra, his voice sounding harsh and loud.

"Yes. It follows the oracle."

Leonidas put his hand on the pommel of his sword. He didn't fancy a fight with the unsteady platform of the boat under his feet.

Cyra lightly touched him on the shoulder. "There." She pointed.

A boat slowly appeared, one unlike any that the Spartan king had ever seen. The first thing he noted was the upthrust prow, with an intricate carving at the tip. Leonidas squinted, making out the details: seven snake heads originating from one body. Then the rest of the boat came into view. It was long and sleek, very different from the short and stubby boats the Greeks and their neighbors favored. Six oars on each side swept into the water in unison, then rose out and came to a halt.

The boat glided smoothly through the water, slowing, until it stopped less than two feet from Leonidas and Cyra, an impressive feat of seamanship. Shields lined the side above the oar holes, and no one was visible.

"Come," Cyra was on her feet. She reached out, and Leonidas noted a set of notches in the side of the ship. Cyra put her hand in one, foot in another, and then quickly climbed on board. He reluctantly followed.

Climbing over the edge, he paused, looking into the ship. The first thing he noted were the twelve oarsmen. They were large, well-muscled men with black skin. Leonidas had heard tales of such dark-skinned men living to the south on the other side of the Mediterranean, but he had never seen one. They wore the skins of animals, but such creatures the king had also never seen: yellowish hides with black spots.

"Come." Cyra was waiting.

Leonidas followed her gaze to the rear of the boat, where long reeds had been woven into a semicircular shape, the interior of which was lit by a dull blue light. It reminded him of the Corycian Cave, as if the best attempt to transport such a place onto a boat had been made. The blue glow came from a stone similar to what he had seen at Delphi. A figure was seated on the other side, a long hood covering the face.

Leonidas followed Cyra along the center plank. The oarsmen ignored them, sitting as still as statues. Leonidas noted their weapons: long, curved swords that looked very heavy. The metal gleamed, and he could tell the weapons were well maintained. He knew by the men's bearing that they were warriors.

Cyra entered the reed cave and bowed her head. Leonidas stood next to her and chose not to bow.

"King and Priestess." The voice was low and sensual, as if from a girl in her prime. But when the figure pulled back the hood, a lined, old woman's face was revealed.

"Oracle," Cyra acknowledged.

"You called me here," the Theran oracle said.

Leonidas glanced at Cyra. How could she have summoned the oracle?

"We were both called here," Cyra said. "I fear we will not be able to make it to the Gates of Fire in time."

The oracle looked at Leonidas. "Because he is true to his laws, he does not follow your advice." She held up a hand, forestalling Cyra. "It is as it must be, for his laws are what makes him what he is. And what he is, is what is needed."

"But if he is not at the Gates in time"—Cyra began, but she was cut off.

"Why do you think I came? I will show you a way, using the hidden paths. It is a perilous journey, but I will give you a weapon that will help."

At the word *weapon,* Leonidas's interest perked up, only to have it dashed with the oracle's next words.

"I will also tell you some things I know that you need to know. Things I was told by my mother."

Leonidas waited impatiently, his eyes scanning the surrounding mist.

"The Shadow is strong and can move along the hidden paths. As you must, now that you are late." She glanced at Leonidas briefly. "But the paths sometimes can be influenced. That is why the Gates of Fire, the Persians, and you Spartans must all come together there."

"I don't understand," Cyra said.

The oracle touched her head lightly. "We are much more powerful than we realize. And enough minds brought together, working at a very high level of activity, can affect the paths, change them for a little while."

"A high level of activity?" Leonidas repeated. "Such as in battle?"

"Such as in battle," the oracle confirmed.

Leonidas had an idea what she was talking about. He never felt more alive than when he was in combat, every nerve ending on fire, his time sense of the world slowing down so that every second seemed to stretch out many times its normal length.

"What you experience is not imaginary," the oracle said to him, as if she could read his mind.

Leonidas said nothing, trying to determine the value of what she was saying.

The oracle turned to Cyra. "There is a woman that is with Xerxes. Her name is Pandora."

Cyra nodded. "I know."

"Do you know what she is?"

"An adviser to the Persian king," Cyra said.

"She is a Sibyl," the oracle said.

"A Sibyl?" Leonidas asked.

"A priestess who has been suborned by the Shadow," the oracle said. "She advises the Persian king. Fortunately, he follows her advice about as well as our king here."

"I'm here, aren't I?" Leonidas said.

The Theran oracle focused on Cyra. "What do you know of Ahura Mazda?" she asked Cyra.

"That is the name of the god that Xerxes—and the rest of the Persians—worship," Cyra replied.

"What else?"

Cyra shrugged. "No more."

"Too bad," the oracle said. "You must remember that there is some degree of truth in all things, even lies."

Leonidas shifted his feet. The mist was getting thicker. He wished the old lady would give them the weapon and tell them the way and be done with it.

"Those who worship Ahura Mazda believe he created the world."

"All beliefs say their god created the world," Leonidas interjected, trying to hurry her to the point.

"Ah, but the priests—called magi—of Ahura Mazda say he created *seven* worlds, all branching from him. The oldest of these worlds is called *Asha,* or the Fire World. Fire is worshiped by the followers of Ahura Mazda as the sacred channel to eternal light. To get to the eternal light, one must pass through the infinite darkness."

Leonidas had no clue what she was speaking about, but he remained quiet, realizing nothing he could say or do would hurry the old woman along. He noted that the ship was moving very slightly, as if now riding on a low swell.

"And the end of the world," the Theran oracle continued. "Do you know how those of Ahura Mazda say it will end?"

Cyra remained silent, indicating she didn't.

"Purification by fire." The old woman reached inside her cloak and pulled out a roll of parchment. She unscrolled it slightly and read, "'And a great river of blazing fire will flow across the land and will consume everything, land and ocean, man and creature, even unto heaven and hell. The entire world will be scorched and the human race annihilated except for the chosen ones, the angels of white, also known as the light travelers.'"

Leonidas thought of the Valkyrie—easily an angel of white to the unknowing eye.

The Theran oracle opened the scroll a little further, then looked up. "What is interesting, as near as I can make out from this translation, is that the followers of Ahura Mazda believe the world goes through a cycle of destruction and re-birth. Thus the world has been destroyed many times."

As with the rest of it, that made little sense to Leonidas. He noticed that the forwardmost two rowers had stood up, swords in hand, and were peering over the bulwark. The oracle spotted him noticing. "Yes. They come."

"Valkyries?" Leonidas drew his sword.

"Yes." She pointed to her right. "Take that."

Leonidas noted what appeared to be a pole in the shadows. When he stepped forward to grab it, he paused. It was a weapon, one end of which was a wide spear blade, the other, like the prow of the ship, a seven-headed snake.

"You may use that against the Valkyries. It will cut their skin easily. But I must have it back." She looked at Cyra. "After you have the golden sphere, you must bring the Naga staff back to me. It will be needed later."

Leonidas hefted the spear. It was surprisingly light. He held the blade close to his eyes and was amazed at the workmanship. It was beyond any edge he had ever seen, and the metal was something no blacksmith he knew had ever worked with.

"Tell me," the oracle said to Cyra, "have you been properly taught the four stages of awareness?"

"Awareness of self. Awareness of others. Awareness of the world. Awareness beyond the world."

"Very good. Because you will soon face the fourth stage."

One of the oarsmen at the front of the boat called out in a strange tongue, but there was no mistaking his alarm. Leonidas strode forward. Behind him, Cyra leaned close to the Theran oracle, who handed her a piece of parchment.

Leonidas came up between the two oarsmen. They glanced at him, noted the staff in his hand, and then turned their attention back to the fog. Leonidas felt cold, a strange sensation, considering it had been warm just moments earlier. He glanced over his shoulder and noted that the other oarsmen had all given up wood for steel. A half dozen were arrayed in front of the oracle and Cyra. The rest were facing the sides of the ship.

The man to Leonidas's left hissed something. The king turned in that direction and saw two white figures float out of the fog toward the ship. They paused about twenty feet away, suspended about ten feet above the water, just barely visible.

A scream from behind caused Leonidas to spin about. One of the oarsmen was being held in the air, run through by a tentacle with teeth on the end that had gone in his back and punched out his chest. More of the arms appeared, blindly grasping for targets. The men hacked at them with their swords.

Leonidas turned back toward the Valkyries. The two hadn't moved. He ignored the sounds of mortal battle behind him and remained focused on the two white creatures, the Naga staff at the ready. For the first time, he noted that they were holding something between them—a black cylinder about five feet long that tapered to a point—which was pointed directly at the boat. Leonidas frowned as the cylinder began to transform at the rear, the black becoming gold, moving slowly forward.

"No!" The strength of the old woman's yell surprised Leonidas. He turned. The oarsmen were having some success keeping the kraken arms at bay; the deck was littered with severed arms. The oracle was coming forward, Cyra helping her. The old woman held something glittery in her hands, out of which a bright light was emanating. Leonidas blinked when he realized it was a skull, but one made of a clear material, not bone.

"No, you don't," the oracle hissed as she reached the

middle of the boat. She held the skull up in her wrinkled hands.

A flash caused Leonidas to spin to his right. A golden ball was heading directly toward the Oracle. He watched as it struck her, enveloping her in the glow. The oracle was highlighted in gold for several seconds, standing rigid, her mouth open in a silent scream. Then the gold was pulled into the skull, absorbed completely. Cyra caught the oracle as she collapsed. Leonidas turned back to the sea, but the Valkyries were gone, along with the krakens, the fog dissipating.

. . .

Xerxes sat on his throne, looking down at the canal that cut through the isthmus that led to Mount Athos. His fleet was passing through, one by one, a long line. Each side of the ditch was lined by soldiers holding torches, spaced five feet apart.

As if to mock the effort of years of digging, the weather was perfect, not a cloud in the sky, the stars sparkling overhead. The fleet could have gone around the Mount, but Xerxes would not hear of it. The canal had been dug, and therefore the ships would use it.

Pandora had started to say something when Xerxes issued the order to his fleet commander, but he had chopped his hand to let her know he didn't want to hear anything she said. She stood silently to the rear of his chair, her eyes on the back of the seat.

. . .

"Is she all right?" Leonidas asked.

Cyra had her hand on the oracle's forehead. "She's alive."

"What happened?"

"You saw as much as I did," Cyra said.

Leonidas had noted that the boat—and the oarsman—who had brought them out to the ship were gone, most likely victims of the kraken. "Did she tell you this secret path?"

"Yes."

Leonidas stood, waiting.

Cyra finally looked up. "So now you are in a rush?"

"It does us no good to remain here."

One of the oarsmen came over and easily picked up the oracle. He carried her back to the reed cave and laid her down on a mat, covering her with a blanket. Leonidas pointed at his own chest, and then toward the shore, or at least where he thought the shore was in the darkness. His army was marching for war; there were no fires to delineate where the Spartan camp was.

The warrior nodded and yelled orders in his language. The surviving men bent to the task, and the ship began moving. The man who had carried the oracle went back and retrieved the skull. He placed it under a blanket next to her body.

When the ship was close to shore, the rowers pulled their oars up, and the ship glided to a halt, the keel lightly hitting. Leonidas carefully climbed over the side with one hand, the other clutching the Naga staff. His feet entered the water, and he paused, then he lowered himself very slowly until he touched bottom. He stepped away and held up his free hand to help Cyra, but she ignored the assistance.

By the time they had walked up on shore, the ship was already pulling away. Leonidas headed for camp, Cyra hurrying after him. When he was challenged by a sentry, he called out the proper password, then began issuing orders for all to awaken and the march to be resumed, even though dawn was several hours away.

13

The Present

Every human being on the planet, except for those on board aircraft in flight, felt it. It started almost 5,000 kilometers inside the Earth, along the transition zone between the solid crystalline core and the molten inner core. The solid core turned, adjusting to the power coming down from the Nazca fault and in doing so, sent P compression waves rippling through the inner core. The solid lower mantle dampened the effect somewhat, as did the upper mantle, but every person in contact with the surface of the planet felt the ground tremble under their feet.

The readings all over the planet were exactly the same, which told shocked scientists the source and foretold of much worse to come. Those same scientists were brought before heads of states and solutions were demanded.

The replies, to say the least, were unsatisfactory, especially given recent events over the Nazca plain and at Chernobyl.

• • •

"Do you still have the portal pinpointed?" Dane asked Ahana. He was bone tired, having flown from the carrier, across Central America and a large part of the Pacific, back to the Devil's Sea gate. He'd not felt the planet move, but he'd received the reports while in transit. The grim looks on Ahana's, Marsten's, and Foreman's faces confirmed what the numbers had reported.

Ahana nodded. "Yes. The probes we sent through are still transmitting."

"I'm going in."

"What are you going to do?" Foreman asked.

The Naga staff was leaning against the conference table, and a large metal case holding the crystal skulls was on the floor. "I'm going to find Amelia Earhart first," Dane said. "Then I'll figure out the next step."

"Not much of a plan," Foreman complained.

"When you have a better one, let me know," Dane said. He turned to Dr. Marsten, who had yet to speak. "Is Rachel ready?"

"Yes."

"Have you translated any more of the dolphin cries that the *Connecticut* picked up?"

"As near as I can tell, it's the same message, repeated over and over again. That's all Rachel's given back to me."

Dane had been thinking about that. "What kind of map are they referring to?" he asked the room.

"It must be a map that shows the connections of the various portals," Ahana said.

"But even if we get such a map," Dane said, "how will that help us change the path of the power?"

There was no answer to that question, nor had Dane really expected one. He stood and picked up the Naga staff

"Give me a hand with that," he asked Foreman, indicating the case with the skulls.

They walked onto the deck of the FLIP. A *Deepflight* submersible was waiting.

"You sure you want to go alone?" Foreman asked.

"I'm not going alone," Dane said. He indicated a gray dorsal fin cutting through the water next to the submersible. He climbed down onto the deck of the craft and stored the staff and skulls inside.

Deepflight was a radical departure from previous submersibles. It was designed more like an airplane than a submarine. It was forty feet long with a wingspan of fifteen feet. The compartment Dane would ride in was a titanium sphere in the very center. Wings with controllable flaps extended out from each side, giving the craft excellent maneuverability. Forward of the sphere was a specially designed beak that reduced drag when the submersible was moving forward. In the rear were two vertical fins right behind the dual propeller system that complemented the wings for three-dimensional flight.

The crew sphere was solid, with just two holes in it: one the hatch that screwed out and a second, smaller one that accessed control and command cables. To see outside, Dane would use various cameras and radar. Powerful spotlights were bolted all around the craft. Dane paused in the hatch when Ahana spoke.

"There's something interesting one of the Navy people found when they ran a maintenance check on the submersible. It appears as if it passed through both high temperature and a strong radioactive field."

Dane nodded. "We know some of the portals are hot." It was one of the confusing aspects of the entire gate-portal system. Some were radioactive and had high temperatures, while others had neither characteristic.

"It had to have happened on the last trip in," Ahana said.

"And?" Dane was anxious to be going.

"Then how did she get through unscathed?" Ahana was pointing at Rachel.

That gave Dane pause, but it was just one of many things he didn't understand and didn't particularly have time to ponder. "I don't know. Let's just be grateful that she does."

He grabbed the hatch. "I will see you when I will see you." He ducked down into the sphere and swung the hatch closed, then began screwing it shut.

The Space Between

Earhart almost collapsed from exhaustion as she put down the man she had carried from the Valkyrie cave. Asper, a U.S. Navy assistant surgeon who had been aboard the USS *Cyclops* when it ran into the Bermuda Triangle gate in 1918 and disappeared, knelt next to the man.

"How is he?" Earhart asked.

"Seems all right," Asper said as he examined him. "Shock, mostly."

Earhart had seen it before. New arrivals to the space between were often so stunned by their abduction that it took a day or two for them to regain their bearings. She noted the man's clothing.

"U.S. Navy?"

Asper nodded. "Looks like. But not from my time." He touched the silver eagle on the man's collar. "A captain."

Earhart noted something on the man's chest—an insignia shaped like a dolphin. "What's that?"

"I don't know."

"Curious," Earhart remembered the dolphin that had accompanied Dane. "I think . . ." She paused and turned her head toward the inner sea. "He's here." She smiled. "And so is she."

"What?" Asper asked. "Who's here?"

She turned to Taki. "Come."

    •   •   •

The touch of the inner sea's water on his skin sickened Dane. Everything was slightly wrong with the elements in the space between. The air smelled funny, the water felt and tasted strange, and the black soil was unlike anything Dane had ever seen on Earth.

The case containing the skulls was waterproof, and he was able to half lie on it as he kicked for shore, Rachel at his side, the Naga staff in his hand. He'd left *Deepflight* anchored just outside of the portal he'd come through. There were at least a dozen portals in view

Rachel cut across in front of him, rolling on her side, rubbing against his legs, and Dane stopped kicking as a vision flashed into his brain: rows of men in armor, spears leveled, advancing across a plain. Then it was gone.

Dane wasn't surprised to look up and see Amelia Earhart standing on the shoreline, her samurai guards around her, waiting for him. His feet touched bottom, and he walked up to her, carrying staff and case, water dripping off.

"I knew you would come back," Earhart said. "And we need that," she added, pointing at the Naga staff.

"For what?" Dane asked, not surprised that she needed it.

"To capture some Valkyries."

"And what do we do with them?"

"Take their armor suits."

"And then?"

Earhart put her hands on her hips. "I thought you would tell me that."

Dane slowly nodded. "Let's get the Valkyries first. One step at a time."

She paused. "There's something else—actually, a couple of things."

"Yes?"

"My navigator arrived here not long ago."

"Noonan? I thought you said you saw him die."

"I did say it, and I did see it," Earhart said. "But he arrived here alive—seriously injured and sick, but alive. His message was that we had to get some Valkyrie armor. And that someone would come with"—she pointed—"a Naga staff to help us do that."

"Are you sure he died?"

"A kraken punched a tentacle through his chest," Earhart said. "There's no evidence of a wound at all on the man here."

"You don't think its Noonan?"

"No, it's him."

"How can that be?"

"I thought you might tell me."

Dane didn't have a clue. "You said there were a couple of things?"

"We also rescued a couple of castaways. They appear to be from the U.S. Navy, from around your time, probably."

Dane nodded. "We just lost one of our submarines near the Devil's Sea gate."

As Earhart led the way back toward her camp, Dane filled her in on everything else that had happened since he'd left her and returned to his own world and time. Behind them, Rachel slowly circled, then sprinted off toward the visible portals.

The Present

Some places on the planet's surface are less stable than others. When the core shifted a second, more powerful time, several of these gave way. The most significant was in the Rift Valley in Africa, the longest continuous land crack on the surface of the planet. Along the 6,700-kilometer length of the Great Rift was the lowest land point in the world—the

Afar Depression at 510 feet below sea level—and along its flanks were some of the highest and largest volcanoes, including Mount Kilimanjaro, the highest peak in Africa.

From the north, the Rift starts in southern Turkey, running from there to Syria, then splitting Israel from Jordan with the Dead Sea, then along the full length of the Gulf of Aqaba and the Red Sea, where it splits going both north and south. The northern branch runs along the Gulf of Aden to the Indian Ocean, separating the Arabian tectonic plate from the Indo-Australian plate.

Southward, it cleaves the eastern half of Africa, forming the Galla Lakes of Ethiopia, into Kenya, where it cuts through a place called Kino Sogo, a vast plain of lava sheets that the Rift is continuously tearing apart. From there it continues, producing Lake Turkana, then into land so barren no one lived there, which was fortunate, considering what was coming.

Given fossil discoveries such as that in the Olduvai Gorge, it was widely suspected that humankind originated in the Rift. As the crystal moved for a second time, it appeared as if it would be the beginning of the end of mankind.

As the inner Earth shifted below, the entire right side of the Rift Valley, which represented the western edge of the Somali African tectonic plate, dropped a quarter mile in less than fifteen seconds. The drop was destructive enough for those living in those countries from the eastern half of Mozambique to Ethiopia, killing almost a million people immediately as the Earth buckled and spasmed.

Worse followed. The drop put the majority of the land below sea level. The Indian Ocean poured in, creating a 1,000-mile-long waterfall, the likes of which the planet hadn't seen since the Mediterranean Basin opened to the Atlantic Ocean and began to fill millennia ago.

Millions more died as a wall of water over 800 feet high roared forward, destroying and submerging everything in its path until it smashed up against the mountains forming the left side of the Rift Valley, which were now the east coast of Africa.

A tidal wave, nothing compared to the incoming one but still over 100 feet high, headed back out to sea after the collision. It devastated Madagascar, swept over the Seychelles, and deaths would be recorded as far away as India and Australia.

The face of the Earth had been changed in less than a few minutes' time.

14

480 B.C.

Leonidas stared across the narrow strait that was the only opening from the outer sea to the Gulf of Corinth. He was on the walls of the city of Rhion, and he could clearly see the walls of Antirhon across the way. Dawn was coming from the right, the rays glinting off the small waves that danced on the surface of the water. On the near shore, the sailors of Rhion were preparing their ships to ferry their troops and the Spartans across. Antirhon was not a sea power, for which Leonidas was grateful, as the crossing would not be opposed.

He felt loose and ready for battle. He'd been up for several hours already, and Xarxon had spent a considerable amount of time working the king's muscles, rubbing oil into the skin, loosening scar tissue. Leonidas's armor was shined to a mirror finish, and his weapons had been sharpened.

He could see that the city proper was set back about a mile from the coastline. Several docks and warehouses lined the shore, then behind them, a long, sloping plain led up to the walls of the city. That was where he wanted the battle to take place, even though the enemy would have the high ground. It would be better than laying siege.

If he were the enemy commander—and this was something Leonidas had been taught in his agoge to consider—he would choose neither the town nor the plain to fight. He would mass his troops on the shore and take down the invaders as they disembarked, before they could form ranks or mass strength. But there was no sign of the Antirhonians issuing forth, and Leonidas's advance party of rangers—Skiritai—were already on the far shore, two hundred men strong, waiting in a thin red line that was his toehold. He'd sent them over under cover of darkness, and they had landed unopposed. How to draw the Antirhonians out of their city was the next issue. Leonidas smiled. There were ways.

"What makes you happy on this grim morning?" A woman's voice startled him out of his tactical musings.

Cyra had her cloak wrapped tightly around her body, her face lined and drawn.

"What is grim about this morning?" Leonidas gestured at the sun. "It looks to be a fine day."

"There will be much death today."

"Not ours, Priestess, not ours." He extended his hand toward the stairs off the wall. "Shall we?"

"Are you not afraid?" Cyra asked as they headed down.

Leonidas smiled once more. "Yes. I am afraid. Any man who does not feel fear before battle is not right in the head, and he is a danger to his companions."

"Then how can you smile?"

They passed through the city gate and walked toward the waiting boats. "From my first day in my agoge—training barracks—fear was something we worked with all the time. *Worked* is the wrong word; we lived with it. Did you know we Spartans have made a science of fear?

"The key to it is not the mind but the muscles. You cannot change the mind's reaction to the potential of death or being horribly wounded. Indeed, one would not want to, because that reaction brings forth the extra energy that gives a warrior superior strength.

"The muscles, though, can be disciplined. And not in the way other armies train. Any fool can be taught to march in step and hack and slash. Before a boy in an agoge is allowed to touch a sword, he is first taught to control the fear muscles."

Cyra was interested despite herself. They reached the docks, and Leonidas led the way to one of the boats. She waited until they were on board and the boat cast off before asking, "The fear muscles?"

Leonidas's right hand was like the strike of a snake, smacking her lightly on the left side of her face before she had a chance to move back. When he did it a second time, she stepped back in shock and anger. "Why did you do that?"

"To show you the two types of muscles: fighting muscles and fear. Your fighting muscles made you step back. Your fear muscles made your face react. Tell me. What part of the body do you protect most instinctively?"

Cyra wasn't certain whether to be angry at being struck or to be impressed that he was talking so much to her. "I don't know. Why don't you tell me?"

"Didn't the oracle teach you anything worthwhile?" Leonidas tapped his right eye. "The eyes. Think how quickly we can blink if something comes at our eyes. The lids are shut before we are even aware there is a threat." He drew his dagger and extended it to her, handle first. "Take it."

Reluctantly, Cyra did so and held it in her hand.

"Strike at my eyes," Leonidas said, "but do not actually touch me. After all, I have a battle to fight soon."

"I don't—"

"Do it!"

Cyra jabbed, point toward his eyes, and was amazed to see he didn't blink. She handed the dagger back to him. "How did you do that?"

"Many, many hours and days and years of learning the discipline of the body. Of the fear muscles. I was hit many times around my eyes for many years before I learned the control of these muscles. And once I learned those, I was taught the others in the body until I could achieve physical control."

"Fearlessness," Cyra translated. They were halfway across the strait, and Cyra could see the lead ships were already landing, scarlet-cloaked Spartans scrambling ashore, forming in ranks behind the screen of Skiritai.

"Not exactly. As I told you, I am afraid."

Cyra was surprised that Leonidas made no attempt to keep his voice down nor showed any concern that the nearby warriors heard him.

"What I control," the king continued, "is my reaction to the fear. I feel it but don't react to it."

"And that is what makes the Spartans the greatest warriors in Greece?"

"In the world. Partly. There are other important factors, but I am afraid I do not have time to discuss them right now." The keel of the boat hit the bottom with a grating sound, and men began jumping off. "Watch and learn," Leonidas said as he moved forward.

Leonidas yelled orders as he passed through the troops. He halted at the front, looking up the slope at the city. He could see the helmets of soldiers lining the walls, but the gates were still shut.

As the rest of the Spartan army landed, the docks and warehouses were put to the torch. Parties of Skiritai ranged out around the city, and lines of smoke began to dot the air as they burned farms and houses.

The rest of the Spartan army arrayed itself in formation and waited as the sun rose along with the smoke.

Cyra stood near the water, behind the army. She could sense the collective desperation rising from the walled city. Thousands of people watched their livelihoods being destroyed, their homes in flames.

Cyra felt a similar despair. Most of those inside the walls had no idea why this had happened. The Spartans were here only on the possibility that the Persians might swing their fleet wide and pass through the strait behind her and threaten the Spartan homeland. She wondered if a person counted for anything.

She was surprised to hear chatter and laughter among the Spartan ranks. Although their formations were perfectly aligned, the men were at ease. She could sense the fear among them, but at nowhere near the level she would have expected, given the numbers involved. She noted that Leonidas was walking to and fro, stopping every now and then to talk to someone.

The chatter paused as the gates to the city opened, and soldiers began filing out. Leonidas's ploy had worked, and the Antirhonians were coming out to challenge the Spartan army. While the Spartans had aligned in less than ten minutes after the last troop was ashore, it took their foe almost an hour and much yelling and hands-on positioning by officers.

To Cyra's unpracticed eye, it appeared that the Spartans were outnumbered at least three to one. But even she could tell the difference between the two armies. The Spartans were silent now, their ranks perfectly aligned so that when she looked down a line, not only were the men shoulder to shoulder, their spear points appeared as one. The spear points in the Antirhonian ranks, on the other hand, trembled and shivered as if a stiff breeze were blowing among them.

Some among the enemy ranks began slamming the butts

of their spears into the ground and smacking the wood haft against their shields. The racket increased, men yelling curses at the Spartans now. Still, the red-cloaked lines remained deathly still and quiet.

An officer moved to the front of the enemy lines. He had a high purple plume on the top of his helmet, and the edges of the helmet were rimmed with gold. He was pumping his arm and trying to yell an order that went unheard among the blustering racket of his troops. Some of the men saw him and began moving, producing a very uneven start to the Antirhonian advance.

Still the Spartans remained motionless.

The enemy commander had his spear held parallel to the ground, dashing from side to side in a most undignified manner, trying to align his battalions. Looking at the Spartan lines, Cyra saw that Leonidas was now out in front of his formations, leaning on his spear, watching the approaching enemy as if viewing a harmless parade.

Cyra frowned as she noted that the Antirhonian line was sliding to the right and also becoming more uneven. Then she realized the rightward movement was an unconscious attempt by almost every man to get closer to the protection of the shield of the man to his right. The more brave—or foolhardy, Cyra thought—were moving to the front, while others held back slightly. She saw officers in the rear of the Antirhonian lines with swords drawn, smacking men back into line. She even saw one man cut down as he broke ranks and tried to flee. The ground was trembling at the approach of so many armored men. Their cries were louder, and, if her ears heard rightly, more desperate than threatening.

The Spartan main body remained still and quiet.

Leonidas made a gesture, and Cyra saw several companies of Skiritai begin moving on the flanks, swinging wide to get around the advancing enemy. The bravest of the Antirhonian troops were less than a half mile away. Cyra could see the sweat on the men's faces as they labored to advance against the dual hindrances of their fear and their heavy armor, which, unlike the Spartans, they weren't used to wearing.

Leonidas gestured for a second time, lifting his spear up high so the point was toward the heavens. A ripple ran through the Spartan lines. Cyra felt her heart beat quicker. Slowly, very slowly, Leonidas brought the spear down. She noted that the left foot of every Spartan was lifting at the same pace that the spear lowered. When the king's arm locked into place level and pointing at the enemy, the entire Spartan main body took a step forward, their heavy oxhide battle sandals slapping the ground at the exact same time. The army was moving in rhythm, the cadence having been pounded into each man since his first day in the agoge. Sixty steps a minute, a slow march.

The Antirhonians were now less than 600 meters away, but Cyra could see the men were slowing, from both fear and exhaustion. She saw the wisdom of Leonidas, allowing his enemy to cover most of the ground, putting distance between them and the safety of the walls. The Skiritai had now flanked the enemy on both sides but held their places, bows at the ready.

Leonidas was walking in the lead, spear still held level, when he pumped his left hand once. The pace doubled to a quick march, 120 paces a minute. The ground thundered from the rhythmic march. The spears of all the men were in the three-quarter position, angled exactly between upright and parallel to the ground.

The Antirhonian king could no longer control his troops. The ranks broke as men lost all reason and charged forward all out but much too soon. Cyra could see that more were trying to run to the rear, and there were more summary executions by the trailing officers. The front of the two lines were less than 200 meters apart.

Leonidas pumped his hand twice, the order mirrored along the rank by other officers. The Spartans increased the charge to 180 paces a minute. The king fell backward into his place in line, his spear in one hand, the shield handed him by Xarxon in the other, half protecting the man to his left, presenting a solid wall.

No command was given that Cyra could see for the next action on the part of the Spartans. She could only assume, like everything else she was witnessing, that it was something that had been drilled until it was instinctual. With the Antirhonians at just 100 meters away, the spear points of the Spartans snapped as one from three-quarters to horizontal, glittering blades pointed directly at their foes.

She could almost hear the moan of fear from the ranks of the enemy at this fearsome maneuver. At least half of those in the Antirhonian front rank stopped and tried to form a shield wall, but the weight of the ranks behind shoved them forward, many falling to the ground.

Cyra knew the battle was over already, and the Spartans had yet to taste blood with their blades.

Those who fell became obstacles to those behind, their spears tripping their fellows, their shields catching on others' shields. It was chaos and then a massacre, as the Spartan line smashed into the Antirhonians.

It produced a sound unlike any that Cyra had ever heard in her worst nightmare. Metal on metal, metal on flesh, a sickening sound as spears punctured flesh, bones cracked, the mortal screams of the dying, and perhaps worse, the triumphant yells of the Spartans, who finally let loose with sound as they struck with their spears.

The Antirhonians were like ants under the wheels of a heavy ox cart. Immediately upon reaching the enemy, the Spartans had shifted gears once more, again without a command, but by dint of their training, going from the charge to the slow advance. Eight-foot spears jabbed into flesh, puncturing and ripping. Given the length of the spears, the front three ranks of the Spartans all were engaged in the killing.

Then, to add to the mayhem, the Skiritai began firing their bows, striking the rear ranks of the Antirhonians from the flanks.

The Antirhonian line, not very solid to start with, broke, and the slaughter rose to a new level. Cyra was beginning to truly understand the Spartan advantage in this type of warfare. Yes, the individual Spartan was a superior warrior, but it was the ability to work in unison that took their abilities to another level. Without order, the Antirhonians were nothing more than a mob, their shield wall nonexistent, each man fending for himself.

The Spartan advance picked up the pace, and the spear was exchanged for the sword. Shield and armor were designed to protect when the man holding and wearing it faced the enemy. With backs turned as they ran, the Antirhonians were presenting the Spartans with flesh covered only by leather.

Blood flowed, and men screamed in agony. The ground was churned, turning into mud from the blood and urine let loose by frightened bladders. Cyra began walking forward and passed the first of the bodies. She was surrounded by Spartan squires who finished the work their masters had begun, slicing the throats of wounded Antirhonians while recovering the few wounded Spartans they found and marking bodies.

She saw Leonidas, his armor splattered with blood, walking among his men. A large cluster of Antirhonians, the remainder of their army, was begging for mercy, tossing away weapons and armor. Leonidas was restraining his men from slaying them, speaking soothing words to his angry warriors, who wanted revenge for a few slain comrades.

The gates of Antirhon were open, and now the Rhionians, whose troops had held back during the battle, surged forward. Cyra could feel their blood lust against their ancient enemies. She saw that Leonidas sensed it also as he turned from keeping his troops from massacring prisoners to intercepting the column of warriors heading for the gates. The king stood alone in the dusty trail, covered in blood, his shoulders slumped in weariness and held up his left hand.

Amazingly, the Rhionians halted.

Cyra moved close to the front of the column.

"Blood begets blood," Leonidas said. "You can massacre everyone in the city . . ." He jerked his thumb at the open gate behind him. "But what of those who have hidden in the forests and the hills? Won't they have children and tell them stories of revenge? And one day, your children or your children's children will have their gate open and an Antirhonian army ready to enter and massacre them."

There were mutters of dissent among the Rhionians.

Leonidas held up his sword, not in a threatening manner but to show the blood on the blade. "This is what we have done for you. And it is Spartan blood that soaks this field as well as that of your enemy. Sack this city, and do not call for our aid again."

. . .

King Xerxes saw mountains ahead, filling the horizon. His army had crossed the Plain of Thessalia without any resistance from the Greeks living there. His fleet was offshore, something that made his admirals less than happy as the island of Euboea lay within sight, meaning they were pinned between the mainland and island with little maneuvering room. But Pandora and his spies told him the Athenians and their ships weren't moving.

His throne was set in the center of the camp, a ring of Immortals guarding him. A cluster of generals waited on his orders. He signaled to one of the slaves, who brought forward a table with a jade top and placed it in front of him. Then he turned to Pandora, tapping the table. She had a tube in her hand, with stoppers on both ends. She pulled one out and then retrieved a rolled document.

She placed it on the table, laying small gemstones on each corner to keep it in place. The paper was something none had ever seen, with a shiny sheen and impervious to water. It showed the known world in fine detail and so far had been valid during their march to the west.

Pandora put a thin finger on a spot. "We are here."

Xerxes crooked a finger, and his top generals came forward. No Persian army had ever penetrated this far into Greece, so they were on unknown ground. There were plenty of Greeks among the army, but Xerxes would not trust them this far into their homeland.

"Is there room for us to move along the coast?" he asked Pandora.

She ran her finger farther south. "As you can see, My Lord, the mountains ahead come close to the coast, here, at Thermopylae. But there is a pass there right next to the ocean."

"How wide?" Xerxes asked.

Pandora leaned over and looked closely. She tapped the spot. "Almost a mile wide at the narrowest."

Xerxes scanned his generals. A mile wasn't much room to push his army through.

"Are there any alternatives to going through this pass?" he asked Pandora.

"Here at Brallos to the west," she said, "but then your army will be in the mountains. You will not have the fleet on your flank. The Greeks will have many places where they can ambush you."

Xerxes slapped his hand on the map. "We will go through this pass." He looked at Pandora. "What did you call it?"

"Thermopylae."

"Thermopylae. Move the army."

• • •

The 300 had marched hard, the land becoming more and more desolate and deserted as they got closer to Thermopylae. It never ceased to amaze the warriors how word of pending disaster could pass so quickly among people whose entire world consisted of their farm and the nearest village.

At the very head of the column marched Polynices, in command until Leonidas brought the rest of the army. He did not march like an old man; indeed, several of the younger warriors had complained among themselves about the brutal pace he set. They feared they would be too worn out to fight, to which Polynices had loudly observed it would be better to arrive in time and fight tired than to be too late and not have the glorious opportunity to fight. He told the warriors they could come at their own pace and that the rest would try to capture a Persian or two for them to spar with. After that, there were no more complaints.

But they all felt the eyes of the countryside on them as they moved north. The people were hiding in the hills, afraid even to come when they saw the scarlet cloaks of the Spartans, which indicated an extreme level of fear and the power of the rumor of the Persian strength. Usually, all it took was the sight of a single Spartan knight, and a Greek would feel he was safe.

The road began to climb as the way narrowed. Polynices walked ramrod straight, a 120-pound pack containing his shield, sword, and supplies on his back. They passed several hot springs. To the right they could see the Malian Gulf; to the left, the terrain rose abruptly, leading up to a spur of Mount Oeta.

"This is good!" Polynices spoke loudly, his voice echoing off the rock to the left. "Do you feel it, men?"

The road curved slightly left, then right. Polynices finally halted. From the cliff to sea was less than fifty meters. A pile of stone lay ahead, the remains of an old wall. In front of the wall was an open, level space. Polynices smiled as he saw that: a perfect killing field.

"I feel death here!" Polynices turned to face the small column of Spartans. "Do you feel it?"

There was a murmur of assent, and being the veteran of many campaigns that he was, Polynices could also sense the unease among the men. This *was* a place of death. Any fool could feel it. "I think many Persians will see their last sunlight here," he continued. "There will be so much blood flowing from them, the sea will turn red."

The 300 had gathered round. Polynices was done with the attempt to raise spirits. They would fight when the enemy arrived. He detailed scouts to check the plain to the north to see how close the Persians were. Then he instructed others to begin rebuilding the rock wall, known as the Middle Gate.

As the men followed his orders, the old man finally sat down on a boulder. Reluctantly, he removed one of his oxhide sandals. It was soaked in blood, and he saw white where one of the bones on the top of his foot was exposed, the skin worn off during the march. He quickly wrapped the injury and then went back to supervising the preparation for defense of the Hot Gates.

"Ah!" one of the men cried out. "Look at this."

"What is it?" Polynices walked over to the man who had rolled over a large stone.

"Look," the man pointed.

There was a carving etched into the stone. A very old carving to judge by how the stone was worn down. There were warriors, spears in their hands. The points of the spears were pointing at an array of finely drawn creatures, most of which Polynices didn't recognize, but all appeared to be quite fearsome.

"A great battle was fought here in ancient times," Polynices said.

"Between who?" the man who had found the carvings asked.

"Man and beast." Polynices noted something else. Behind the beasts were a pair of figures, almost human, but with straight lines, almost floating above the battle. "And these, whatever they are."

"And who won?"

Polynices laughed and slapped the man on the back. "What does it matter? It was a great battle."

. . .

Cyra was praying over the bodies of the dead, Spartan and Antirhonian alike, when she felt such severe pain in her left eye that she wondered if she'd been shot with an arrow. She staggered back, hand reflexively going to the eye. She looked at her hand, half expecting to see blood, but there was just flesh. She went to her knees and bent over, eyes tightly shut.

She saw a scorched plain. Wide and open, ocean on one side. Thousands and thousands of troops, all moving forward. Toward mountains. A pass. The Gates of Fire—she knew it.

She opened her eyes and staggered to her feet. She saw Leonidas issuing orders, still covered in dried blood. She pushed her way through the people around him.

"What is it?" Leonidas asked, surprised at her sudden appearance.

"The Persians are close to the Gates."

"How close?"

"Less than a day's march."

"It is too soon."

"There was no resistance to their advance across Thessalia," Cyra said.

Leonidas nodded, as if he expected this bad news. "You know the path the Theran oracle gave you?"

Cyra's face went white as the blood drained from it. "Yes."

"We will take it."

"And your army?" Cyra asked.

"The three hundred are already there, if I know Polynices. The rest of the army will follow as quickly as they can. Which way?"

Cyra pointed to the mountains to the north and west. "The entrance is that way."

15

The Present

"How many do you think there are?" Dane whispered. He was lying next to Earhart, peering down at the huge cavern full of tables holding human bodies. Underneath the clear wrap he could see muscles, bones, and ligaments. He saw one woman near the edge who'd had both legs amputated, and there was an open cavity in her chest where a lung had been removed.

They'd only stopped by Earhart's camp to drop off the crystal skulls. They discovered that Noonan had succumbed to whatever was ravaging his body and that the Navy men were still unconscious, but Dane had confirmed they were from his time—part of the crew of the *Connecticut*.

"Thousands and thousands," Earhart replied. "At first we would raid the cavern and put some of the people out of their misery but . . ." Her voice trailed off, and Dane knew what she meant. There were simply too many people in too much agony. The aura that was sweeping over him was worse than even going into a gate. His stomach spasmed, and he rolled to the side, heaving, but nothing came up.

When he turned back, Earhart offered him a water bottle. He took a swig of the slimy inner lake water and then spat it out. "Why are they doing this?"

Earhart shrugged. "I don't know. Maybe they're trying to figure us out. What makes humans tick."

"They've had a long time to do that," Dane said, realizing, even as he spoke the words, that he couldn't be certain how long the Valkyries had been doing this to people here in the space between, given that time was very much a variable here.

"You know," Dane said, "it looks like . . ." He searched for the vision that had just flashed through his mind, but he couldn't draw it up. He shook his head and focused on the task ahead of them. "How do we find a Valkyrie in there?"

"We draw them to us," Earhart said as she got up. She signaled, and Taki and his men rose to their feet. Dane stood but paused when Earhart put a hand on his arm. "Can you handle that thing?" she indicated the Naga staff.

Dane hefted it uncertainly. "I was pretty good with an M-60 machine gun, but this . . ." He shook his head. "You have a suggestion?"

"Taki is a samurai," she pointed out. "Trained in many different weapons."

"It's all his then," Dane said. Earhart said something in Japanese, and Taki took the staff from Dane, bowing slightly at the waist as he did so. In turn, he handed his sword to Dane. The samurai leader then spun it about in his hands so fast, Dane lost track of which end was where. Taki jabbed, sliced, and shadow-fought for a few seconds, getting a feel for the weapon; then he nodded and turned toward the cavern.

Dane didn't feel very reassured with the sword in his hand. He hefted it as Earhart said something to Taki.

"I told him not to damage the suits too much," she translated.

"Let's hope they feel the same way about our skin," Dane muttered.

"If you have to, go for the eyes . . . the red crystal," Earhart suggested.

Dane followed Earhart and the samurai down the slope, and they entered the cavern. Dane looked at the first person on a slab that he passed and was shocked to see the woman's eyes following him, her head locked in place, a number of thin wires with small lit bulbs stemming up out of the exposed top of her brain. He started to step toward her, sword half raised, but Earhart gave him a slight push.

"Not yet."

Taki had reached an intersection among the slabs and paused, looking in all directions. Dane felt as if a ring of barbed wire was wrapped around his head, and it was being tightened. The pain was overwhelming as he absorbed the agony of the multitude of tortured humans around him. Writhing through the pain was the awareness that many of these people could no longer really be called human, as their minds had snapped from the pain and nightmarish situation.

Taki moved along a row and summoned some Valkyries by the gruesome method of killing a dozen of the most hideously disfigured of the humans in one row. He paused, then hissed, pointing to his right. He held up two fingers and ducked behind a slab.

"Two Valkyries," Earhart whispered as she edged Dane into a hiding spot.

The person on the slab they hid behind had his ribs spread wide open, revealing the inner chest cavity. As he hid, Dane noted that most of the man's intestines had been removed. The opening was covered with the same clear material, which must provide some protection from infection, he realized. A black tube was wrapped in a tight coil in place of the intestines, and Dane could only assume it performed the basic functions needed to keep the man alive.

Dane forced his attention toward Taki. The Japanese warrior had the Naga staff in his right hand, and he had his back to the rear of the slab. A white figure floated past his location, then a second one. Just as the second one cleared, Taki sprang out, spinning, the Naga staff level.

The blade struck right at the creature's neck, slicing through cleanly, cutting through the front half of the neck. The body came to a halt, floating, the arms limp at its side, black gas issuing out of the wound. Taki was already attacking the second. He jabbed, the blade hitting the creature in the left shoulder, punching through. Black gas hissed out of the hole.

The creature swung its clawed hand at the samurai, narrowly missing. Taki ducked under its second blow and jabbed the point of the blade into the center of its chest. He twisted the haft of the staff, using the Naga heads for leverage, and rotated the blade 360 degrees inside the Valkyrie's chest. Its arms dropped to its side, and it was still like its headless companion, bobbing slightly.

Earhart was moving, gesturing for the samurai to grab the bodies. Dane ran to the one whose neck was cut. He found he could move it by himself, just pushing it. Earhart grabbed the other, and they headed out of the cavern as quickly as they could, Taki bringing up the rear.

The Present

It is a common saying that those who forget history are doomed to repeat it.

History records that the winter of 1811–1812 was a very difficult one for the handful of settlers who braved the frontier and had settled in the Mississippi River Valley. The Shawnee chief Tecumseh was organizing the tribes of the area to push back the whites and, counting numbers, it looked as if it were a very real possibility come spring. And as if that weren't enough, on the morning of December 16, 1811, the Earth shook terribly numerous times, and the sky filled with ash, blocking out the sun. Throughout the winter there were many more earthquakes, culminating on February 17, 1812.

That was the day the Mississippi reversed its course.

Along the New Madrid fault line, which roughly followed the line of the Mississippi between Tennessee and Kentucky and Arkansas and Missouri, the surface of the planet split. A twenty-mile section of the mightiest river in the continent simply dropped through the opening.

Crewmen on the first steamboat launched on the river, the *New Orleans*, which was on its inaugural voyage, woke to the amazing spectacle of the island they had anchored to having disappeared under the water, and the ship being pulled upriver as the water raced in that direction.

No one knows how may thousands of Native Americans, mainly Chickasaw, died. Where there had been forests, there were now lakes. As the Mississippi resumed its flow, there were miles and miles of it in a new channel, gouged out by the earthquakes.

Few who lived in that area in present day knew of those events in their history. The devastation of the southeast coast of Africa had stunned the world. Still, as extreme as the event was, there was a tendency in the United States and Europe to feel that it had taken place far away, and life went on, most people unaware of the ticking time bomb deep inside their planet because the various governments didn't see a need to spread panic and chaos.

That changed abruptly as the Earth's core shifted slightly, and the New Madrid fault gave way once more. Unfortunately, the area that was sparsely populated less than two hundred years before was now inhabited by several million people.

Seventy miles north of Memphis, where the Mississippi made a sharp bend opposite the town of New Madrid, a hole opened: a hole over twenty miles in diameter, that dropped almost a half mile down. It took with it a twenty-mile section of the Mississippi River along with the countryside all around.

The mightiest river in North America flowed backward once more as water surged upstream into the hole. Even before the water overwhelmed them, the majority of the thousands of people who lived and worked there were dead or dying from the devastation of the violent planet below them.

The rest drowned as the Mississippi filled the hole. The ripple effect from the earthquake resonated outward. In Saint Louis, to the north, the Arch collapsed. Thousands died as buildings followed.

Like a punch to the solar plexus, America now knew the threat. But still, the government refused to release the information that worse was to come.

The Space Between

"How do they stay in the air?" Earhart asked as they circled one of the two suits.

"Something must be built into them," Dane said. He was looking for any sort of opening. "There's no blood," he noted. He reached up and pulled down on the suit with the neck wound. He looked inside. "There's a body, at least," he said as he saw flesh. And he also saw the reason for no blood; the wound was covered with the same clear material that was on the bodies in the cavern. The wound was capped off by the material, but the damage to the flesh at the time of the strike had been too great. "This stuff must have snapped in place when the neck was cut. Pretty effective wound control, except not when you get half your neck cut through. Looks almost human," he added. He wondered if the Shadow used humans inside the suits to do their bidding.

There was something strange about the body, although Dane couldn't tell exactly what it was by the little he could see through the wound in the suit. Earhart put her hand in the wound on the other one's chest. "Feels like the same thing; the wound was covered."

Dane closed his eyes and tried to concentrate. There had to be a way the armor came off the bodies. Dane opened his eyes and checked the claw hands on the closest one. He noted that the claws could retract back, leaving the armored fingers free to work. The white armor was cool to the touch, and judging from where it had been penetrated, extremely thin. Yet Dane had seen it resist all blows except those from a Naga staff.

He noted something on the inside of the left forearm—a small series of slight indentations. Two rows of five. Each indent was about the size of a dime. He pointed them out to Earhart.

"What do you think they are?" she asked.

"I think this is an external control pad for the suit," Dane said. "Ten, one for each number, one through ten."

"So there's a code?"

Dane nodded. "Most likely."

"That doesn't do us much good."

Dane rubbed his chin, noting that he had a stubble of beard. He tried to remember the last time he'd taken a warm shower or shaved. "Let's step back from things for a second and consider what's going on," he suggested.

"What do you mean?" Earhart asked.

"You saw Noonan die when your plane went down, yet he shows up here alive—mortally wounded from passage through a portal—but alive. He tells you that you'll need to get some Valkyrie suits. But that you'll need to get a Naga staff in order to do that. So I show up with the Naga staff. I don't know why exactly I took it from the Bermuda Triangle gate other than that I sensed it was the next thing to do."

"And?" Earhart wasn't following his thoughts.

"It seems to me . . ." Dane tried to figure out exactly what it was that was troubling him. "It seems as if there's a plan to all this. As if we're being nudged in the right direction, to take the next right steps. Or maybe the wrong steps. I don't know," he ended in frustration.

"The Ones Before?" Earhart asked.

"Most likely," Dane agreed. "They sent my team sergeant to me in the Angkor gate and helped me there. I'd say they sent Noonan to you the same way."

"But I saw him die," Earhart insisted. She turned and looked at the body of her navigator, the face covered with a shirt. "And now he's died again. How can that be?"

"I saw Robert Frost die and Washington, D.C., destroyed in an atomic war," Dane said, almost to himself. A war that didn't happen. He felt a tingling along his spine, as if he was very close to something, but it was still just beyond his grasp. The feeling extended to his fingers. He held his hands out, as if seeing them for the first time.

He turned to the Valkyrie suit. He ran the fingers of his left hand lightly over the indented keys. He paused, then did it once more. Then he pressed a half-dozen keys in rapid succession. There was a click; then, with a hiss, the suit split open, hinged on the right side. A body tumbled out, the head rolling back unnaturally.

"God," Earhart whispered as she saw the condition of the body. It was like one of those on the slabs: skin gone, covered with the clear material. She looked up at Dane. "How did you do that?"

"I just let my fingers do it," Dane said, as if that explained it. He was examining the inside of the suit.

"They're humanlike." Earhart nudged the body with the

toe of her boat. The body was that of a human without its skin, but the muscles were atrophied, and it probably weighed no more than a hundred pounds. There were no genitals that they could see.

"Or they use humans," Dane said.

"Look at this," Earhart pushed the flopping head slightly with her boot, exposing the right side of the face. There was skin underneath the clear wrap. Unblemished, almost pink skin running from just below the ear to just shy of the nose. "That's strange, don't you think?"

Dane went over to the other suit and punched in the same combination. It split open, and another body spilled out. This one had unblemished skin on the upper half of its body, and Dane knew what he was seeing.

"They're grafting skin they take off people in the cavern," he said. He looked at the interior of the helmet. A slightly curved, smooth surface was on the inside of the ruby eyes. He went back to the first suit.

He backed into the rear half of the suit, stepping up backward and placing his feet in the heel, six inches above the ground. As soon as he was pressed against the rear, the suit swung closed. He felt it press against his skin, conforming. Dane blinked as everything went dark for a second, then the screen came alive with an outside view. He knew he was in technology that was far advanced of what was even on the drawing boards on Earth.

He looked down. He flexed his fingers. When his fingers went back as far as they could go, the claws snapped forward. He bent the tips forward, and the claws flipped back. He felt strange, floating above the ground. He tried to swing one leg forward, and the entire suit moved him a couple of feet ahead. He did the other leg, and it moved forward the same distance.

"Interesting." He tapped the open code, and the suit released him.

"We have the suits," Earhart said. "Now what?"

"Now we get the map."

"Which is where?"

"Why do you think we need the suits?"

"To go into a portal," Earhart said. "But which one?"

"Whichever one Rachel leads us to."

16

480 B.C.

Leonidas left his army with orders to march northeast toward the Gates as soon as they consolidated after the victory at Antirhon. Then he and Cyra headed in that direction, both mounted on the fastest steeds they could cull from the conquered city. When they reached where the road went over a mountain pass beyond the city, Leonidas halted briefly and looked back. He could see his army, the red cloaks easily visible at this distance. The sun was low in the western sky.

He turned his horse and followed Cyra, who had not halted. The track she was following headed into mountains, the peaks of which were shrouded in low-lying clouds. A cold wind was blowing steadily into their faces as they wound their way upward.

"A great victory," Cyra said, the words whipped away by the wind so quickly that Leonidas barely heard her.

"You fight well with words," the Spartan king said.

"So it was not a great victory? You were outnumbered."

"The Antirhonian army was militia," Leonidas said.

"They drill twice a year, between their time in the fields. Their commander was a fool to charge; they aren't used to running that far with armor. But he had no real choice, once he opened the gates. We would have outwaited them, let the fear grow in their bellies, until they would have broken without a fight."

"Even though he knew he would lose, he ordered the charge anyway?"

"Yes."

"That's insane."

"It's war."

"Men." The way Cyra said the one word indicated a wealth of feelings, none of them good.

"Did you see the women lining the walls of the city?" Leonidas asked. "Waiting to see the blood? It is not just men."

"True," Cyra acknowledged. "Your women lined the road and sang a hymn as you led the army off to battle. Perhaps the problem is that men have something that women need and women have something men need."

Leonidas turned in the saddle. "What do you mean?"

Cyra tapped her chest. "I don't think we're complete. We're all lacking something."

"And that is?"

"I don't know. But I do think that if we don't change, there is no future for mankind."

* * *

Jamsheed had just finished relating to Xerxes what Leonidas's response to the Persian offer had been. The Persian king had expected that answer, although he had hoped to gain more time.

"And their army?" Xerxes asked.

"Half has moved to the west. Half remains in Sparta."

"The west?" Xerxes was puzzled. He was seated in his

throne at the head of his dining table in the imperial tent. His generals were gathered around the table, and Pandora was to his right rear. The army was stopped for the night, with thousands of campfires around the tent, like a field of stars, indicating the expanse of the army. They had encountered no resistance and had already crossed a third of Greece. The pass was not far ahead.

"They secure the entrance to the Gulf of Corinth, My King," Jamsheed said.

"And none move north?"

"Three hundred, My Lord."

"Three hundred?" Xerxes laughed. He had more than three times that number of Immortals gathered around his imperial tent. "What of this Spartan king?" he asked. "What kind of man is he?"

"He killed one of his own men in front of me, Lord."

Xerxes leaned forward slightly. "Why?"

"The man presumed to speak for Sparta. Leonidas killed him without any warning."

"So he is a man prone to rash action?" Xerxes asked.

Jamsheed frowned as he considered that. "No, My Lord, I do not think so. I believe he is a man prone to bold and decisive action if it is required."

Xerxes laughed. "That may well be, but he marches west instead of north."

"There is something else, My Lord," Jamsheed said nervously.

"Yes?"

"There was someone with Leonidas, Lord. A priestess. From Delphi."

"And?"

"Delphi is the home of an oracle—a seer—a very famous one in whose words the Greeks place great weight. Leonidas was coming from Delphi when I met him, which was strange to start with, as the Spartans are the least likely of all the Greek states to listen to oracles."

Xerxes was picking at the food on his golden plate. "The point?"

"This Delphic priestess knew of Pandora," Jamsheed said.

Xerxes arched an eyebrow and half turned in his throne. "She did? And what did she know of Pandora?"

"She said you should not trust her, Lord."

Xerxes raised a hand as Pandora was about to speak, silencing her. "Did this priestess say why?" He turned back to Jamsheed.

"She said that the entire future of the world, east versus west, was in the balance."

"That much is true," Xerxes said, "but what does that have to do with Pandora?"

"The priestess also said that you should weigh the words of Pandora very carefully, My Lord. And that Pandora does not speak for Persia nor for Greece, and that you should find where her true allegiance lies."

Xerxes nodded. "Wise words." He twitched a finger, indicating for Pandora to come in front of him. "What do you say in response to the words of this Greek priestess?"

Pandora's answer was quick. "She seeks to sow discord in your camp, My Lord."

"And you?" Xerxes asked. "What do you seek?"

"Your victory over the Greeks, Lord."

"But you also plan other things," Xerxes noted. "Taking the child out of that town was one. What else do you have planned that I do not know about?"

"Nothing, My Lord. The Greek priestess lies."

He turned back to his ambassador. "The three hundred Spartans. Where do they march?"

"I do not know, Lord. I received a report from a spy while

I was on my way here. The spy only said they left Sparta and were moving to the north and east."

"So they could be going to Athens? Perhaps a delegation?"

"No, My Lord. This morning, I received another report positioning the three hundred north of Athens and marching hard. That report is several days old."

Xerxes looked down the table to his senior general. "How long until we get to the pass?"

"We will be there tomorrow, Lord." The general cleared his throat. "Three hundred Spartans cannot hold a mile-wide pass," he added.

Xerxes shifted his gaze to Pandora. "True, they couldn't."

• • •

Polynices's fingers were torn and bleeding, yet he still joked as he lifted stones and put them in place. Blood oozed through his sandals, but he showed no sign of discomfort as he moved about. The wall was now chest high and spanned the entire width of the narrowest part of the Gates of Fire. Torches were spaced every ten meters and sputtered in the growing darkness.

The old warrior paused in the work as a well-mounted Skiritai came galloping up the pass from the north. Polynices sat down on top of the wall, his feet dangling, as he waited for the scout to ride up.

"Report," Polynices ordered as the man dismounted.

"The Persians are less than a day's march from here. If they march in the morn, they will be here before nightfall."

"Have they sent out patrols?"

"No."

Polynices found that strange. He could only assume that the Persians were so confident in their numbers that they felt no need to scout their path. The Skiritai was looking about, first at the wall, then up at the sky.

"What is wrong?" Polynices asked, noting the strange look that had come over the man's face.

"The sky was clear when I entered the pass," the ranger said, "but now it is overcast and it appears as if it will storm."

Polynices looked up. He could see no stars, and the moon had not yet risen. There was a flicker of lightning inside a cloud above them. Polynices could have sworn the sky was clear just a moment ago when the scout arrived. A gust of wind blew off the mountain, causing the ache in his old bones to match the pain from his feet and hands. He slid off the wall, wincing despite his best efforts, as his feet hit the hard ground.

"Back to work!"

As if to emphasize the command, a long peal of thunder echoed off the mountainside above the 300.

· · ·

Leonidas pulled his cloak tightly around his body, but the thin material did little to stop the freezing wind that found every niche in his armor and swirled underneath.

"Come on!" Cyra was ten feet ahead of him, gesturing. "Hurry!"

Leonidas dug the hard edge of his ox-hide sandals into the side of the horse. The animal was loath to move forward, fighting him as it had been for the past mile. They were on a narrow track in the mountains. To the left, a rock face reared up almost vertically, disappearing into the black clouds. To the right, the slope was almost as steep into a narrow valley.

Leonidas sensed that something wasn't quite right about the land, and as he tried to keep the horse moving, he opened up his five senses to coalesce into the sixth sense he had been taught—the sense that was the unconscious mind pick-ing up something from the five collective senses that the conscious mind hadn't yet acknowledged. After a few mo-ments, he realized what was wrong. There was no sound of water. Leonidas had been on many, many mountain paths that paralleled a ravine or valley, and there was always the sound of water making its way downhill inside the low ground. He cocked his head to the right, thinking perhaps the sound of the wind was too much, but he realized there was no water in the low ground to his right.

The horse finally stopped dead, and no amount of kick-ing or coaxing could make it go farther. Leonidas leaped off, noting that Cyra's horse had also refused to move.

"Do they know something we don't?" Leonidas asked as he moved up next to the priestess. Both animals bolted back down the trail and were immediately out of sight.

"We're near the gate," Cyra said.

"Gate to where?"

"Gate to the tunnel that will take us to the Gates of Fire." Cyra began walking forward into the stiff wind, still moving up the path.

Leonidas felt the same sense of dread he had experienced at Delphi and on the Gulf when they met the Theran oracle. He drew his sword and followed the priestess closely. The path was narrowing. From the worn stone beneath his feet, he could tell it was an old path, but the untrampled vegeta-tion that grew among the cracks indicated it was rarely if ever used in the present.

The path appeared to end abruptly in a cliff face. Leonidas almost bumped into Cyra when she halted. The priestess turned to the right, and the king now saw that a nar-row set of stairs were carved into the side of the mountain, leading down. He stayed right behind Cyra as she de-scended. He counted as they went down, and they reached the bottom after 120 steps. They were in a streambed, but as

Leonidas had noted, there was no water. Cyra turned to the left.

"This way," she pointed.

"Where's the water?" Leonidas asked.

Cyra shrugged. She began climbing through the stones and boulders, moving in the direction of what would have been upstream. The feeling of dread was growing stronger, and Leonidas peered ahead into the darkness, searching.

Cyra abruptly halted. "There."

At first, Leonidas couldn't discern what she was pointing at. Then he realized that there was a blacker circle in the darkness ahead. The blackness seemed to absorb even the night air about twenty feet ahead of them.

"The gate?" he asked, hoping that she would answer in the negative but knowing better.

"Yes."

Leonidas started to move toward it, but Cyra put a hand out and stopped him. "Not yet."

Leonidas then realized something; he could hear water now. Splashing against rock, making its way downslope close by. But the trough underneath his feet was still dry. While he was still puzzling over this, the landscape was lit by a bolt of lightning. Leonidas could see that the black circle was about eight feet in diameter and at the lowest part of the streambed. He blinked because he could have sworn that behind the circle and to the left, where the notch in the side of mountain curved slightly, he had seen a waterfall coming down. A second bolt of lightning confirmed that, which confused Leonidas, because the water had to be going somewhere.

"Soon," Cyra had her hand on his shoulder, and they edged closer to the circle.

"Where does this go?"

Her eyes were glazed over, and her mind seemed elsewhere. "To the Gates of Fire, eventually."

"Eventually?"

A third bolt cut the sky.

Cyra nudged him and stepped forward. "Now."

Leonidas had advanced toward enemy lines bristling with steel several dozens of times in his life, but he was surprised to find his legs reluctant to move, as if they had picked up some degree of common sense from the horses. Still, he forced his way forward behind Cyra. She reached out a hand, and it disappeared into the black. She glanced once over her shoulder at him, nodded, and then stepped into the circle and was gone.

Leonidas took a deep breath and then followed. The blackness hit his skin with icy coldness, far chillier than the cold wind, which was suddenly gone. All was black, and he felt pressure all around his body. Then, the next thing he knew, he was almost waist deep in water.

He blinked, looking about. There was light coming from above, but he couldn't see the source. He was standing in the middle of a stream that also came out of the black circle just behind him. On either side was black land. The stream ran straight ahead toward a body of water so large that he could not see the other side.

"Come." Cyra was to his right, standing on the black soil. Leonidas stepped through the water and then looked back. Seen from the side, the black circle had almost no thickness, less than a finger's width. The water just came out of the one side, with nothing flowing on. Leonidas realized he was seeing the water that had been coming down the mountain on the other side of the gate, yet both streams had come out facing the same way. He was confused, but he had no time to ponder this bizarre situation.

"Hurry." Cyra was tugging at his arm and speaking in a low voice. "This is a dangerous place."

"Where are we?" Leonidas realized he was whispering also, a strong sense of dread tightening his guts.

"The oracle called this place the space between." Cyra was heading along the shore of the dark sea.

"Where is this?"

"I don't know," Cyra said. "I think we are between our world and the world of the Shadow."

"Where are the Gates of Fire?" Leonidas asked.

"We must pass through another gate like the one we just traversed to get there," Cyra said.

Leonidas paused as he noted a pillar of black ahead and to the left. "What is that?"

"Another kind of gate," Cyra said.

"The one we seek?"

"No."

Leonidas grabbed Cyra and pushed her down into the black sand. "Valkyries," he warned, as two figures in white floated across the black sand about a quarter mile in front of them, heading for the water.

17

The Space Between

Dane was finding moving inside the Valkyrie suit most annoying. He moved his legs as if walking, but instead of actual leg movement, the suit simply moved forward. To change direction, he had to twist at the waist, the upper body pointing in the correct direction, the suit following. It didn't take much effort to move the suit, and he realized that was necessary, given the atrophied condition of the bodies they'd taken out of them. He had the Naga staff, while Earhart carried a backpack with Sin Fen's skull tucked inside.

"This isn't much of a plan," Earhart's voice was a low buzz, coming out of a speaker inside the headpiece. They'd discovered they could communicate with each other simply by talking. Dane had to assume that the transmitters and receivers were built into the skin of the suit, again indicating a high level of technical proficiency.

"It's as much of a plan as you had before I got here," Dane noted. He could see the inner sea now and a portal column ahead and to the right. He headed straight down to the water. He immediately saw an advantage to the suits as he floated out over the black surface. He stopping moving his legs and came to a halt, Earhart floating next to him.

Dane concentrated, mentally projecting an image of himself. He was rewarded by the sight of a gray dorsal fin cutting the smooth, black surface a quarter mile ahead and racing toward them. When Rachel was close by, she leaped into the air, clearing the water completely and flipping over onto her back with a tremendous splash. She then rose up out of the water about two feet, regarded the two floating white figures for several seconds, bobbed her head as if nodding, and then began swimming off farther into the inner sea.

"Let's go," Dane said as he set off after the dolphin. Just for a moment, he sensed a presence nearby and paused and turned. But then a blast of urgency from Rachel overwhelmed that sense, and he turned back and followed her.

．　．　．

Cyra was watching the two Valkyries move. Leonidas raised his sword slightly as one of them paused and turned in their direction, but then the creature turned back and followed the dolphin away. In a couple of minutes, the two white figures disappeared around the black column.

"That was strange," Cyra said as she got to her feet.

"*That* was strange?" Leonidas was dusting black sand from his cloak and armor. "What *isn't* strange in all of this?"

"The dolphin being with the Valkyries is strange," Cyra clarified. "I was taught that the dolphins are our brethren in the sea. Why would they be with our enemy?"

Leonidas had no answer. "Let's find this gate and get out of here," he suggested.

"Come." Cyra strode off.

．　．　．

"Did you feel that?" Dane asked as they skirted around the black cylinder of power.

"What?" Earhart asked.

"Someone was back there. On the shore. Someone with the vision."

"I didn't feel anything," Earhart said.

Dane could see a half-dozen portals ahead, the black columns varying in width from a few feet to one over three-quarters of a mile wide—large enough for the sphere to travel in. He wondered which one was the Nazca power portal and if placing Sin Fen's skull into it would disrupt it. Earhart was right; he didn't have much of a plan. Despite those misgivings, he felt as if he were on the right path.

Rachel swam between two portals with Dane and Earhart following. Dane noted that some of the portals were different. In several, he could see swirls of colors, mainly red, gold, and blue. These colors came and went so quickly, it was hard to get a read on them.

Looking ahead, Dane saw that the inner sea stretched as far as he could see with numerous portals visible. The dolphin paused and rose half out of the water, head turning to and fro. Then she dove forward. Dane noted that her course was taking her directly toward a portal a quarter mile ahead. This portal was about 100 meters wide. Rachel came to a halt right in front of it and once more rose out of the water. She jerked her head toward the portal a couple of times, then slid back into the water, disappearing from sight.

"I guess this is it," Dane said.

* * *

"There," Cyra pointed at a black circle that hovered above the water about ten meters offshore.

"Are you sure?" Leonidas asked.

"As sure as I am about anything else we've done," Cyra answered, which did little to reassure the Spartan king. Still, he led the way, wading out from shore until he was just in front of it. The water was knee deep and the portal at his waist. He sheathed his sword, then laced his fingers together, forming a step for the priestess. Without hesitation, she put one foot in it, stepped up, and fell forward into the circle, disappearing.

Leonidas backed off a few feet, then ran forward and jumped, arms extended, into the portal.

・　・　・

Dane was less than a foot from the shimmering black surface of the portal. Every so often, there was a flicker of red in the black, similar to what he had seen in a few of the others on the way to this one.

"After you," Earhart said.

Dane nodded and then realized the gesture couldn't be seen. Without a word, he moved forward into the blackness. The screen in front of his eyes blacked out for a second, then came back.

"Oh, my God," Dane whispered as he took in the scene the screen displayed. He wasn't even aware as Earhart materialized beside him and her own gasp of dismay echoed inside the helmet.

Dane was floating less than two feet above the Reflecting Pool on the Mall in Washington, D.C. Except there was no water in the pool and the concrete was blistered and blackened. But what held his attention was the view directly ahead. The Washington Monument had been sheared off about fifty feet up, the broken stub of the base pointing into the air, the bulk of the remainder lying cracked and smashed on the ground next to it. Beyond, on a rise, the dome of the U.S. Capitol had been blasted away, leaving only the shattered remains of the building.

"We're too late," Earhart whispered, her voice hoarse.

18

480 B.C.

Polynices heard the cries of alarm and hurriedly grabbed his shield and sword. He ran to the yells and skidded to a halt, feeling no pain in his feet for the first time in days as he saw what had caused the disturbance. A black circle had appeared just in front of the wall, and a half-dozen Spartans were around it, weapons at the ready.

They took half a step back as a woman came flying out of it, tumbling to the ground. As she rose to her feet, dusting herself off, a second figure came through. This one did a complete tumble, then was on his feet, weapon at the ready.

"Hold!" Polynices cried out as several of the Spartans stepped forward to engage the newcomers. The man removed his helmet, and all dropped to one knee as they recognized their king. The black circle snapped out of existence.

"My Lord," Polynices walked up to Leonidas. "I don't understand . . . How?"

Leonidas shook his head, more to clear it than to let Polynices know he had no clue exactly how he made it here. He blinked and looked about, noting the stone wall and the men with weapons at the ready.

"I cannot explain it," he said in a loud voice so that all nearby could hear. "Suffice it to say I am here. How far away are the Persians?"

"Less than a day's march," Polynices informed him.

Leonidas glanced at Cyra. He knew she had been right; there would be no time for the rest of his army to arrive. More and more of the Spartans were circling around the king until all 300 were within earshot. He could hear the buzz among the men about the strange mode of arrival and the woman who was with him.

Leonidas held up his hand, and quiet descended in the Gates of Fire. The flickering light from the torches on the wall cast long shadows from the men facing the king and lit his scarred face intermittently.

"This"—he indicated Cyra—"is a priestess sent to us from the oracle at Delphi. As you all have heard through the soldier's line"—this brought a low chuckle from the men as the king referred to the rumor mill that often kept the men more informed than their commander—"I was given a prophecy by the oracle when I traveled there. I will tell you now what she told me."

There was absolute quiet; even the breeze had stopped.

"I was told we were to win a great victory here. But that in order for that victory to occur, I—we—must assist her and her priestess"—he again pointed at Cyra—"in a task they have that involves the gods. We traveled here, as you saw, via a pathway of the gods through the under-world."

Leonidas scanned the faces, but as he expected, they were inscrutable. He imagined most of the men were still mulling over the prophecy of victory, trying to believe it in face of their numbers and the reports of the scouts about the size of the Persian army that would be here the next day. Leonidas knew most of the men were like him. They had seen men praying as fervently as the most possessed priestess, and they had seen them cut down.

Still, there was the factor of his mode of arrival. Leonidas knew that added an edge of the surreal to not only what he was saying, but the setting provided a backdrop that he could tell was unsettling even the most hardened warriors. Lightning flickered, highlighting the rocky mountainside, the stone wall, and the sea—and the faces of the men.

He knew what question was foremost in their mind, and it wasn't what the gods were up to. "We defeated the Antirhonians yesterday."

The news of the victory wasn't what they focused on but the timing. Yesterday. Antirhon was a long march away. Leonidas took a deep breath. They were Spartans, but they were men also.

"We will face the enemy. The three hundred of us. We will hold them here. The six lochoi will be here in five days' time hard marching. Anyplace else, you and I know it would be impossible. But . . ." He let the word hang in the air; then he walked to the exact middle of the pass in front of the wall.

"Shoulder to shoulder, a line." He extended his arms out from his side, indicating what he wanted. The men moved. A line formed from the mountain to the cliff. A second one behind it. And a third. And most of a fourth.

"Three deep. We fight here three deep as we fight anywhere. Spear length. The Persians can only bring the same against us." He smiled and indicated the men in the last rank. "And we even have a reserve."

"Yah!" Polynices slammed the pommel of his sword against his shield. "I have fought many places, but this . . . this is the best by far. This ground will run with Persian blood. We will make a wall in front of this wall"—he indicated the stone wall he had so laboriously worked on—"with their bodies. And that will be so much easier on my poor hands," he added.

The men laughed.

Leonidas walked over to the Middle Wall. He slapped a stone. "This is good. But this"—he held up his sword, the blade glinting in the torchlight—"is better. You have done well. I think sleep is more important now. The Skiritai platoon will maintain security to our front."

The men slowly broke ranks. Leonidas walked over to Cyra. "Well?"

The priestess shrugged. "Good talk."

Leonidas laughed. "Wait until tomorrow. There won't be any talking."

• • •

The Persian scout was brought before Xerxes and his general, his clothing covered in mud, his face pale and tired. It had taken him four hours to make his way up the chain of command, giving his report to each level as he progressed. Now he stood in front of the king himself, but he was so tired he felt little other than a burning desire to find his bedroll and curl up under his blanket.

"Report!" the king's senior general ordered.

The man kept his eyes downcast from the king. He had heard stories of what happened to those whose reports displeased Xerxes. "Your Majesty. I was sent forward to scout the route into and over the pass at Thermopylae. I was accompanied by an Ionian who had traveled this path in previous years on trading missions."

Xerxes's left hand gave a rolling motion, which the man barely saw, but he recognized it as a signal to get to the point.

"There are Greek troops in the pass, My Lord."

The general stepped forward. "How many?"

"I could not tell. I saw the lights of torches and glimpses of troops. Not many torches, maybe twenty at most, Lord."

"Twenty?" the general laughed, considering the camp that surrounded the imperial tent had as many fires burning as stars in a clear night sky. "Most likely a feeble attempt by some local militia."

"We have encountered no resistance so far," Xerxes noted. The general's laughter was abruptly cut off. "Could this be the three hundred Spartans that Jamsheed told us about?"

"Perhaps," the general allowed, "but even if it is, three hundred could not hold that pass for more than five minutes against an assault by the Immortals."

"Make your plans," Xerxes ordered. "I want these Spartans dealt with swiftly and harshly."

"Yes, My lord."

The scout stirred, almost lifting his eyes, desiring to say more, but he didn't.

Xerxes left the main chamber, retiring to his quarters. Behind him, his generals pored over Pandora's map, making their plans for the next day's action.

Most of the camp was asleep or attempting to get to sleep. Soldiers spent the majority of their career sitting around doing nothing. The next largest amount of time was spent training. The least amount of time was spent in actual combat. Although no official word had been passed, all in the camp already knew that they would meet Greek forces the next day. Around the fires, men talked or sat in silence, whichever their angst forced them to. Veterans talked in low voices to each other in whispers, the word that the enemy were Spartans also having been passed.

Inside his quarters, Xerxes slept deeply.

• • •

"The first day," Leonidas said as the sun hung low in the eastern sky.

Cyra was next to him, wrapped in her red cloak, but she said nothing.

"Why four days?" Leonidas turned to her. "Why couldn't it be two days? Or today?" He laughed. "That would make things easier. But four days . . ." He shook his head. "My scouts tell me there are almost a quarter million troops facing us."

"We cannot control the timing," Cyra said. "We can only control our actions."

"We can't control our actions if we are dead," Leonidas noted.

A scout came running in from the north, across the open space in front of the Middle Gate.

"Yes?" Leonidas asked as the ranger came to a halt in front of him and gave a half bow.

"My Lord, the Persians are moving. An advance guard has just begun to enter the trail at the base of the pass."

Leonidas slid his helmet on, putting his face into a dark shadow. "It is time."

• • •

A contingent of Egyptian troops, over four thousand strong, began their way into the pass. Xerxes's scouts did not lead the way. After all, he had the report from the scout the previous evening and Pandora's map. Instead, they had been deployed on the crucial mission of finding a vantage point from which the king might view the coming action. They had located such a place on the mountainside to the northwest, where the angle was just sufficient to see into the pass and the Middle Gate. As the Egyptians had assembled, the scouts had laboriously carried the heavy throne up into position.

While the advance guard of the Egyptians entered the beginning of the pass, Xerxes, surround by his guard and most of his generals, slowly rode up a steep track to the small, level notch where his throne was set. Pandora walked behind him and to the right. They reached the throne, and Xerxes settled in, then got his first view of the pending battlefield.

He jerked to his feet, a vein throbbing in his forehead. "What is this?" he screamed.

"My Lord?" the head of the scouts cowered in front of him.

"The pass." Xerxes was pointing to the southeast, the hand shaking with anger. "Is that it?"

"Yes, My Lord."

"But . . ." He turned to Pandora. "Explain."

She was slowly shaking her head. "I cannot, My Lord."

"Your map shows the pass to be over a mile wide," Xerxes shouted. "That is less than a hundred meters wide at the top."

They could all see the narrowness and also the lead Egyptians less than a half mile from a slightly wider spot and the stone wall in the center. There was only one man present on the wall, a Greek in full armor who stood tall, looking straight at the king.

Xerxes spun to the head of his scouts, signaling as he did so to his master-at-arms. "Seize him." Once the man was in chains, Xerxes drew his dagger and walked up to him. "Why did you not tell us how narrow the pass was?"

The head scout swallowed hard. "My Lord. You did not ask."

Xerxes slid the razor-sharp blade across the man's throat and stepped back out of the way, as blood gushed out. Then he walked over to Pandora. "Your map is wrong."

"My Lord"—Pandora took a step back. "I did not make the map. I was given it."

"By who?"

"By those who seek to aid you. They might not have known the map was"—She paused as if something occurred to her. "My Lord, the map is of a different time. When the pass is wider. We could not have known."

"A different time?" Xerxes placed the blade against her throat. "I am—"

"King." One of the generals was pointing to the pass. Xerxes turned, keeping the metal in place. A woman had joined the Greek warrior on top of the wall. They were about two miles away, but it was obvious they were looking at him.

Pandora spoke quickly. "They wish me dead, Lord."

"I wish you dead, right now," Xerxes said through gritted teeth.

"There are only three hundred Spartans in the pass," Pandora continued. "Your army can make short work of them."

"You were the one who told me how dangerous the Spartans were," Xerxes noted.

"They are. But there are only three hundred. You have four thousand marching toward them right now. And many thousands more behind."

"The problem," Xerxes enunciated each word slowly and clearly, "is that in that narrow place, their front and our front will be the same width and depth. You made light of my military knowledge, but I do know that much." He pressed the blade, drawing a trickle of blood.

The Greek warrior held up a staff, as if in salute to Xerxes. The king's eyes narrowed as he peered at the weapon—a Naga staff. "Interesting," he muttered.

"That is Leonidas, sire," Jamsheed reported.

Xerxes removed the dagger from Pandora's throat and

turned to his master-at-arms. "Bring me the staff." When it was in his hands, Xerxes lifted it, returning the gesture.

.   .   .

"That is Pandora?" Leonidas asked Cyra as he lowered the staff.

"Yes."

"Xerxes does not seem pleased with her."

"She is just a pawn, as is he. When such pieces are allowed to think, sometimes they make the wrong move."

"And am I just a pawn?" Leonidas asked.

"I hope not," Cyra said as another scout ran up and reported the current status of the Egyptians moving up the path.

Leonidas looked down on the Spartan troops assembled in front of him. "I want fifty men. Each squad leader give me one man. We are going to meet the enemy."

Leonidas leaped off the wall as the chosen men quickly lined up. He led the way, across the open space in front of the wall and then into the trail that descended to the north. He went about two hundred meters, then halted. The trail was only twelve feet wide, with a precipitous drop to the right and a cliff wall to the left. It went down about twenty meters in a straight line before curving out of sight to the left.

"Three deep," Leonidas ordered.

Without further instructions, the Spartans formed three ranks, completely blocking the trail with a wall of metal, leather, wood, and flesh. The three rows of spears bristled, points level. Leonidas stood in the exact center of the front line, the Naga staff blade shining more brightly than the spears to the left and right, but held up straight into the sky, not level like the others.

The first rank of Egyptians appeared around the bend in the trail and came to an abrupt halt at the sight of the Spartans. There was confusion for several moments before an officer made his way to the front and surveyed the situation. Leonidas could clearly see the man, less than fifteen meters away. His cheeks were rouged, and he wore silk over his finely wrought armor. But the man's eyes were sharp as they swept across the Spartan line and took in the tight terrain. He yelled orders in his tongue, and his soldiers began to awkwardly fill the space.

Leonidas had expected this and had prepared his men. He snapped the Naga staff down to the horizontal, and the front two Spartan lines, without an order yelled or any other sound, charged forward, reaching full speed in less than five strides. Even as they moved, the left side of the Spartan line edged ahead of the right, so that when they smashed into the as yet unformed Egyptians, the left hit five paces ahead of the right. It was like a housewife sweeping her porch of dust mites.

Those not immediately slain were pressured back against those behind. The angle of the attack pushed them back toward the drop-off, and Egyptians began to tumble off, many screaming on their way down the rocky face before being silenced when crashing into the thin shoreline below.

Leonidas met the Egyptian commander. With a swing of the Naga staff, he sliced through the man's shield and into his chest. The man fell to the ground, dead, and Leonidas pressed forward. Within twenty seconds, the pass to the bend was empty of live Egyptians.

Leonidas went to the bend and peered around. He could see the rest of the trail—over a mile—to the plain below. It was crammed with more Egyptians. "Follow me," Leonidas yelled over his shoulder as he spitted the closest Egyptian with the Naga staff.

The Spartans charged down the path eight across, killing everyone in their way or knocking them off the cliff. Some of the enemy fought, but many were killed from behind as they turned and tried to run but found their way blocked by their own forces.

Leonidas kept the advance under control, rotating out the lead eight men every twenty meters or so, insuring fresh arms in the front rank to thrust spears and swing swords. They made their way almost three hundred meters down the path and had killed uncounted Egyptians when the entire remaining column panicked.

"Hold," Leonidas ordered, seeing the mayhem as the Egyptians' advance had turned into a disorganized rout. He leaned on the Naga staff, watching. The battle had taken perhaps an hour, but he knew that the Persians would have to spend the rest of the day getting the Egyptians off the path and trying to reorganize another assault.

Leonidas turned and slowly began walking up the path toward the pass, his feet almost slipping at times from the slick blood that coated the trail. Cyra was waiting for him as the trail opened up at the top.

"Day one is ours," Leonidas said. "Day two will be different."

19

Beyond the Space Between

Dane had no idea how long he and Amelia Earhart had been motionless, floating above the Reflecting Pool, looking at the ruins of Washington, D.C. The extent of the devastation was beyond overwhelming. Without a word, they floated toward the remains of the Washington Monument.

They passed the monument, continuing toward Capitol Hill, when they both stopped and turned to the left. The White House was gone. Scorched earth was all that remained.

"Oh no. Oh no." Earhart was repeating the phrase as if by doing so, she could keep the horror of what they were seeing at bay.

Dane paused, slowly turning inside the Valkyrie suit to look at something less than ten feet away: a car, the metal twisted and scorched but the make still recognizable. He blinked. But the screen showed the same thing. His heart accelerated.

He could be wrong.

He twisted slightly. Another car. Then another. He studied each one.

"Amelia."

She was still muttering her mantra.

"Amelia!" Dane's voice was sharp. "Listen to me."

She was silent for a few moments. "What?" she finally asked.

"This is . . ." Dane was at a loss for words. "The cars," he finally got out.

"What about them?" Earhart turned toward him.

"They're old," Dane finally said.

"Old? I don't recognize them."

"They're after your time," Dane allowed, "but they're not my time. Thirty years before my time. Late fifties. Early sixties." It clicked then for Dane. "This was the vision. The one I saw with Frost. The Cuban Missile Crisis. The Russians launched. The bomb went off." Dane spun about. Where the Lincoln Memorial had been there was a crater.

Dane moved forward. And there was a cab, the yellow burnt off it, but in the exact spot outside the White House where he had seen Frost stop it. Floating in the air a few feet above the ground; seeing Washington destroyed; having traveled through the space between; all that had happened to him recently from the Angkor gate through the Bermuda Triangle gate to the Devils Sea gate; Dane's brain was beyond overwhelmed.

He began hyperventilating, and the suit's air processor couldn't keep up with the demand, given that someone inside had no real physical exertion. Darkness swept over him like a tidal wave, and he passed out.

The Space Between

Captain Stokes blinked several times, trying to get oriented. A man was leaning over him, silhouetted by a light that wasn't the sun.

"Are you all right, sir?"

"What? Who are you?" Stokes tried to sit up, and the man put a hand behind his shoulders, helping him.

"Assistant Surgeon Asper, USS *Cyclops*."

"*Cyclops*?" Stokes frowned, trying to place the ship. The Navy was down to less than 300 ships in the post–Cold War era, and Stokes had served for over twenty years, but he couldn't fix the name with a ship he knew.

"Fleet?" Stokes asked.

"Naval Auxiliary Force, Caribbean."

"What?"

"Sir, the *Cyclops* was collier."

"A what?"

"A coal ship."

"Coal?"

"Sir, the *Cyclops* was lost in March 1918, while returning from Brazil. We were northwest of Puerto Rico, when a cloud appeared off our port bow. The captain . . ." Asper paused, and Stokes could hear the disgust in the man's voice. "He decided to stay on course, and we went into the fog."

"The Bermuda Triangle?"

"Aye, I hear that's what you people call it."

"And here?"

"The space between, sir."

Stokes's head felt clearer. He slowly got to his feet. He noted the other members of his crew who were still unconscious. His executive officer. His chief petty officer. His engineering officer. His chief sonar man.

Why those of all his crew?

Then he realized. If he had to run his ship with an absolute minimum of personnel, they were the ones he would choose.

The Present

Foreman had a stack of reports in front of him, ranging from damage reports concerning the "disaster on the Mississippi" as the press was calling it, to classified Pentagon updates on the modification of cruise missiles to go through the gates/portals.

He was startled out of his reading by Ahana sliding a single piece of paper on top of the document.

"What is this?" Foreman asked as he picked it up.

"An update on the time line."

The numbers were bleak. "Forty hours?"

"Yes, sir. And there will be other activity before then."

"What exactly happens then?" Foreman asked.

"The core will explode."

Beyond the Space Between

"Goddamn it, wake up."

The voice was insistent. Dane tried to block it out, but it was bringing him back to consciousness.

"We can't hang around here forever," Earhart was right next to him, hovering six inches above the street. Dully, Dane noted that the asphalt had melted and then re-formed.

"I'm OK," he murmured.

"Geez, don't do that again," Earhart said. "You were just hanging there."

"How long?" Dane asked.

"Who knows how long," Earhart said. "I haven't had a sense of time since my plane went down."

Dane looked up and for the first time noted that the sky was a uniform gray and he couldn't tell where the sun was.

The sight of the destroyed buildings had been so strong that
he had overlooked the other effects of the nuclear war.
"God, we sure screwed things up, didn't we?" Then another
piece of reality snapped in. "This place has got to be hot."

"Hot?"

"Radioactivity. This is the result of a nuclear war," Dane
said. "The bombs leave behind an effect that is deadly."

"I know what radioactivity is," Earhart said.

"The suits"—Dane nodded, once more realizing it
couldn't be seen. "They must protect against it somehow."

"What do we do now?" Earhart asked.

"Why did Rachel send us here?" Dane wondered out
loud, not responding to her question. "This didn't happen."

"Then what are we seeing?" Earhart asked.

Dane was completely confused. He pushed aside the
questions hammering at his mind and concentrated on the
first question she had asked: what to do now?

"Let's go back to the portal in the Reflecting Pool." He
turned and moved back toward the Mall. His sense of dread
grew as he got closer, and when the Reflecting Pool came
into sight, he knew that his fear was well grounded; the portal was gone.

"Oh, this is good," Earhart said.

"Shh." Dane closed his eyes. Rachel had to have sent
them here for a reason. Was it just to see this or . . . "There's
got to be another portal nearby."

"Where?"

"Let me listen."

"Listen?" but Earhart fell silent, waiting.

Dane remembered the vision of Frost. The meeting with
Kennedy. Leaving. Getting in the cab. Getting out of the
cab. Dane felt a pang of excitement. Frost had forgotten
something! Dane turned to the south. Looking across the
Tidal Basin. A dome stood, the marble scorched and blackened.

"There," Dane said.

"The Jefferson Memorial?"

Dane was already moving, forcing the suit forward, floating across the mall. He went in a straight line, right over the Tidal Basin. He noted that the cherry trees that had graced the way were nothing but stumps.

He floated up the stairs and into the center, where the statue of Jefferson loomed over him. And at the base was a black circle. It was their way out, they both knew, but both halted, looking up at the statue for several moments.

Then they went through.

20

480 B.C.

"You can never fight the same way against the same enemy," Leonidas said. "You can never take the same path back from the fight that you took going toward it; it's setting yourself up for ambush. These are basic rules of warfare."

"So what will be different today?" Cyra asked. They were behind the Middle Gate, Leonidas's squire, Xarxon, helping him put his armor on.

"They will be ready for us on the path. I imagine Xerxes will have his best troops—his Immortals—leading the way in battle formation. The good news about that is that they will take the path slowly, expecting us to come charging down. So they will waste most of the morning getting up here."

"You will not meet them on the path?"

Leonidas shook his head. "No. That would be playing into their plan. We want them to play into our plan."

"And we have one?"

"Of course."

"When did you brief your officers?" Cyra wondered.

"They don't need to be briefed on this," Leonidas checked the blade of his sword, then slid it into the scabbard. "It will be straightforward today. Nothing fancy—at least not for us. Standard battle tactics."

. . .

As he sat down on his throne set on the side of the mountain, Xerxes reached out a hand whose fingers glistened with rings. A slave handed him a goblet of wine, and he drank deeply, trying to soothe his sore throat. He had spent many hours screaming at his generals the previous evening, and in the end, his voice had given out. The head of the commander of the Egyptian contingent decorated a pole outside his imperial tent.

He had brooked no arguments nor sought any advice from his generals. His order was simple. The Immortals would lead, and they would take the pass. Today.

Xerxes relaxed for the first time in many hours as he saw the line of his best troops making its way slowly up the trail. There was no sign of the Spartans, either waiting on the trail or even at the Middle Gate. For a moment, Xerxes wondered if they had retreated and given up the pass. But then he saw a scarlet-cloaked figure climb up onto the stone wall, a Naga staff in his hand. The Spartan king. Xerxes's eyes narrowed as Leonidas dipped the staff in salute toward him. He could swear the Greek was smiling. Xerxes spat out his wine. He hoped the smile was still on the man's face when his head also adorned a stake.

"My Lord."

Xerxes turned slightly. Pandora was to his right, the cursed map in her hands.

"What?"

"I have been studying the map. I know it is wrong about the pass for some reason, but . . ." She paused, waiting, trying to gauge his reaction.

"But what?"

"It indicates a path over the mountain to the west of the pass. A very small path and apparently a treacherous one, but still a path."

"And I am to believe this?" Xerxes asked. His voice hurt even speaking at a normal tone. He took another deep drink of the wine.

Pandora began to open the map, but he stopped her with a wave of her hand. "The pass will be ours today. I do not need your map. Out of my sight, Priestess."

Pandora moved back into the ranks that surrounded the king.

. . .

Leonidas sat on the stone wall, his feet dangling. The sun felt nice on the little skin he had exposed, and he enjoyed the feeling. He'd always found it fascinating that pending battle made the smallest things seem so significant. Given there was a chance that today was the last time he could enjoy such a simple pleasure, all his senses were heightened. He wondered what it would be like to live every day as if there were a pending battle but to not have the battle.

A scout came running up to him from the northern trail. "A quarter mile away, Lord."

It was just before noon. Leonidas smiled as he stood. The Persians had wasted half their daylight simply getting here. And he knew their column must be hot and tired. The latter not so much from the climb, although it wasn't easy, but from the stress of moving forward, not knowing if their enemy waited behind every turn. For most of the morning, he had had his Spartans rest in the shade of the wall and mountain, helmets off, armor half unbuckled. He'd given the order to gear up when a scout reported the Persians were a half mile away.

"Form up," Leonidas ordered. The 300, minus two dead

and three seriously wounded in the previous day's battle, formed two long, perpendicular lines behind the stone wall.

Leonidas looked to the north, waiting. The first rank of Immortals appeared around the turn in the pass, entering the narrow, hundred-yard-long space in front of the Middle Gate.

"Two ranks in front of the wall!" Leonidas cried out.

The two lines of Spartans quickly poured through low places in the stone wall, forming into shoulder-to-shoulder ranks as they deployed. Leonidas was watching the Persians. Their commander appeared disconcerted by the lack of space, and the column was halted, the first two dozen ranks of four in the open area.

The Persians were still trying to decide what to do when the two lines of Spartans were in place. Leonidas glanced to the northwest once more, noting that Xerxes was still on his throne, watching. Then the Spartan king jumped down and moved through his lines to the forefront.

"Count off," Leonidas ordered. From left to right, each man counted until it reached the last man on the end of the line above the sea.

The Persian commander was quickly beginning to deploy his men, spreading his line. It was obvious to Leonidas that the Immortals were much better trained than the Egyptians as they swiftly formed up.

Leonidas held the Naga staff straight up in the air. The Spartans snapped to attention. With his free hand, Leonidas held up one finger. He was in the immediate center of the Spartan line.

Slowly, Leonidas brought the spear down toward the horizontal. The left leg of every Spartan in the front rank lifted at the same rate, and their spears lowered. The rear rank kept their feet still, but their spears moved forward into the quarter-down position, above the heads of their comrades in front of them.

Leonidas's arm locked horizontal, and the front Spartan rank took a step forward. Then another and another behind their king. The Immortal commander noted the movement and screamed commands. Leonidas wasn't going to give him time to complete his deployment. The Spartan king pumped his left hand once, and the rank broke into a quick march. Leonidas then poked one finger into the sky, pulled his hand down, then poked it up into the air a second time, holding up two fingers.

Every odd man in the advance line paused for two steps, then continued, effectively doubling the single rank into two and narrowing it as the open space grew tighter toward the path the Persians were on.

The lead Immortals were quickly forming, leveling their short spears, locking their wicker shields in place. The two forces were less than twenty meters apart when Leonidas held up one finger, pumped his left hand twice, held up two fingers, and spread the hand open. The front rank of advancing Spartans broke into a charge, a split second later snapping their spears into the horizontal, slapping the haft against their chest armor, the sound an ominous one. The second rank froze in place, weapons also at the ready.

The heavily armored front rank smashed into the Persian line. Screams of pain and anger rent the air. The Immortal line, not quite ready, quivered, held, wavered, then staggered back several paces under the onslaught. Leonidas was in the center, the Naga staff slicing through shields as if they weren't even there, cutting flesh and bone. Inside his head he was counting, as was every Spartan in the rank, even as they fought for their lives and to take the lives of their enemy.

When the mental count reached ten, Leonidas jabbed at the nearest Persian, the Naga blade piercing deep into the man's chest, then he disengaged, rapidly walking backward twenty paces, as did every other Spartan who had been fighting. Then they dropped to the ground, prone.

The second rank charged forward, right over the backs of their comrades, sandaled feet hitting the armor, and then the rank crashed into the dazed Persians. The front rank stood up, re-forming. Leonidas took several deep breaths, scanning the line. They had lost a few men, and squires were scurrying about the fighting in front, trying to drag away the downed Spartans, even as the second rank pushed the Immortals farther back, narrowing the field, leaving their enemy only about ten meters of space.

The Persians' bodies were piling on top of each other. Wounded who were passed by the rank of Spartans were killed by Spartan squires who slit their throats, the blood adding to the gore covering the ground. Through this, Leonidas had been counting once more, the rhythm of the count beaten into him for years on the plains of Sparta. When he reached fifteen, the rank that had passed them began disengaging. Leonidas counted five more beats, then he charged forward along with the rest of his line, passing over the prone bodies of the second rank, stepping on the armor of one of his comrades and sprinting into the enemy line.

The Immortals who faced them were disoriented, not used to the maneuver. They were trapped between the charging Spartans and the thousands of Immortals crowding the pass behind them. They couldn't retreat, and they couldn't hold their ground. The result was murder.

. . .

"Pull them back," Xerxes ordered. "Now!"

His lead general issued the orders, and flag bearers gave the appropriate signals, the order then being translated to sound as trumpets blasted the call for retreat. Slowly, much too slowly for those Immortals engaged with the Spartans,

the rear of the column began backing out of the pass. The
king's face was flushed with anger as he watched his Immortals try to extract themselves.

He stood and walked to the edge of the small ledge. He
crooked a finger, and his senior general joined him. "Now
that you know the terrain and know what you face, tomorrow will be different; you must come up with a different
plan."

"Yes, King."

Xerxes headed down the narrow track toward his imperial tent.

• • •

Leonidas halted the advance at the path, allowing the Persians to escape, despite the protests of his men. He knew
they could pursue down the path, slaying many more of the
enemy, but he felt it was better to regroup after this first en-
gagement. Also, there was a good chance the Immortal commander had prepared an ambush for just this contingency.

Leonidas walked among the bodies, noting the squires
pulling the few wounded and dead Spartans from the piles.
His experienced eye estimated about a dozen of his men
down. And about two hundred Persians. A very good kill
ratio, but one he knew they wouldn't be able to sustain for
many more engagements.

"They are done for the day," Cyra said, surprising
Leonidas, who had not heard her approach.

"There is still at least three hours of light," Leonidas
noted.

"Once more, they were not ready for you," the priestess
said. "Tomorrow will be different."

Leonidas knew that. "Then tomorrow we must be different."

"You must hold for two more days," Cyra said.

Leonidas pulled his helmet off and wiped his sweaty forehead. "And then?"

"Then we will have the map."

"And you will leave," Leonidas noted.

"Would you prefer to be back at Antirhon?" Cyra asked. "The Persians would still be here."

Leonidas began unbuckling his armor. "True. There is work to be done. It will be a long night."

21

Beyond the Space Between

This place is worse. That was the thought that resounded through Danes mind as he took in the environment around him, slowly turning the Valkyrie suit so he could survey his new surroundings. The sky overhead was covered with black clouds with swirls of red and yellow in them. Lightning flickered inside the clouds, producing a dull thunder as if even sound were defeated by the bleakness surrounding Dane and Earhart. The land was scorched clean, the ground blistered and buckled yet covered with a layer of ice and blowing snow. He had no idea where they were as there was no apparent sign of civilization.

"We might be on another planet," Dane whispered, as if by speaking in a normal voice he would become part of the desolation.

"We can breathe," Earhart said.

"There are filters—or some sort of rebreather—built into this suit," Dane said. The portal was behind them, and he was tempted to simply turn around and go back through it to the devastated Washington—at least that held a degree of familiarity. "Or maybe it's a planet with an atmosphere like ours," he added uncertainly.

"Wrong portal?" Earhart asked.

Dane controlled his desire to flee. "I don't think so." He could feel the cold through the suit's armor.

"There!" Earhart was pointing with a white arm.

Dane turned in that direction, and a small, moving speck was visible on the screen inside the helmet. It took him a moment before he recognized what it was: another Valkyrie suit, moving toward them.

"Friend or foe inside?" Dane wondered out loud.

"We'll find out soon enough," Earhart said as she flexed her fingers, extending the claws on both hands.

As the figure got closer, Dane could see that its white armor was blackened and dirty. Dane focused his attention, trying to mentally probe through the suit and determine who, or what, was inside.

"Friend," he said as he picked up an aura. It was familiar, almost as if he had met whoever was inside the suit. He could now see that the armor was damaged in a couple of places, much like theirs was.

The figure came to a halt ten feet in front of them, both hands held up, palms out, claws not extended. "Welcome to hell."

The voice was female, one Dane knew. He felt a wave of shock pass through him as he recognized it. "Ariana? Ariana Michelet?"

"Yes. I've been waiting for you."

"But . . ." Dane struggled to get the words out. "You're dead."

The voice was low and almost melancholy as she answered. "Sometimes I wish I were. And I will be soon. But first, I must accomplish what I have been tasked to do."

"I don't understand," Dane said. "How can you be alive?"

"It's like Noonan," Earhart cut in. "I saw him die, but then he came to me."

"Come," Ariana gestured. "Come with me. I will show you and explain."

Despite not being able to see her, Dane knew it was Ariana in the suit. The aura was the same as he remembered. He had not recognized her right away because he considered her dead.

"Where is here?" Dane asked.

"This is Earth. Washington, D.C."

"It can't be," Dane said. "We just left Washington. And even that Washington wasn't"—He tried to process all that had happened. "Is this the future?" But that didn't make sense, he realized, because the Washington they had just left had been the past. Or his past. And Earhart's future. He felt as if a spike was being driven through the center of his brain as he tried to assimilate the paradoxes and the situation.

"The future," Ariana repeated. Dane could almost see her shaking her head inside her helmet. "Yes. In a way. We are at about the same place where you went through that"—She pointed at the gate behind them.

"Things got worse?" Dane asked.

"This isn't the same Washington," Ariana said. "This is a different time and place."

"But you just said this is Washington in the future."

"In my future—or more accurate to say my present. Not yours."

"But—"

"Your Ariana died," she said.

Dane was totally confused. "Then who are you?"

"Ariana Michelet. But a different Ariana. As the Washington, D.C., you just came from was different from the Washington, D.C., in the world you initially left, and this one is also different from those other two," Ariana said. "This"—she held out both arms, slowly turning—"is Earth in a different time line. Parallel to the one you know, but one that took a different path at a certain time in the past. I am Ariana Michelet, but not the Ariana Michelet you knew in your time line. She died in your time line. In this time line, I failed in stopping Erebus from erupting. Because I failed, I survived. I was taken by the Ones Before as the world—this world—collapsed around me into destruction." She dropped her arms. "Then they sent me here. To wait for you."

"Why?" Dane asked, trying to understand.

"So your Earth doesn't end up like my Earth."

Dane took in the swirling snow and ice-covered ground. "Ice this time," he whispered to himself.

22

[faint offset text from facing page, illegible]

480 B.C.

The dead bodies of the Persians were tossed off the cliff, tumbling down and splashing into the water. The seven Spartan bodies were laid out behind the Middle Gate. The severely wounded were being tended to. As far as Cyra could tell, severely wounded meant a lost limb or partial evisceration, as those who had wounds not that severe were standing with the rest around Leonidas in front of the wall. Torches sputtered from their niches on the rock wall as the Spartan king addressed his men.

"They will come first thing in the morning. They know the land now, and they know their enemy. We will not have the advantage of surprise as we have had so far. But we still have the advantage of terrain and of arms." Leonidas turned to the oldest member of the 300. "Polynices, what do you foresee?"

"Archers. So many that the sky will turn black with their arrows' flight." The old man smiled. "It will shade us from the sun, so we will be able to fight in the shade."

The assembled men chuckled.

Leonidas nodded. "I agree. They will try to fix us with arrows. And then?"

Polynices tugged on his beard. "They will mass as many men as possible in the open space and attack. And attack. And attack."

"Recommendations?" Leonidas threw the question out to all.

"They will expect us to fight the same way," someone yelled out.

"True," Leonidas acknowledged. "So we must do something different."

Polynices stirred. "You started by saying they know the terrain and the enemy. Why not change one of those?"

Leonidas smiled. "My thoughts exactly."

• • •

Xerxes never received a casualty report. Those killed during the day's fighting were Immortals. He knew that every man killed or wounded had been replaced immediately, and the Immortals were at strength, ten thousand strong. Thus, in a way, there were no casualties, therefore no need for a report.

He sat in his dining throne, the Naga staff on the table in front of him. His generals were gathered round the long table, their eyes downcast. Pandora was not behind the king, but to one side, the master-of-arms next to her. Her map was in the center of the table, a half-dozen daggers slammed through it. They had been there when Xerxes entered the tent, and he assumed that had been done by members of his staff who had friends and relatives among those slain during the two days of fighting. The head of the lead scout was mounted on a spear outside the entrance to the tent, along with that of the Egyptian leader.

"Do we have a plan for the morning?" Xerxes finally asked.

The general slowly got to his feet. "Yes, My King."

"And that is?"

"We will deploy a front line of heavily armored Scythians at the top of the pass. Behind them we will mass archers. We will fire all morning and then withdraw the archers, reinforce the Scythians, and assault."

Xerxes nodded, then waved a hand. "Everyone leave. Except Pandora."

The tent cleared quickly.

"I have shown much restraint with you," Xerxes said. He ran his fingers along the smooth metal on the haft of the staff. "You arrived with this and the map. The latter has proven false. What is the purpose of this?" he tapped the staff.

"I do not know, My Lord."

"My patience is exhausted," Xerxes said. "If you do not tell me now, I will have your head on a pole outside my tent within the minute."

"It is to be used to destroy something, if necessary," Pandora said.

"What?"

"Another map."

"Of?"

"I do not know. Truly!" she added as he started in anger. "I only know what I have been told in visions."

"Visions from where?"

"The gods, My Lord."

"There is only one god, the true god, Ahura Mazda."

"Then the vision came from him."

"You lie."

"I am telling you all I know. I was taken from my home, which was being destroyed by earthquake and fire. To a dark place. I remember being on a table. Tied to the table. Figures in white all around me."

Xerxes leaned forward, chin on hand, interested in spite of the situation. "Angels?"

"I do not know. There was much pain. I could not see clearly. And I had visions. They told me to seek you out. I did not want to. But I have had no choice in all of this. If I tried—and I did once, if you want honesty—to escape from your camp, there is so much pain in my head that I could not continue." She spread her hands helplessly. "I have no control over my life."

"And this other map? Where is it?"

"As far as I know from the visions, it will be in the pass in two days, My Lord."

"Who will bring it there?"

"I do not know."

"What about this priestess from Delphi? The Spartan king next to her had a staff like this," he tapped the Naga staff.

"I do not know."

He let go of the staff and indicated the map. "That was not very useful. Why were you given it?"

Pandora closed her eyes. "It is supposed to help you defeat the Greeks and gain the pass."

"But it doesn't even show the pass correctly." Xerxes leaned back in his throne. "I do not pretend to question my god—the god. I do not think you come from him. And if you do not come from him, then perhaps you come from evil."

Pandora shrugged. "That might well be." She took a step forward. "But the map shows a trail over the mountain and coming in behind the Greeks. I have talked to some locals that your troops captured. One of them says there is such a trail, confirming what the map indicates."

"I cannot waste troops on such a thing."

"I will reconnoiter the trail, My Lord. Verify that it does exist. You can send someone you trust with me to confirm what I see."

Xerxes shook his head. "There is no need. We will have victory tomorrow."

. . .

Leonidas took his place in the long line of men. He was stripped down to his tunic and sandals, and the night air felt cool on his skin. He was surprised when Cyra slipped into place next to him.

"This will be man's"—he paused, and rephrased his comment—"hard work."

Cyra smiled, her white teeth glinting in the dim light from the torches on the wall. "You think you know all there is to know about hard work? About controlling pain and fear?" She shook her head. "Men. Try having a child. Then you will learn about pain. And maybe you will learn something about love, also."

Leonidas was about to say something when the first stone came down the line, passed from hand to hand. He grabbed it with both hands on his right side and swung to the left. Cyra's hands were ready, and she took it from him, passing it on to the next Spartan in line.

They worked on through the darkness. After several hours, a rider came galloping up the pass from the south, and Leonidas left the line. He took Cyra with him, even though she protested that she was fine.

"Report," Leonidas ordered as they came up to the courier. The horse was sweating, even though the night was cool.

"King." The man nodded. "Your six lochoi march swiftly, but they are still four days away."

Leonidas had expected as much. "And the Athenians?"

"Sit behind their walls and argue."

"Are there any Greek forces on their way to join us?" Leonidas had sent out a dozen emissaries to the closest city-states.

"Two hundred archers from Mellos are coming. They are led by Lichas."

Leonidas smiled. Lichas was a wily old warrior, and his men were skilled with the bow. "When do they arrive?"

"In the afternoon, sire. At best."

"That is all?"

"Yes, sire."

Leonidas dismissed the courier to get some food. He ran a hand through his dirty hair as he pondered the situation. He could sense Cyra's presence next to him. "The smart move would be to withdraw, since the people who live behind us obviously don't care enough to send troops to save their own skin. We could link up with my six lochoi and hold the isthmus at Corinth. That would also force the hand of the Athenians."

"We must"—Cyra began, but Leonidas cut her off.

"I know we must hold until tomorrow. And not just for your map. We must stay here because we said we would."

23

Beyond a Portal

"Where's the water?" Dane asked.

They were on what had been the bank of the Potomac, but the riverbed was dry, except for some thin, blowing snow.

"The Shadow took the water," Ariana said. "All of the fresh water they could tap through portals. And quite a bit of the oceans, also. The shore of the Atlantic is about sixty miles that way; that's how much water the Shadow has taken. In your time line, the Shadow takes power and people, but it wants more. Once it has sucked a world dry of those two, it moves to other materials. Water. Air."

"Who is the Shadow?" Dane asked.

"I don't know," Ariana replied. "An intelligent race, if doing this to planets can be considered intelligent. One that has learned to move in both time and space using the portals and gates. Who understands how to use laws of physics we were just beginning to learn existed."

"Slow down," Dane said. "What do you know about the

portals and gates? What's the difference between the two? Why is there just a portal in some places"—he pointed at the black circle they had come through—"and sometimes the portal is hidden inside a gate?"

"I don't exactly know," Ariana admitted. "My best guess, from what I've seen and learned, is that the Shadow can open portals between worlds. Gates are a by-product, most likely occurring when some of the Shadow's world spills through the portal into the other world. When that happens, some of the creatures from the Shadow's world come through also, such as the kraken."

That made sense to Dane, the first thing that had in quite a while. "So the Shadow attacks various Earth time lines via portals to scavenge them?"

"Yes. There must be many parallel Earths, each a little different from each other, changed at some point in their history, and the Shadow has been pillaging them. I remember reading a research paper where the author postulated an almost infinite number of parallel universes, existing side by side but separated slightly by time and space."

"How do these Earths differ from each other?" Dane asked.

"A decision or different action by someone here and there that changes the course of history," Ariana said.

"Could the Shadow be causing these differences?" Dane asked. "To maintain their supply of worlds?"

"I never thought of that," Ariana said. "It's possible."

Earhart's voice cut in. "And the Ones Before? Have you met them?"

"No. I've received visions of what I am to do."

"And that is?" Dane asked.

"I've done it—most of it—by showing you this world and telling you of the time lines and parallel worlds."

"We need the map of the portals," Dane said.

"There's something else I need to show you first," Ariana

said. She turned toward the west and began moving, Dane and Earhart hurrying to keep up.

There were many questions running through Dane's head, but he didn't know which one to ask first. There was a high ridge ahead, and Dane tried to remember if there had been such a terrain feature west of Washington in his time line world, but he couldn't recollect one.

When Ariana reached the top of the ridge, she paused and waited for them to catch up. Dane slid to a halt next to her, bobbing in the air for a few moments before the suit came to a stop. His questions were forgotten for the moment as he took in what had caused the ridge.

The top edge of a massive black sphere was all that could be seen, but from the quarter-mile-high ridge he was standing on, and from his experiences, Dane knew he was looking at one of the spheres that was used to traverse the large portals and capture ships and planes. It must have struck the ground hard, given how far it was driven into the earth, but it appeared to be intact.

"That's what captured me," Earhart said.

"It is one of the Shadow's craft," Ariana said.

"What happened?" Dane asked.

"I don't know. I was given a vision of it here, and I knew I needed to show this to you."

"It looks like it crashed—hard," Earhart added.

As far as Dane could remember, all contacts with the spheres had been in the water. "It can move in the air?"

"Obviously," Ariana said.

"Would the portal map be on board?" Dane asked.

"No. I didn't see it there."

"But it might be?"

"My vision said you must go through another portal for the map."

Dane felt a surge of frustration. "Where is the map?"

Ariana must have picked up his mood. "You need to

know what the map is of—what the portals are. There are indeed several portals that lead to the Shadow's world, but the vast majority are between parallel Earth time lines."

"OK," Dane said. "I understand that now. But my—our time line"—he pointed at Earhart—"is running out of time."

"I know," Ariana said. "When the Shadow activates the core portal via the Nazca plain, it is the last stage of scavenging. It has happened to other Earths. They no longer exist."

"We don't have much time to get back to our Earth and stop the core," Dane said.

A strange noise echoed in the Valkyrie helmet, almost as if Ariana had laughed. "The time you spend here might or might not equal the same time elapsing on your Earth."

Dane remembered the crew of the USS *Scorpion,* which had reappeared over thirty years after disappearing, yet none of the men had appeared to have aged at all.

"We have time for you to learn." She headed toward the sphere.

The Space Between

"Where do the ships go?" Captain Stokes asked Asper. The rest of the survivors of his crew were gathered behind him in Earhart's camp. They were all battered and bruised but functional, and that was all that Stokes was concerned with. Several of the samurai, including Taki, were also standing close by.

"There's a graveyard, a couple of them as far as we know, on Earth," Asper said. "Deep under the ocean. A big cavern."

"How do we get there?" Stokes asked.

"I imagine through a portal," Asper said. "The problem with that is that there is a good chance the portal is hot, and you'll get fried and die like"—he pointed at Noonan's body—"that poor fellow."

Stokes turned to Taki. "This Dane fellow—he came through on a ship, didn't he?"

Taki stared at him blankly, and Stokes cursed. He knelt down and drew a rough outline of a submersible in the black sand. He pointed at it. Taki nodded and pointed toward the inner sea.

"But you still won't know which portal to go through," Asper pointed out.

Taki was kneeling and drawing something next to Stokes's sketch. Stokes frowned. "A shark?" he asked as he noted the fin on top of the form that was drawn.

"No, a dolphin," Asper said. "Last time they came through, they had a dolphin leading them."

"Is it still in the water with the submersible?" Stokes asked.

"Only one way to find out," Asper said as he gestured to Taki, then pointed toward the inner sea.

The Present

Deep underneath Lake Tahoe straddling the California-Nevada border, the Earth cracked and then belched. A rude term for the hundreds of thousands of tons of molten lava that surged up through the sudden crack and met the cold water at the bottom of the lake. As the front edge of the lava solidified, the mass behind it continued to press forward, breaking through, solidifying, then being broken in turn.

Hundreds of miles and the width of California away from the nearest ocean, people living on the banks of Lake Tahoe had never considered the possibility of a tsunami. Their first warning was when a sixty-foot wave of water, displaced by the crack and surging lava, came sweeping across the normally placid surface of the lake, heading both east and west.

Thousands died staring at the water in shock and amazement. The survivors were treated to a rather unique event, one unknown to those who had survived ocean tsunamis. Trapped in the borders of the relatively small lake, the tsunami waves recoiled off the shorelines and both oscillated. As they went back and forth, sometimes they canceled each other out; sometimes they hit the shore at the same time and doubled the strength.

This was to continue for almost twenty-four hours, the dual waves gradually losing power, but long enough to completely decimate all living things around the lake.

. . .

The Russians had known there was a gate inside Lake Baikal ever since they'd become aware of the existence of what their early scientists termed Vile Vortices in the late forties. The discovery had been shocking, both for the fact there was a gate and the location.

Baikal was a place that was held close to the heart of Russians; even for the vast majority in the east who had never seen its waters. It was as if the people had always known what scientists had discovered about it—that it was the world's oldest and deepest lake. It also held a fifth of the world's fresh water within its 700-kilometer length in southern Siberia. That was more water than all of North America's Great Lakes combined.

The lake drew its extreme depth from the unusual fact that it was at the joining of three tectonic plates, plates that were spreading apart from each other, producing a fissure in the planet. This had been going on for over thirty million years, and the fissure was estimated to be over forty kilometers deep, although the lake, at its deepest, was only just over a kilometer and a half deep. The rest of the fissure was filled with sediment brought into the lake from more than 300 rivers and streams that fed it. This was the planet's deepest land depression, far deeper than that of the Rift Valley although not as long.

The entire area, because of the moving plates, was rocked by mild earthquakes almost daily. In 1861, a large quake had caused over 310 square kilometers of land on a peninsula to simply disappear into the dark water.

The lake even had species of life in it that were found nowhere else in the world. How these life-forms came about had been a mystery until Professor Kolkov arrived in the area in the early fifties to try to pinpoint the location of the Vile Vortice he believed to reside somewhere near the shores of the lake. After locating the gate, Kolkov had postulated—in classified papers read only at the highest levels in the Soviet Union—that some of the unique creatures had come through the gate from the Shadow's world.

The aborigine people who had lived around the lake before the arrival of the Russians from the east were called the Buryat. They believed that gods dwelled in the depths of the lake. The most feared of those was Doshkin-noyon who stole ships and the men who crewed them from the surface of the lake during times of storm and fog. Buryat fishermen still made a toast of vodka to the demon god, a cupped handful tossed into the water, before venturing onto the lake.

While it has many feeders, the lake has only one outlet, the Angara River. It was estimated that there was so much fresh water in the lake, that even if all the inlets stopped, the lake would still take over four hundred years to drain out via the Angara.

A second outlet was now opening up at the very bottom of the lake. Inside the Baikal gate, a massive portal, over a mile wide, opened. And into it poured the water. The opening of the portal was noted by the superkamiokande in Japan, and the information was forwarded to Kolkov. He accessed his monitoring stations at Baikal, and it only took a minute before the change was noted. The water level had dropped over a foot in that short amount of time, an astonishing amount, given the size of the lake.

All along the shoreline, the Buryat and others who lived there could see the water level dropping.

. . .

Ignoring the quiet hum of activity in the FLIP control center, Foreman glanced at the clock, noting that only thirty-two hours remained before the planet's core went critical. The reports of disaster were flowing in: the Mississippi, Lake Tahoe, Southeast Africa, and now the news that Lake Baikal was being drained. There was no sign of Dane, and the power flow through the Nazca fault continued unabated. For almost fifty years, Foreman had studied the gates, and now he sat, impotent, as they were active all over the world, draining his planet of power and water.

"Another portal has opened," Ahana announced.

"A new one?" Foreman had mapped out sixteen gates over the years, but in recent days, new ones were popping up all over the place.

"Yes."

"Where?"

Ahana was looking at a piece of paper she had just pulled out of the printer. "The stratosphere just above the Antarctic."

Foreman didn't understand at first. "The what?"

Ahana pointed up. "The stratosphere. Just south of Argentina."

"How high is that?" Foreman asked.

"Over fifteen kilometers up."

"What the hell is it doing there?" Foreman wondered aloud as he pulled out his SATPhone. "There's only one thing I can think of that can get there quickly and go that high. I'm going to scramble *Aurora* to check it out."

. . .

The remote location in Nevada was known by many names: Area 51; Dreamland; Groom Lake; S-4; the Ranch; and a half-dozen others. The Air Force insisted it didn't exist, even though satellite images of its runway, the longest in the world at seven miles, were posted on the Internet.

It was where the SR-71, the B-1, and B-2 bombers, and the Stealth fighter had been test-bedded and first flown. Located northwest of Las Vegas, it was in one of the most desolate and isolated parts of the United States. The base was set alongside Groom Mountain, and the long runway stretched along a dry lake bed.

Responding to Foreman's call, strange-looking craft rolled out of a hangar cut into the side of the mountain. The shape of the plane, if it could be called that, was untraditional, as there were no wings. The body was a solid V, long and sleek. It was more than 250 feet long and 100 feet at its widest. Its official, classified Air Force designation was the SR-75 Penetrator, but it was more commonly called *Aurora*. There was even a Testor model on the market that was a very good approximation of the craft.

The skin of the aircraft was dull black and consisted of a special composite that could handle extreme temperatures, both cold and hot, and was radar absorptive. There were two small windows up front, more of a solace to the human pilots than necessary for flying the craft, as its velocity at top speed was so great that by the time a pilot saw something with his eyes, it would be too late to maneuver.

The SR-75 had a crew of three: a pilot, navigator, and systems officer. All were tightly strapped into form-fitting crash seats with a plethora of displays and controls within easy reach. Each man wore a suit similar to an astronaut's and breathed oxygen from an onboard supply.

The pilot, Colonel Richards, received a go from the Area

51 tower and gradually began accelerating the aircraft using the plane's conventional turbojet engine. It took over three miles of runway before the unique shape of the plane produced enough lift for the plane to separate from the ground.

Richards pointed the nose upward at a sixty-degree angle, while turning the plane to the south. The acceleration pressed all three crew members deep into their seats. As the SR-75 passed through ten kilometers' altitude, it also broke the sound barrier. Richards kept the craft angled up, gaining altitude as it accelerated. When they reached twenty kilometers, he began to level them out. His display indicated they were moving at Mach 2. The conventional turbojet engine was beginning to struggle to get enough oxygen at this altitude.

"Switching to PDWE," Richards announced over the intercom.

He moved his finger over the stick and pressed a red button. The entire plane shuddered as the high-speed engine kicked in. PDWE stood for pulsed-detonation-wave engine. Underneath the conventional engines, the PDWE consisted of a series of high-strength compression chambers. A special fuel mixture, including oxygen, was being pumped into them. An explosion occurred in each chamber in sequence, which formed the high pressure pulse they had just felt. The pulse was sent out of specially designed vents on the rear of the aircraft, providing propulsion.

As the explosions occurred faster and faster, the shuddering almost settled into a steady rumble. *Aurora* passed through Mach 3, then 4, and was still accelerating. The plane was already over Mexico and only eight minutes out from Area 51.

Richards kept a tight eye on the controls, and when a display indicated relative speed at Mach 7—over five thousand miles an hour—he finally locked down the throttle. They were covering a mile and a third every second.

"Nav, give me a fix," Richards asked. His screen flickered for a second, then a green line indicating their planned route appeared. A moment later, a red line, indicating the craft's true position updated via ground positioning satellites, appeared on his main screen. The red was right on top of the green from Nevada through their current location.

"Right on track," his navigator confirmed what the screen displayed.

"What are we heading toward?" Richards asked his systems officer, Major Rodriguez.

"Target is located one hundred twenty miles east of the Falklands," Rodriguez reported. "It is moving on a northward course at a speed of two hundred miles an hour. Target information is originating from muon transmissions being tracked by the superkamiokande in Japan."

Richards frowned. He'd read the classified reports on the gates, and they'd been told upon alert that this had something to do with that, but he preferred hard targeting data. "Anything from satellites?" he asked.

"No current coverage of that area," Rodriguez reported.

Other than the British during the Falkland War, Richards knew, no one much cared about what hapened in that part of the world, so it made sense there would be no spy satellites covering the area.

"Nav, ETA at target?" he asked.

"Twelve minutes thirty-six seconds and counting."

"What the hell is out there?" Richards wondered out loud.

• • •

The water level had dropped over fifty feet already in Lake Baikal. Stunned Russians lined the shore, watching.

Stunned Americans looked out over a massive lake eighty miles long by twenty miles wide, stretching from New Madrid up- and downstream. The current of the Mississippi ran through the center of the lake. Corpses continued to surface.

. . .

"Let's take this slow," Richards said as he throttled *Aurora* back from Mach 7. They were over Bolivia with the Paraguay-Argentina border rapidly approaching. Piloting *Aurora* was vastly different than even a jet fighter. When Richards thought of turning, he had to consider entire countries to be crossed. He wasn't worried about violating sovereign airspace; they were so high no radar would pick them up as no one would think of painting their altitude. By the time Richards had them slowed to Mach 3, they were over Buenos Aires and then over the South Atlantic.

"Range?" Richards called out. Technically, he could glance at his display and see the readout, but he was old school. He believed they were a crew, and each man had to be responsible for his specific area. It was also good for morale if the other two crew members felt like they were pulling their weight. He continued to slow the plane below Mach 2.

"Two hundred klicks," the navigator announced. "ETA in two minutes."

"Paint me something," Richards told Rodriguez.

"Extending imaging pod," Rodriguez announced.

From the belly of the SR-75, a small door slid back. A hydraulic arm extended downward, holding a cluster of sophisticated cameras that could pick up infrared through ultraviolet and thermal images. If they were traveling any faster, the entire array would be ripped off, another reason for Richard's throttle back.

"One minute thirty seconds," the navigator reported.

Richards glanced down. Next to his forward-looking display, a smaller screen showed the imaging.

"What the hell?" Richards muttered. A black rectangle

filled the screen, almost from top to bottom and extending beyond the left and right limits. "Wide angle," he ordered.

"That is wide angle," Rodriguez said.

"Geez." The word came out of Richards's mouth without conscious thought, even as he automatically pulled back on the throttle. "How big is that?" he asked, even though he had no idea what it was.

"Radar indicates over two hundred miles wide by twenty high," Rodriguez reported.

"What is it?" Richards asked as he checked his speed. Almost down to Mach 1.

"Thirty seconds," the navigator announced.

Richards pushed his stick hard left, beginning a turn. He ignored his screens and looked out the small, thick windows in front of him, twisting his head to the right as the plane turned.

He saw it.

He would have been blind not to.

Stretching from horizon to horizon, left to right, a latticework of black struts supported panels of gray material. The scale was beyond what Richards or his two crew members could comprehend. And in the very center was a black sphere a half mile in diameter. Even as they watched, more panels were unfolding at the ends, extending it further and further.

About a mile behind the black sphere was a portal, and a stream of ionized matter was flowing from the panels toward the portal and being sucked in. Lightning crackled around the panels, and even forty kilometers away, the men aboard *Aurora* could feel the hair on the back of their necks tingle and raise.

"What the hell is that thing doing?" Richards wondered as he completed the turn.

• • •

On board the FLIP, Foreman echoed Richards's question. And he received an answer.

"Water and air," Ahana whispered, staring at the image relayed from *Aurora.*

"What?" Foreman demanded.

"The Shadow is draining Baikal, getting fresh water." Ahana pointed up. "We have a better idea of the layers of the atmosphere surrounding the planet than the layers inside the planet, given the simple fact that man has traveled through all those layers on their way into space. That doesn't necessarily mean that any intelligence has been attached to the knowledge gained." She tapped the imagery. "From the surface of the planet reaching up to fifteen kilometers is the troposphere. The next five kilometers—where this thing is—is the transition between troposphere and stratosphere, which extends outward from twenty to fifty kilometers. A relatively small constituent element of the stratosphere is made of three oxygen molecules bonded together. It is called ozone.

"Oxygen came into the Earth's atmosphere approximately two billion years ago as a by-product of photosynthesis of early forms of plant life. Enough by-product was produced over time to make oxygen a large component of air, which extends upward almost three hundred kilometers from the surface. At the top, in the rarefied upper atmosphere, high-energy ultraviolet radiation from the sun hits circulating O_2 molecules, splitting them into their constituent atoms. The single atoms swirl together to form O_3, or ozone, which in time breaks down to oxygen, which in a perpetual dance circulates up and is split down to individual atoms and then back into ozone.

"There isn't much ozone in the stratosphere. If it were at surface level, the layer would be no more than a tenth of an inch thick. But it is a very important tenth of an inch because it screens out long-wave ultraviolet-C light and most ultraviolet-B radiation. Both of these are extremely harmful to living organisms.

"It was only in 1974 that we began to realize both how important this layer of ozone is and how damaged something that had taken a billion years to develop had become in less than a century. It started in the 1930s when man invented chlorine, fluorine, and carbon compounds, known as CFCs, for industrial applications. CFCs react with practically nothing and thus once used, float into the atmosphere, rise up to the ozone layer and above, where the UV radiation finally breaks them down, releasing chlorine or bromine, which does react with ozone, destroying it. It isn't just man that affects the ozone. Erupting volcanoes spew ash that also interacts with ozone, depleting it.

"It appears to me that the Shadow is using this thing to take in both oxygen and ozone. Notice the discharges. Hell, that thing could be breaking the O_2 and O_3 down to single molecules for transport back, then reconstitute them when it goes through the gate."

Ahana sat down wearily, rubbing her fingers against her temples. "The Shadow is stripping us of our most precious resources. Even if we stop the core destruction, there might not be anything to save."

24

480 B.C.

Cyra lay still on the hard ground, slowly taking inventory of her body. She felt as if she had been severely beaten. Every muscle ached, and her fingers were torn, the wounds still oozing blood. She slowly sat up, grimacing in pain. As she expected, the Spartans were already awake and moving, even though dawn was an hour away. She could see Leonidas ten feet away, his squire slowly rubbing oil onto his skin, then kneading the muscles underneath, loosening them.

"It will be a clear day," Leonidas said in a low voice, as if respecting the darkness.

Cyra glanced up. The sky was clear, thousands of stars sparkling overhead. She heard muted laughter from a group of warriors as she gathered her cloak tightly around her shoulders.

"How do you feel this morning?" Leonidas asked, his teeth flashing as he gave a quick smile.

"Fine."

The smile was gone as rapidly as it had appeared. "It will be a long day," the king said.

"You must hold until tomorrow," Cyra said.

"And then we can die?"

Cyra wasn't certain whether it was a question or a statement. She noted a red tinge on the horizon, but in the wrong direction, to the north.

Leonidas must have noticed her looking that way. "The Persian camp is like a false dawn. They burn much wood. An army on the march is like locusts, devouring everything in its path."

"It is a waste," Cyra said.

"Yes, it is." Leonidas wasn't looking to the north though but rather at a cluster of young Spartans who were sharpening their swords. "I want you to stay behind the wall this morning. I don't want the men to see you once they form."

"Why is that?"

"You remind them of home. Of their families. Their wives."

"Isn't that a good thing?" Cyra asked.

"They know why they fight," Leonidas said. "I want their focus on battle."

Cyra nodded. "I will tend to the wounded. Those who cannot fight."

"Stay close to the wall, on the south side, near the wounded," Leonidas said.

"Why?"

"You will see."

• • •

Metal on metal, leather creaking, men cursing. The Persian army began to stir and move. The orders had been issued, taking hours to trickle from general down to squad leader. Those chosen to fight this day, their fates decided by a few old men sitting in the king's tent the previous evening, began to gird themselves for battle. Those not called up said their silent prayers at being spared for this day at least.

Stories circulated the camp from those who had met the Spartans in battle, mostly from the Egyptians, but even some of the Immortals had told tales late at night. And, as with most armies, the stories became exaggerated. The Spartans were seven feet tall. They fought with limbs cut off. It took a dozen normally mortal blows to kill one. There was even a story there were only 300 of them in the pass. Men shook the heads, disbelieving this last story. Three hundred could not hold for two days, not fight off the Immortals.

. . .

The real dawn came with a blazing red sun rising over the Gulf. Leonidas had his armor on and was pacing along the top of the Middle Gate, deploying his men. The Spartans formed a double line as they had the previous day, directly in front of the diminished stone wall. The sound of bugles and drums echoed up the pass, indicating the Persians on the march.

A squad of Skiritai came jogging back, and their leader went directly to Leonidas. "Five hundred foot of Scythians—heavy infantry—lead. Behind—archers. At least four thousand. Different nationalities. Some I've never seen before."

Leonidas nodded. "Join the squires," he ordered the rangers. He raised his voice so all could hear. "Knights! Listen. The Persians come, just as we expected. A wall of heavy infantry and behind them archers. We are ready for that. As your aching backs can tell you."

That brought a low chuckle from the men.

"But we must stand fast for most of the morning before we implement our plan. I do not want any of you to fall asleep from boredom."

Leonidas waited out the laughter. "As you already know

from the soldier's vine, the rest of our army is two days' march away. And the only reinforcements closer are two hundred archers under Lichas."

There was no laughter. From her place with the seriously wounded, Cyra was surprised that Leonidas would tell them such negative information, yet he didn't want her in front of the wall for fear of affecting the morale.

"That is the state of things," Leonidas said simply. "Are there any questions before the Persians arrive and we begin our day's work?"

There were none, and Leonidas hopped off the wall and walked the line, checking his men, paying particular attention to those who had been wounded the previous day, making sure they were up to the task.

"Hey, old man," he stopped in front of Polynices who sported a blood-soaked bandage poking out from underneath his helmet. "Did some Persian try to knock a little sense into you?"

Polynices laughed. "If he had achieved that, I wouldn't be here, would I?"

"True, true," Leonidas agreed. "I assume you sent whoever dealt you the blow to his gods?"

"I parted his head from his body," Polynices said. "His gods might not recognize him."

The Spartan king edged closer and lowered his voice. "What do you think? Can we hold the day?"

"If their generals are stupid—yes."

"If their generals are smart, what would they do?" Leonidas asked, even though he knew what he would be ordering if he were the Persian leader.

"Heavy infantry in assault after assault all morning, regardless of casualties, to keep us engaged in the pass while using the fleet to land to our rear."

That was Leonidas's greatest fear—that the Persians would simply land troops behind them. He had rangers posted to watch the Persian ships, and so far, the fleet remained still, the only activity barges landing to bring food and supplies to the massive army. Perhaps the Persians thought there were more Greeks marching this way and such a maneuver could turn into a rout, with the landed troops caught between the pass and the reinforcements.

"Do not worry," Polynices said. "The Persian army is too large for a general to think straight. It takes enough brainpower simply to move the entire thing and keep it fed. Not much left over to figure out how to employ it in battle."

Leonidas looked around now that he could see. He noted the Persian ships in the Gulf to the north. And the contingent of finely garbed soldiers surrounding their king as he made his way to the throne set on the mountainside. And then up the steep mountain to the top, noting the scrub-covered slope, then back down to the pass.

"I feel as if I am forgetting something important," Leonidas confided in Polynices.

"You would not be a good commander if you didn't feel that," the old man said. "We have a good plan for today. That is enough for now." He nodded toward the pass. "We have company."

The first rank of Scythian heavy infantry marched into the open space, the commander deploying his men, doing a much better job than the Immortals had the previous day. Eighty wide, six ranks of Scythians locked in place, shield to shield, thick spears pointing ahead. Behind those six ranks, bowmen filled the space, packed tightly, with just enough room between the ranks for their weapons to be wielded. The same was true on the narrow path to their rear as more bowmen prepared for battle.

Leonidas went to the center of his line. The Scythians were eighty meters away, and he could see the eyes of his enemies. He slid into the open space in the line and, like the rest of his men, waited.

• • •

Xerxes impatiently watched the preparations. He was tired of this place, of Pandora, of the Spartans. "Why are they not firing?" he demanded of his general.

"My Lord, the bowmen are stacking their missiles," the general informed him. "It will be difficult to resupply them once the battle is engaged. And we want to keep a continuous bombardment going so that when the Spartans weaken from holding their shields over their heads, there will be no respite except that of death."

Xerxes frowned. "Shade," he ordered, indicating his left. A slave quickly ran into place and held up a palm branch, protecting the king from the slanting rays of the early morning sun.

"What will today bring, Pandora?" Xerxes asked.

"I do not know, My Lord."

"No predictions? No visions? No words of wisdom?"

"I am afraid not, My Lord."

"You are not very useful as a seer," Xerxes said loudly, bringing uncertain chuckles from his court sycophants. "I will make a prediction then. I will tell you what I see the day bringing. Spartan blood coating that cliff wall underneath the pass. That is what I see. And I see further than that. I see all of Greece in flames. The cities that have caused us so much trouble, especially Athens and Sparta, razed to the ground, the earth plowed over and salted so that no sign of them remains and nothing will grow in those sites. That is what I see."

• • •

"Shields up!" Leonidas yelled the command in a loud yet calm voice as he noted the archers bring their bows, arrows nocked, to bear at a forty-five-degree angle. He lifted his heavy shield as he went to one knee, locking it in place with the men to his left and right. The shield was at the same angle, in inverse, from the archers facing them.

The sound of the first volley of arrows being released by the Persians was almost musical but very loud, louder than any Leonidas had heard in all his battles. As the sky darkened with the wooden shafts arching up, he estimated they were in range of at least a thousand archers, quite a feat on the Persian's part to get that many in so small a place.

While the first volley reached its apex and began descending toward the Spartan lines, the second volley was launched. Leonidas realized he was tensing and forced his shield hand to relax. The missiles landed with the thud of iron tips striking wood, ground, and rock. Leonidas felt one strike his shield, hit a rivet, and bounce off. His eyes were peering through the slightest of cracks between his shield and the man to his right. The Scythians were leaning on their shields, laughing and screaming obscenities.

The second volley landed. From somewhere to Leonidas's right, a man cried out in pain as an arrow found his exposed foot, pinning it to the ground. The warrior cursed as he lowered his shield and ripped the arrow out of his flesh—a mistake, as the next volley caught him exposed, and three arrows struck his body. Two bounced off armor, but the third caught him in the neck, driving down into his body, severing arteries. The man fell forward, his blood spurting.

All this Leonidas caught out of the corner of his eye. "Hold!" he yelled. "Leave him," he ordered as the men on either side made to retrieve the wounded man. "Lock in place," Leonidas further ordered. The two men slid closer together, keeping the shield wall intact. The wounded Spartan tried to crawl back under the shield wall, but he didn't make it, bled dry. More arrows hit his body.

Behind the Middle Gate, Cyra was seated with her back to the stone wall. The dozen seriously wounded were to her left and right. Eight feet in front of them, the ground was

pin-cushioned with arrows, clearly delineating the safe zone
from the death. An occasional arrow would bounce off the
top of the wall and drop harmlessly into the safe zone. She
couldn't imagine what was happening on the other side of
the wall. She could not believe an ant surviving this, never
mind a man.

• • •

"How long has it been?" Xerxes grumbled.

"Three hours, My Lord."

Xerxes leaned forward, squinting. "Are you sure they
aren't dead underneath those shields?"

The general swallowed. "Sire, they would not still be
holding them up if they were dead."

"Surely they must grow tired soon," Xerxes said.

"That is the plan, Sire."

Behind the king, Pandora stirred impatiently, the rolled-
up map held tightly in her hand.

• • •

"Did you hear the one about the Persian king and the
chicken?"

Leonidas smiled as he listened to the men joke to each
other underneath their shields. Several more men had been
struck, but the wall was holding. His arm ached, the muscles
quivering, but he had held the shield in this position many
times in training for much longer periods of time, while
trainers went down the ranks striking men with wooden
poles, screaming at them. King or not, Leonidas had taken
his place in the training every month.

Leonidas checked through the crack. The Scythians were
still leaning on their shields, but they were neither laughing
nor hurling obscenities. He knew it was beginning to sink in
to them that the Spartans would not be so easily dispatched.
He also knew that his men were beginning to wonder when

he would issue the orders to implement the plan they had prepared all night.

Leonidas raised his voice so that his men could hear above the sound of bow strings twanging and arrows thudding home. "Isn't it nice of the Persians to supply us with so many arrows for Lichas and his men to shoot back at them?"

There was laughter, but Leonidas could tell it was strained. He returned his attention to the front. He edged his shield over slightly so he could see the hillside where Xerxes's throne was set. He could see the Persian king flinging his arms about, mouth wide open, obviously yelling at the cluster of finely armored officers in front of him. Leonidas was tempted to give the order, but he knew that as long as the Persians were content to lob arrows at his forces, the clock was ticking in his favor. And there was the issue of when Lichas and his archers would arrive.

• • •

"You heard me." Xerxes restrained himself from ordering his master-at-arms to lop off the general's head for questioning the order.

The general bowed his head. "Yes, My Lord." He scurried off to pass the order down the chain of command.

• • •

Leonidas had watched the general scurry away and wondered what was next. It was obvious the Persian king was losing patience with the barrage. From the lack of shadows from the arrows sticking into the ground nearby, Leonidas estimated it was noon. This had gone on without change for longer than he had hoped.

He was thirsty, and his bladder was full. Several men had already pissed where they knelt, the urine flowing in small golden rivulets along the rocky ground. And no one said a word about it. What was a little piss when arrows were rain-ing down upon them and a quarter million men waited to slay them?

Leonidas could see the Scythian commander talking to a courier who wore a helmet with a tall plume on it—the same officer that Xerxes had been screaming at.

"Steady, men," Leonidas yelled. "Something's getting ready to happen."

"About damn time," someone yelled in response, which brought a chorus of laughter.

The Scythian commander was yelling orders in his strange tongue, his men lifting their shields. Still the arrows came. The commander went down his line, making sure it was dressed properly, shields interlocked, spears forward.

Leonidas frowned as another arrow thunked into his shield. The Scythian lines began moving forward, yet the barrage wasn't stopping. If anything, Leonidas realized, it was getting thicker. He suddenly realized what was about to happen. He looked through the thin space between his shield and the man to his right toward Xerxes. The Persian king was leaning forward, as if watching some interesting sporting event.

The Scythian commander pointed forward toward the Spartans with his sword. Leonidas could see the fear on the men's faces. He could hear muttering in his own ranks as his men realized the enemy infantry was approaching; yet the arrows still came down.

The Scythians were halfway across the open space. Some arrows, their range short, began to fall into their ranks. Leonidas saw one of the warriors in the front rank collapse to his knees and fall forward, a shaft sticking up out of his back.

When the Scythians were less than twenty meters from his men, Leonidas rose to his feet, bringing his shield from the up to forward position. His heart pounded with pride as the entire two lines of Spartans immediately rose and did the same, ignoring the arrows that showered down upon them.

The Scythians slammed into his lines, both sides jabbing, hacking, and slashing as they fought among the arrows still being fired by the Persian archers. The missiles struck without regard for the side one was on.

Leonidas neatly sliced the head off a Scythian right in front of him, then pointed the Naga staff blade up into the air and pumped up and down three times, before bringing it down to parry a thrust from a Scythian officer.

Hidden in the bushes above the pass, a ranger saw the signal and passed it along. Over two hundred squires and Skiritai were hidden on the slope, crouched under bushes and behind piles of rock, clinging to the steep slope in small hollows they had dug the night before.

Released, they sprang into action, shoving forward stones that had been laboriously carried up the slope from the Middle Gate the previous evening. The heavy rocks tumbled down, smashing into the clusters of archers below.

The squires and Skiritai were too high, but the archers tried to turn their weapons against them. The arrows reached their apex fifty feet below, then many arched over and caused their own mayhem among those that had loosed them.

And at that moment, Lichas and his archers arrived. They announced that by a line of men stepping up onto the Middle Gate and firing point-blank into the Scythians, just over the heads of the Spartans. At such close range, their powerful bows could punch through armor, and the effect was devastating.

The arrows from the Persians had stopped as the archers reacted and died under the rock assault from above, which was becoming a literal avalanche as the hundreds of head-sized rocks, which had once been half of the Middle Gate and had been carried by the Spartans up the slope the previous night, showered down upon them.

The front rank of Scythians were fighting bravely, even as the ranks behind them were spitted by the Greek arrows. Leonidas moved forward, and the Spartan line surged, the men actually happy to be free to move, even if it were toward the enemy, after so many hours under their shields. Their heavy sandals snapped the arrows stuck in the ground as they slashed at the Scythians.

Leonidas howled with the passion of combat as he drove the Naga staff completely through the chest of a warrior in front of him, the thrust so strong it actually struck the man behind that Scythian, killing him also. The entire Spartan line growled, screamed, and yelled as they cut into the Scythians with a vengeance their enemy had never seen and would not see again as they died.

*   *   *

Absolute silence reigned on the hillside around Xerxes's throne. Not a single Scythian escaped. Half the archers were dead, crushed by stones or knocked off the trail to fall to their death below. The others were fleeing down the same path taken by the Egyptian and Immortal survivors of the past two days.

Xerxes pulled his dagger out and stalked forward. His master-at-arms was at the edge of the escarpment. Xerxes slammed the blade into the man's chest, and he tumbled forward. The Persian king spun about. No one would meet his eyes. Except Pandora.

"Go." Xerxes gestured with the bloodstained dagger. "Check the path. Be back by daylight."

*   *   *

"Stop."

Leonidas whirled, Naga staff at the ready, and only managed to halt the sharp blade as it reached Cyra's neck.

"Stop," she repeated, placing her hand on his arm. "It is done for today. It is done."

Leonidas blinked.

"It is done. You have won."

Leonidas slowly nodded. "For today," he whispered, looking at the blood on the blade of the Naga staff.

"For today," Cyra acknowledged.

"And tomorrow?" Leonidas looked around in a daze at the dead and dying that surrounded him, lying in a field of countless arrows. His feet were submerged several inches deep into the mud made of dirt, blood, and urine.

"Ah," Leonidas moaned. He staggered several feet to the right and sank to his knees, ignoring the muck as he dropped the Naga staff and cradled the head of a wounded man in his arms. Cyra joined and recognized Polynices.

"You led well," the old man whispered, blood flecking his beard.

Leonidas was looking about. "We have lost many."

"But as long as there is one Spartan standing . . ." Polynices paused to take a deep breath before continuing. "The Persians will not have the pass."

"You fought bravely," Leonidas said. "I saw"—He stopped when he noted that the blood was no longer bubbling out of the old man's mouth. He reached up and closed the lifeless eyes. "He was my first instructor in the agoge. He was the first to teach me bravery in the face of battle."

Cyra placed her arm across the king's shoulders. "Perhaps—just perhaps—fear is a good thing. Perhaps there are things we should fear. Things we don't understand."

Leonidas shook her arm off. "Can you respect the dead?"

Cyra stood. "We are doing this to respect the living."

"The living?" Leonidas walked away toward the archers. He went up to their leader, Lichas, an old man who still stood tall and strong, a powerful bow in his hand. His men were harvesting the Persian arrows, resupplying their quivers.

Leonidas threw his arms around Lichas. "We thank you. You arrived at exactly the right moment. I couldn't have planned it better."

Lichas was looking around. "Where are the others?"

"Others?"

"The other cities? The Athenians? The Thebeans? The Medeans?" Lichas returned his gaze to the Spartan king. "Where are the rest of your warriors? I don't see many here."

"We started with three hundred knights," Leonidas said. "I have six lochoi two days' march away."

"Two days?" Lichas shook his head. "You Spartans are insane. You will not last three days."

"We've already lasted that long," Leonidas noted. "And that was without your aid. With you, who knows?"

25

The Space Between

"This is ridiculous," Stokes's executive officer muttered.

"You have a better idea?" Stokes asked as he leaned over the edge of *Deepflight* toward Rachel. In his hand was a snapshot of the *Connecticut*. The dolphin raised herself halfway out of the water, leaning toward the image. Then she went over backward, hitting the water with a splash that soaked Stokes.

"Look," he said.

Rachel raced off about a hundred meters, then paused, looking back as if waiting.

"Let's go," Stokes said as he slid inside the submersible, joining the rest of the survivors of his crew.

Beyond the Space Between

The scale of the Shadow sphere was overwhelming as Dane, Earhart, and Ariana got closer. Even though it was over half buried, the curving side loomed high over their heads and to the left and right. Ariana didn't hesitate when she reached the craft but began floating upward, along the side. Dane and Amelia Earhart followed, the black surface just a couple of inches underneath their suits.

Ariana was angling to the right and came to a halt about fifty meters short of the top. Dane could see what had caused her to stop. There was a thin line in the surface that extended as far as he could see. About four inches to the left of the line was a strange-looking indentation.

Ariana pointed at that spot. "Use the Naga staff."

Dane had almost forgotten about the pole strapped to his back. Earhart removed it for him, and he took it from her. He realized the indentation was the opposite of the Naga heads. Making sure to keep the blade away from his suit, he slowly pressed the Naga end into the hole. A golden glow suffused the hole and staff, and Dane felt a shock pass through his body.

He let go of the staff and was buffeted back several feet as a loud noise filled the air. The crack slowly opened several inches along the top half of the sphere. A quarter of the way around to the left and right, similar cracks had opened.

"More," Ariana said.

Reluctantly, Dane took hold of the staff and pressed. He was ready when the shock hit him, and he kept his hold. The crack widened until it was five feet wide where they were, narrowing to the joint at the bottom.

"Come on," Ariana said.

"Just leave it?" Dane indicated the staff.

"I don't think anyone is going to come along and do anything to it," Ariana slipped into the opening. Dane followed with Earhart right behind him. He could see that the skin of the sphere was over three feet thick. The interior was lit by a dim golden glow coming from numerous unseen sources. The inside was as magnificent as the outside. It was completely open, with a floor that bisected the diameter in the exact middle. The floor was canted slightly, indicating the sphere wasn't resting with the top straight up.

"This is what my plane was drawn into," Earhart said.

Dane had seen the video from the USS *Revelle* when it was captured by a similar—or could it be the same?—sphere. Ariana was descending, floating downward. Dane wasn't sure how to do that, but the suit seemed to sense the direction he wanted to go, and he followed. Ariana touched down in the exact center of the floor, Dane landing a second later, followed by Earhart.

"It still has power," Dane noted.

"Some," Ariana acknowledged.

"Have you been in here before?" Earhart asked.

"In the vision," Ariana said. She bent over and placed her armored hand on the floor. She quickly stood and backed up as a hatch irised open. It was five feet in diameter, and she didn't hesitate as she slipped down into it. Dane followed, and they went down a long tube for almost a minute before it opened into a circle, about fifty feet in diameter. Floating in the exact center was a golden sphere that took up about a fifth of the space. The surface shimmered, and Dane was certain the exterior wasn't solid.

He felt drawn to it and innately knew this was the control center for the sphere. But Ariana was moving past it. Dane now saw at least a dozen opening tubes, leading out of the space he was in. Ariana disappeared down the lowest hole. Dane checked to make sure Earhart was with him, then followed.

They descended for several minutes, then entered another large opening. Dane's best guess was that they were at the very bottom of the massive vehicle. This chamber was about a hundred feet across and very dimly lit so that it was hard to see. Poking up from the center was a thick rod with a globe on the top. He could make out that the walls were lined with couches. Strapped into almost half the couches were bodies. Human bodies.

"The Shadow are human?" Earhart whispered.

Dane had seen something like this before. He approached the nearest couch. There was something strange about the body. Then Dane saw it. The head was half solidified—not quite crystal, more a dullish gray mixed with crystal. Turning slowly, he could see that all the couches were oriented toward the center—toward the globe on top of the rod.

"I don't know if the Shadow are human," Dane said, "but their fuel for this thing was."

"Not the fuel," Ariana said. "The channel for the power."

Dane remembered the Theran priestess Kaia going into the portal and disrupting the power. "So we can use the skulls to disrupt the Nazca portal if we can get to it?"

"Yes."

26

480 B.C.

"If the words of your oracle were true, this is my last night." Leonidas was lying on his back, his head resting on his rolled-up cloak, his eyes staring up at the stars.

"Yes." Cyra was seated on a small stone to his side, her own cloak wrapped tightly around her body.

"It's strange. Before every battle I have felt fear—of being maimed, of being killed, of being defeated. But no matter how dire the fight appeared or how terrible the odds, I always believed deep inside that none of those would happen." He turned his head toward her. "I mean, I knew one day I would die, either in battle or some other way, but it always seemed some time in the future. But that future is here, now. It is very strange."

Cyra said nothing, overwhelmed by the atmosphere of the camp. There was a low murmur in the air, many men talking in subdued voices to each other. Telling words that only the prospect of imminent death could bring a man to say.

"When you take this map," Leonidas's voice was stronger, "will you stay with it or do you just deliver it somewhere?"

"I deliver it," Cyra said.

"Where?"

"I don't know yet. I am sure I will be shown the path."

"And then?"

"I do not know my fate."

"If you live and are in Greece, will you do me a favor?"

"Yes, if it is within my power."

Leonidas smiled. "I believe it is indeed within your power. Go to my home. Tell my wife how I died."

"I can do that—"

"I'm not done yet," Leonidas said. "I want you to teach my daughter."

Cyra frowned. "What would you like me to teach her?"

"To be like you."

• • •

Pandora cursed as she stumbled over an unseen stone and fell to her knees, gashing one.

"Silence, whore." The voice was harsh and low. The warrior that Xerxes had sent with her was a man who had no name in the court. He was simply known as Xerxes's Dagger. While the master-at-arms carried out public executions for the king, Xerxes's Dagger was known as the one who worked in the dark, executing those who the king desired dead but could not risk publicly killing.

Pandora had memorized the track as well as she could before they left the Persian camp, and so far, the trail was following the thin line that had been etched on the map. It was narrow, only one person wide, and went up the mountain at a steep angle. At times, she had to cling with her hands to the mountainside. But the bottom line was that so far, the trail was passable.

• • •

Leonidas slapped Lichas on the shoulder, startling the old man who was watching over the Middle Gate, toward the glow from the Persian camp.

"I would ask you to fight until noon," Leonidas said. "Then you are free from any obligation."

"What happened to two days and reinforcements?" Lichas didn't appear surprised by Leonidas's words.

"Today is the last day. You just arrived, and you know it. I've been here three days, and I know it."

Lichas slowly nodded. "You are at half strength. Your men, brave and stout though they be, are exhausted. I would recommend you pull back now, under the cover of darkness. Once you are engaged, you will not be able to withdraw."

"We won't be withdrawing," Leonidas said. "I will send a courier in the morning and halt the six *lochoi,* sending them to defend closer to home."

"You have done more than anyone could have dreamed. Another day won't make much difference in the larger scheme of things. The Athenians still sit and argue. The other cities obviously don't care much about the Persians, even though they will be destroyed once Xerxes gets through the pass."

"That is where you are wrong," Leonidas said. "It will make all the difference." He smiled. "I have been told so by the Delphic oracle."

Lichas spat over the wall. "Oracles."

"There is more than that," Leonidas said. "Wars are won by more than just force of arms. There are other factors."

"Such as?"

"The will of the people. That is why we—the Spartans— are here, and why we will stay."

• • •

Xerxes glanced up from his breakfast to note Pandora being escorted into the imperial tent by his executioner.

"My lord"—she began, but he waved his knife, silencing her.

"You would not be alive if the path did not exist." He jabbed the blade at his general. "I want four divisions of Immortals to take this track. Pandora will be their guide." He turned back to her. "How long will it take?"

"It is a narrow track. One person wide. We will be over the mountain and behind the Spartans by noon at the earliest, King."

"Attack as if we must break through the pass, while my Immortals march," he ordered the general. He wiped his chin with a silk cloth, then stood. "I will be on the hill, watching."

• • •

Leonidas found Cyra slowly walking in a circle in front of the Middle Gate. The sun was just above the eastern horizon, and Leonidas had all his armor on. Cyra appeared to be in a daze, her eyes half closed.

"What are you doing?" Leonidas asked.

Cyra held up a hand, hushing him as she continued to walk. She halted about twenty feet in front of the wall and opened her eyes. "This is the spot."

"For?"

"Where the map will appear."

"And once you have it?" Leonidas asked. "Do you know yet where you take it?"

"I have seen a vision that I will need to confirm with the map. Then I will know where to go."

Leonidas frowned. "We will be forced back behind the wall today." A ranger came running up to him from the north trail.

"The Persians are coming," the scout reported. "As-syrians are in the lead. Swordsmen."

"Archers?" Leonidas asked.

"Just infantry."

The king turned to Cyra. "You must wait behind the wall."

"But"—she began, but he cut her off.

"When your map appears, I will get you to it. I will de-tail some men to get you down the pass."

· · ·

Trumpets blared and drums throbbed, the sounds echoing off the mountain. The entire Persian army was preparing to move. Assyrians were heading up the trail into battle, while Xerxes had issued orders for all the rest of his massive force to be prepared to cross the pass. Tents were struck, pack an-imals loaded, and troops lined up in formation.

And high above the pass, in the folds of the mountain, Pandora led four thousand Immortals along the single track.

· · ·

Leonidas arrayed his diminished forces along the western cliff wall, perpendicular to the killing field. Along the Mid-dle Gate were Lichas's archers, stacks of Persian arrows at the ready, but their bows were hidden, and they wore the armor of those Spartans who had been killed or severely wounded. When the first rank of Assyrians came up the path and into sight, they paused at this unusual arrangement, but the pressure of thousands of men moving from behind forced the officers to deploy their men as best they could. The problem was, they weren't certain whether their front should face the wall ahead of them or the Spartans arrayed against the base of the mountain to the right. There wasn't enough room to form two lines at a right angle.

The decision, as Leonidas had hoped, was made to face

the more immediate threat: the Spartans arrayed on the
killing ground. The Assyrians were well trained, wheeling
into ranks facing the mountain, shields up, long swords at
the ready. Leonidas was in the front center of the first rank
of Spartans. He had barely 140 of his original 300 left that
could stand. He estimated at least a thousand Assyrians were
already in the killing ground with more pressing up the pass.

The Assyrians advanced. Leonidas raised his shield into
place, the Naga staff at three-quarters. The rest of the Spartan line snapped into place in a similar position. The Assyrians were barely ten meters away, when Leonidas
dropped the Naga staff into the horizontal position. One
hundred and twenty spears did the same.

And on the Middle Gate, Lichas and his men reached
down and grabbed their bows, which had arrows already
nocked. In one smooth movement, they brought their
weapons to bear on the left flank of the Assyrians. Every
third man fired, their arrows impacting, mowing down the
flank. The next third immediately fired, then the last third,
by which time the first third had their second arrows ready.

The effect of the rolling barrage on the exposed flank was
devastating. The right flank of the Assyrians, unaware of
what was happening to their left, collided with the Spartan
line in a cacophony of metal on metal. Assyrian officers who
were aware of what was happening were trying to bend back
the surviving left of their line. When the arrows were killing
Assyrians a third of the way into their line, Leonidas
snapped the Naga staff into the upright position. Lichas saw
the signal and fired a flaming arrow across the front of his
archers, who immediately ceased fire.

The unengaged Spartan right charged. They rolled up the
disorganized Assyrian left flank, shoving over 100 of the
warriors right off the cliff, then wheeling left. It was a clas-
sic pincer movement. And for the third day, a massacre en-
sued. Leonidas halted the advance when the killing field was

swept clear of the Assyrians. He drew his Spartans back to their start position, backs against the mountain. Lichas and his men dropped their bows and resumed their original stance.

And the fresh Assyrian troops repeated the mistake of their predecessors, unaware of what had happened. And again. And again as the morning wore on. Blood flowed, soaking the killing field. Hundreds of Assyrians died falling off the cliff. Hundreds more fell to Spartan metal. And here and there one of Leonidas's knights went down in the fierce fighting.

After four unsuccessful assaults, word must have finally reached the commander of the Assyrians. There was a lull in the fighting, and Leonidas took stock. He'd lost over 30 men against at least 1,000 of the enemy. But tens of thousand more waited on the trail, and he knew that the next assault would not expose its flank to the archers. He glanced up at the sun. It was after midmorn. Noon was about an hour, perhaps an hour and a half off.

Leonidas pointed the Naga staff toward the Middle Gate. "The wall, men."

In good order, the Spartans relinquished the killing field and retreated behind the Middle Gate. Squires carried the dead and severely wounded with them. Leonidas was the last remaining in front of the wall, watching as a fresh group of Assyrian warriors deployed at the far end of the killing field. Reluctantly, he climbed over the wall and took his place in the center.

For the first time, he noticed that the sun was no longer shining. Looking up, he noted that dark clouds blanketed the sky. Thunder sounded in the distance, drowning out momentarily the sound of the Persian army drums and horns signaling the advance. Leonidas looked across at the ledge where Xerxes was perched. The Persian king seemed calm, a change from the last three days. Leonidas frowned.

"A storm comes," Cyra was next to him.

"He's up to something," Leonidas said, indicating Xerxes.

"All we need are a few more hours," Cyra said.

"We can hold the wall for a while," Leonidas said. "But once they breach it, it will be over quickly." He turned to Lichas. "You have many arrows. You may fire at will."

The archers opened fire, their missiles slamming into the Assyrians. The bombardment was fierce, but the Assyrian officers marshaled their troops as if on a parade ground, lining them up, moving unlimited reinforcements up to take the place of those struck down.

"They're good," Leonidas allowed, watching the spectacle.

"They're insane," Cyra muttered.

"No. They need a solid front to move forward. It's what I would be doing."

Cyra shook her head. "I never said you were sane, either."

Leonidas laughed. "I suppose we aren't. But you needed us. Still need us."

The Assyrians were finally formed and began moving forward. Their shield wall was up, and the effect of the arrow barrage was almost negligible now. Leonidas went to the right side of the wall and tapped Lichas on the shoulder. "You've done your duty."

Lichas nodded, then passed the word down his line. The archers slowly slipped away, making their way down the south trail until only Lichas remained. There was no time for more farewells, as the Assyrians were just about at the wall.

"I will tell Greece what you have done here," Lichas said to Leonidas before following his men.

Spartan spears were leveled, and the points met the Assyrian's assault along the rocks of the Middle Wall. The front rank of Assyrians died, then the second. The third clambered over the bodies of those in front. Leonidas ran to and fro on the wall, using the Naga staff wherever it was most needed, slicing through shields and flesh. He'd dropped his shield some time during the fighting, the leather hooked on an Assyrian sword.

It was even darker, and the sound of thunder was close. An Assyrian leaped up onto the wall to Leonidas's right. A huge warrior, a four-foot-long sword in his hand. He decapitated a Spartan who tried to push him back. Leonidas jabbed at the man, the blade of the Naga staff punching easily into the man's chest, but the Assyrian still managed a strong blow, which slammed into the Spartan king's helmet, staggering him. Leonidas twisted the haft of the staff, gutting the warrior, then pushed the dead man back over the wall to crash into his fellows.

Leonidas couldn't see out of his left eye. He wiped with a free hand and pulled it away, covered with blood. Someone touched him to his left, and he whirled blade first, halting when he recognized Cyra. She used her cloak to wipe away the blood from the wound on his scalp.

"It is almost time!" she yelled, straining to be heard over the screams of the dying, the clash of arms, and the thunder.

Leonidas shook his head, spraying blood and trying to organize his thoughts. He saw Assyrians on the wall here and there, his Spartans trying to push them back. He looked to the rear. Ten Spartans stood, spears ready, eager to join the fray, their eyes locked on him, waiting for his command.

"There!" Cyra pointed at the spot she had indicated in the morning. A black sphere was forming. Frightened Assyrians stepped back from it, opening a hole in their front. Leonidas held up five fingers and pointed. Half of the ten Spartans he had held in reserve broke ranks and dashed forward.

"Come," Leonidas yelled at Cyra, straining to be heard over the sound of battle and storm.

He jumped over the wall, swinging the Naga staff in a

large arc, clearing space. The five Spartans followed, locking their shields, protecting the priestess. Leonidas pressed forward. The black sphere was just like the one he had gone into to get here, hovering just above the ground. One of the Assyrians stumbled back, fell into it, and disappeared. That caused the others in the immediate vicinity to panic.

The way was open. Leonidas stepped off to the left, just short of the black sphere, feeling the power emanating from it race over his skin. The other five Spartans completed a semicircle around the portal, Cyra on the inside.

Leonidas risked a glance over his shoulder. Cyra was reaching forward, toward the darkness, hands outstretched. And out of the portal came two hands holding a golden sphere about three feet in diameter. The skin on these hands was blistered and raw, but they were steady, holding the sphere. The arms extended out all the way, but whoever it was didn't come through.

Cyra took the globe, staggering as if it was heavy, her body shaking as she stepped back from the portal.

"To the wall!" Leonidas yelled. He took point, the five Spartans flanking him in a wedge. There was little resistance from the Assyrians, their ranks still disjointed. The rest of the Spartans had regained the Middle Gate and stood on top of it.

Leonidas paused at the gap in the gate, allowing Cyra and her precious cargo to pass through. He looked over his shoulder. The Assyrians had pulled back and were re-forming, the task easier now that Lichas and his archers weren't bombarding them. With the reinforcements that were pouring into the killing ground, and the losses his men had already endured, Leonidas knew the next assault would ride over the wall and break his line.

He turned his attention back to this side of the wall. Cyra was reverently holding the golden sphere in her hands, peering into it. He could see that the surface wasn't smooth but appeared to be made of numerous two-inch strands of gold interwoven in a complex pattern. Leonidas blinked, because the strands seemed to be pulsing, as if they were alive, even shifting in place, as if she were holding a nest of snakes.

"You must go," Leonidas said to Cyra.

She didn't appear to hear him, her focus on the sphere.

Leonidas placed a blood-spattered hand on her shoulder. "You must go."

Cyra slowly looked up. "I see . . ." Her voice trailed off.

Then Leonidas saw something beyond her that caused his heart to pause momentarily: Lichas limping up the trail with a half dozen of his men. And they were firing their bows back down the trail. The king held up his free hand, five fingers spread wide. Then he pointed to the south. The five remaining knights broke ranks and dashed to support Lichas. The other five stayed near Cyra and Leonidas.

There were shouts of alarm from the east. When Leonidas looked in that direction, he saw the solid line of Assyrian reinforcements moving forward in step toward the Middle Gate.

A horn sounded to the south, and fifty Immortals came rushing up the path, overwhelming Lichas, his archers, and the five Spartans Leonidas had sent as reinforcements. And in the center of the Immortals was a woman who the king recognized as having been the one next to Xerxes: Pandora.

"We're surrounded," Leonidas stepped between Cyra and the Immortals. He saw that Pandora also carried a Naga staff. His eyes darted about, searching for a way to get Cyra out of the pass, but the Assyrians were charging to the north, the Immortals filled the pass to the south, the cliff and sea to the east and the rock wall to the west. He felt a pang of failure, that despite his best efforts, he had not achieved what the oracle had tasked him to do; the map would be Pandora's.

"King." Cyra's voice was so low, Leonidas almost didn't hear her over the din of battle.

"What?" His eyes were on the advancing Immortals, now less than fifty feet away, Pandora in the lead. At the very least, he figured he could kill her.

"I can open a portal."

Leonidas didn't understand. He held the Naga staff across his body, ready for action. The skin on the back of his neck tingled. He'd felt this before. He turned away from the Immortals, even as the Assyrian ranks smashed into the depleted Spartans holding the Middle Gate. Leonidas saw that Cyra's eyes were closed and one hand was running lightly over the surface of the sphere.

"I see the path." Her hand wrapped tightly around one of the strands. A golden glow suffused her, then extended out about three feet in front, between her and the king.

Leonidas stepped back as a portal began to open there. He heard a female yell and could see that Pandora was leading the Immortals in an all-out charge toward them. His time sense had slowed, as it did in the heat of battle, and every second dragged slowly.

Cyra stepped toward the portal, the map sphere in her hands, still covered in gold. "Come with me."

Leonidas smiled, and held out the Naga staff toward her, drawing his sword. "My place, my destiny is here."

Cyra didn't argue. She took the staff. Leonidas spun about, bringing the sword up, the haft of Pandora's staff slamming into it, the blade stopping just short of slicing Cyra in two. The priestess stepped into the portal, and it snapped shut behind her.

27

Beyond the Space Between

They had crossed what used to be the Potomac, and Dane's best guess was that they were in the vicinity of where the Pentagon had once sat. A black circle hovered a foot over the ground ten feet in front of them.

"Is the map through there?" Dane asked.

Ariana's answer was less than reassuring. "So I have been told through a vision."

Dane felt the urgency of their quest, yet he paused, so many unanswered questions nagging at him. "What happened to this time line?" he asked. "Why wasn't the core—and the planet, this planet—destroyed?"

"The Shadow was able to tap all the energy slowly and under control," Ariana said. "I would guess that your fight against the Shadow in your time line has caused it to act precipitously, with a certain amount of control being lost."

"The crystal skulls?" Dane threw out. "Are they useful?"

"I don't know," Ariana said. "They obviously still have

some residual power and can definitely channel the larger power from the planet."

"Can we travel back in time and save your planet?" Dane asked.

"I don't think so," Ariana said. "As far as I can figure out, and from the visions I have been given, the Shadow can use the portals, but they didn't make them."

"I don't understand," Dane said.

"The walls between parallel universes are thicker in some places and thinner in others. And, in some places there are openings—portals—through the walls. I think the Shadow searches for these and uses its power to open the portal. But what that means is that it doesn't control where and when the portals go in those worlds. The Shadow just takes advantage of what it finds. Also, we affect portals somehow."

"What do you mean?" Dane asked.

"Our minds just don't channel power, they help create it on some level we've never known. When enough minds are in one place, pushed to the limit, I think they can affect the portals."

"Is there anything else you can tell us," Dane asked, "that might help?"

"I don't think so," Ariana said. "It is hard for me," she added. "My world"—her white arm lifted and slowly swept from side to side, indicating the desolation around them— "and everyone I knew, including, you"—she pointed at Dane—"are gone."

"How did I die?" Dane asked, feeling the absurdity of the question as he asked it.

"A tsunami took out the FLIP and everyone on board," Ariana said.

"Are you coming with us?" Dane moved toward the portal, Earhart at his side.

"No. I'm dying. I had to go through another portal to get

this suit. It's sustained me enough to meet you, but I don't have much longer."

"You can go to my camp in the space between," Earhart said.

"No. This is where I belong."

Dane had already experienced Ariana's—his time line's Ariana's—death. To realize it was going to happen again in this time line was ripping the scab off a barely healed wound.

"Do you know what is through there?" Dane pointed at the portal.

"I just know enough to bring you here and tell you it is the next step." The white figure floated a few feet away, as if there were no one inside the suit. "I am very tired." Her right hand went to her left arm.

Dane knew what she was going to do and reached out to stop her.

"No!" her sharp rejection caused him to halt. Ariana's fingers punched in the code, and the suit split open. Dane's breath caught in his throat as he recognized the woman he had first met during a rescue mission in the Angkor gate as she stepped out of the suit. She staggered and this time accepted his arm to help her from falling. Her skin was covered in red lesions and pus was crusted around her eyes. Dane now understood her desire to end it quickly.

Ariana waved toward the portal. "Go. Go now."

"Thank you," Earhart said, then she stepped into the portal and disappeared.

Dane hesitated, reaching with a white-armored hand toward Ariana's face, clearing the yellow gunk away from around her eyes. He realized she was crying.

"We did it wrong," Ariana said, looking up at him. "So far, your time line has done it right. You need to take the next step."

Dane couldn't find words to say what he was feeling. He

turned and went into the portal, leaving Ariana sitting alone and dying on the surface of her devastated planet.

The Space Between

Captain Stokes and his surviving crewmen from the *Connecticut* were stuffed into *Deepflight*. On the video monitor above the controls, Rachel was clearly visible, swimming back and forth slowly as they followed as quickly as they could. They passed between two small portals, heading farther out into the middle sea.

Stokes pushed the throttle forward and increased speed to keep up with the dolphin. After a couple of minutes, there was no doubting their destination. A large wall of black, a massive portal, was directly ahead. When they were less than fifty meters from the portal, Rachel stopped.

Stokes didn't hesitate. He kept the throttle at full speed, and they went into the blackness, each man on board instinctively flinching as the screen went dark for a moment. When it cleared, they were on the surface of a circular body of water with a large, black portal over three-quarters of a mile taking up the center directly behind them. And on the black beach that delineated the edge of the water were thousands of craft: ships mostly, with planes, and even two dirigibles.

But Stokes was only interested in finding one craft. He threw open the hatch and climbed on top of *Deepflight,* the other members of his crew joining him. They scanned the shoreline, searching among the multitude of ships.

"There." The executive officer was pointing to the left.

The *Connecticut* was half beached, bow first, near a Spanish galleon.

"Let's go," Stokes ordered.

The Present

Dane's suit floated six inches above the ground. A wall of fire was less than a foot away. Amelia Earhart was to his right, slowly backing away from the flames.

"Where the hell are we?" she demanded.

The wall of fire was over 200 feet high and stretched as far as he could see left and right. There was a similar wall about a quarter mile behind them. The ground beneath their feet was rocky and sandy.

"Nazca," Dane said. The portal they had come through was shrinking, and as he watched, it snapped out of existence. He turned back to the wall of fire. He could see it was being pulled left to right. And in the distance, about two miles away, he could see a massive portal, about a half mile wide, sucking in the flame from all the lines on the plain. He knew it was doing the same thing on a much larger scale from the interior of the planet.

"What's Nazca?" Earhart asked.

Dane pointed at the large portal. "That's what we have to stop."

"How?" Earhart asked.

Dane instinctively knew that even if he had the crystal skulls with him, they would make no difference, given the amount of power that was being drawn from the planet. This was beyond the scope of what a priestess could do. He reached with his one hand and opened the suit and stepped out on the Nazca Plain. Earhart hesitated, then followed suit. He felt relieved to see her face. The air felt good against his exposed flesh.

Dane staggered as the ground beneath his feet rumbled and shifted.

. . .

The crew of *Aurora* watched as the end panels began folding in on themselves. The flow of ozone through the trailing portal was slowing, but given that the craft was now over the Gulf of Mexico, it had stripped Earth's atmosphere of a considerable percentage of the critical material.

• • •

"Fatal failure in the core in less than thirty minutes," Ahana announced.

"And then?" Foreman asked, even though he knew the answer.

"Initially, the core will implode," Ahana said. "Then it will explode. The end of the planet."

Foreman looked out the portal toward the Devil's Sea gate. No sign of Dane. Something nudged against the back of his legs. Chelsea. The golden retriever seemed quite unperturbed about the pending end of the world. Foreman reached down and rubbed the dog's head.

• • •

"Wait," Dane said, holding out his arm as Earhart moved back from the fire.

"What is it?" she asked.

The answer came as a portal opened in the same location as the one they had just come through. A woman stepped through, her red cloak spattered with blood, a golden orb in her hands. She had red hair cut tightly against her skull. Her eyes widened as she took in the walls of fire, then she shifted her gaze to Earhart, then to Dane, where it lingered. She reached out one hand, and Dane took it in his. He felt a shock race up his arm. She pulled his hand toward the golden sphere. The surface writhed and moved, each strand pulsing. But of the dozens of strands, there was one that was suffused with red, and Dane didn't hesitate, allowing her to place his hand on it.

Pain seared into his flesh as if the strand were red hot, but he didn't let go. The world around him, the Nazca plain, the walls of fire, were gone. He saw worlds, many Earths, portals connecting the parallel worlds, all running through the space between. But his focus was on the portal his hand was on: the power line from his world to the Shadow's.

All he could make of the Shadow's world was a black wall, as if it were protected in some manner from the various Earth time lines, but the power line plunged into it, pouring energy through. There was a portal right next to it, and Dane could tell something was getting sucked through it—not power but something else.

A voice was in his head, the voice of the woman in the red cloak. It wasn't exactly a voice because what was coming to him wasn't words but images. He saw what to do. With one hand on the red strand, he reached with the other, pushing into the sphere. His skin recoiled as if he were reaching into a nest of writhing vipers, but he persisted until his fingers closed around another strand. He knew it was the portal line next to the power one, leading from his time/world to the Shadow's world.

Dane squeezed with both hands, the pain spiking so that he cried out, but still he held on, exerting power. The second line gave way, snapping.

* * *

The panels had all folded in and been tucked inside the sphere. The crew of *Aurora* watched as the large black sphere slipped back into the portal and disappeared, the portal shrinking out of existence.

The Space Between

The three-quarter-mile-wide column of black snapped out of existence, causing a shock to reverberate throughout the space between. And momentarily caught in the air, a quarter mile above the inner sea, the black sphere was revealed.

Then it free-fell, slamming into the water with a huge splash, causing a forty-foot-high tidal wave to race outward toward the surrounding shorelines.

The sphere went underwater briefly, then bobbed to the surface, floating aimlessly.

A mile away, the prow of the *Connecticut* appeared out of a portal, the rest of the submarine sliding through.

The Present

Dane's right hand was on fire, the pain unbearable. On his own, he would have let go, but he felt power coming from the strange woman, enough to keep the pressure on the strand. His fingers closed in, tightening on it. He felt heat all around him now, but he dared not open his eyes and lose his concentration.

The strand snapped, and Dane was thrown backward, away from the map. He lay on his back, staring up at stars in a night sky. Then he realized he could see the stars because the walls of fire were gone. The Nazca plain was as it had been, marked but inactive.

Dane leaned up on his elbow. The priestess was still there, holding the portal map. She smiled at Dane, reached into the map with one hand, and a portal opened behind her. She pointed, indicating for Dane and Earhart to enter it.

Earhart went through, followed by Dane. He wasn't surprised to find himself on the shore of the Inner Sea. He turned as the woman came through, the portal map in her hands. The portal disappeared.

A clicking noise caught Dane's attention. Rachel lifted out of the water forty meters offshore and landed on her back with a splash. Dane could pick up the dolphin's happiness. He blinked as farther out in the sea, the conning tower of a nuclear submarine appeared as the craft surfaced. And behind that, he could just make out, among the various portal columns, the top part of a black sphere, the majority of it submerged. He blinked, then looked once more. It made sense to him, each piece, part of a whole that was to come.

He turned back to the two women standing next to him.

Amelia Earhart's face was pale, a thin sheen of sweat covering her skin.

"What just happened?" she asked.

"We saved the world. My world," he amended, glancing at the strange woman.

She was reaching into the portal map again, her eyes closed as her hands searched. She paused, nodded to herself, then removed her hand from inside the map. She tapped her chest and then pointed to the right along the beach.

"What's she trying to say?" Earhart asked.

Dane had no doubt what the gesture meant as he picked up the emotions/thoughts of the woman. "She's going home."

Dane nodded and spread his hands wide in a gesture of thanks. The woman smiled briefly, then began walking away.

"Shouldn't we keep the map?" Earhart asked.

"Others need it," Dane said. "We're not the only world that the Shadow threatens." He faced the Inner Sea and waved at the man in the conning tower of the submarine.

epilogue

The Present

The Earth was still.

In eastern Africa, the central United States along the devastated Mississippi region, around Lake Tahoe, the survivors struggled to stay alive.

In capitals around the world, scientists met with world leaders, but there were many more questions than answers.

On board the FLIP, Ahana studied the data her computers were spitting out while Foreman hovered over her shoulder.

"Well?" the CIA agent asked.

"Good news. And bad news."

"The good?"

"The core is stable; the Nazca portal is closed."

"The bad?"

"The Shadow sphere took so much ozone out of the atmosphere, the surface of the planet will become unfit for human life."

"How long?"

"Two years."

Foreman slumped down in a chair, rubbing Chelsea's head. He seemed relieved. "Two years is a long time."

"And there is also the radioactivity from Chernobyl," Ahana added. "It will reach Moscow in less than a week."

A sailor stuck his head in the door of the control center. "The *Connecticut* has emerged from the gate."

Foreman ran onto the bridge wing. He could see the conning tower of the submarine coming toward them. His hands gripped the railing, waiting for torpedoes and missiles to strike out as he remembered the *Wyoming*'s assault when it came out of the Bermuda Triangle gate. His body sagged with relief as an American flag unfurled from the periscope.

The *Connecticut* slowly came alongside the FLIP, and lines were thrown, connecting the two. A gangplank was extended, and Foreman was the first to greet Dane as he came across.

"Welcome back!"

"Nazca's shut down," Dane said.

"We know," Foreman said. "All muonic activity is stable and low."

"But?" Dane asked. Earhart had decided to stay in the space between, and Dane hadn't bothered to try to dissuade her. This wasn't her time. And her people, the refugees, needed her.

Foreman's summary was succinct. "The Shadow has scavenged a high amount of ozone with a black sphere, and the radiation from Chernobyl is spreading."

Dane nodded as if this was expected. "There is more work to be done. I think I know a way we can fix both those problems."

"How do you know?"

Dane smiled. "I've seen it in a vision."

480 b.c.

Cyra held up the portal map and placed it in the leather sling held by one of the rower/warriors on the Theran oracle's ship. She was standing waist deep in water, and the oracle was just barely visible as a hooded figure in her cave in the rear of the ship. After the map was secure, she passed up the Naga staff to a second man.

The men carried the portal map and Naga staff to the oracle, and Cyra briefly saw her face in the golden glow as she lifted the cloth Cyra had wrapped it in, then once more she faded into darkness.

"Why do you need it?" Cyra called out.

The oracle's voice was low but carried easily over the water. "I don't. Others do. Other places. Other times."

"Where did it come from?" Cyra asked, unwilling to let the oracle fade away so quickly.

Surprisingly, the oracle laughed. "I don't know. And not just where; when is important. In fact, I think . . . well, it is beyond me." The oracle waved in farewell and stepped back into the shadows of her cave.

The ship was moving, and Cyra waited until it disappeared into the darkness. Then she waded back to shore. There was a track from the Gulf of Corinth that led south, and she wearily walked along it, into the high country.

• • •

King Xerxes, son of Darius, grandson of Cyrus, king of Medea and Persia, ruler of Libya, Arabia, Egypt, Palestine, Ethiopia, Elam, Syria, Assyria, Cyprus, Babylonia, Chaldea, Cilicia, Thrace, and Cappadocia, and most blessed of god Ahura Mazda, held a perfumed kerchief over his nose as he stood atop the ruins of the Middle Gate and looked out over the ground strewn with bodies. It was almost impossible to walk without stepping on a corpse.

"Where is the Spartan king?" he asked Pandora. The

priestess was splattered with blood, the Naga staff held tightly in her hands.

She pointed at a mound of bodies—most of them Immortals—just south of the Middle Gate. "The Spartans made their last stand there. I killed him myself." She didn't add that she had accomplished this only after he'd been severely wounded several times by Immortals.

"Did you succeed in your quest?" Xerxes asked.

Pandora wearily leaned on the Naga staff. "No."

"Then whoever sent you will be displeased," Xerxes said.

"This war goes far beyond what you can imagine," Pandora said. "There will be other times and places."

"But not for you," Xerxes said.

Pandora stiffened as a blade entered her back. She saw a figure slip away—Xerxes's Dagger—even as she knew he had delivered a fatal blow. "You are nothing," she said to the Persian king. "You will fail in this. The Greeks will defeat you."

"Is that a prophecy or a wish?" Xerxes asked.

Pandora collapsed on the Middle Gate, adding her body to the multitude.

• • •

The women of Sparta mourned their dead men in much the same manner in which they had sent them off to war. The sound of the mournful hymn they sang rose above the city-state and echoed into the surrounding forests and mountains.

Cyra heard the song as she sat in the shade of a tree near the parade field where Spartan boys sparred, preparing for the next battle. She got to her feet as Thetis approached. The king's wife wore a thin strip of black cloth around her forehead to mark her loss. To her right was Briseis.

Thetis bowed her head slightly. "Greetings, Priestess."

"Your husband asked me to come here," Cyra said.

"For what reason?" Thetis asked.

Cyra looked at the young girl. "To teach your daughter."

Thetis smiled through her grief. "He asked that? A Spartan king concerned about his daughter's future? Perhaps things can change." She reached out and took Cyra's hand and placed it in Briseis's small hand. "Teach her well."

The Present

Alluvial waters have widened the pass at Thermopylae over the centuries since the battle between Spartans and Persians. It is now over a mile wide, as represented on Pandora's map. It was indeed an epic battle, as Xerxes turned back to Persia the following year, never completing his conquest, and the forces he left behind were routed by the Greeks. The entire history of the western world was changed as a result.

Near the mountain, where the pass was tight in days of old, etched on a monument are two lines in memory of the battle:

> *Go tell the Spartans, thou who passest by,*
> *That here, obedient to their laws we lie.*

Greg Donegan is a pen name for a bestselling writer. He is a West Point graduate, former Infantry officer, and Green Beret A-Team leader. He currently lives on Hilton Head Island, South Carolina. For more information, go to www.BobMayer.org.